C000132905

David Sheph
Lancaster. H
and
After University   w,
West Lothian a   al
College in Edinburgh. He was Chaplain of St Paul's
Cathedral, Dundee and Anglican Chaplain
in the University of Dundee.
He is now Rector of St Mary Magdalene's
Church in Dundee.

Twelve detective novels have now been published.
In chronological order, they are:

WHO KILLED SOPHIE JACK?
MURDER WITHIN TENT
A MISHAP IN MAJORCA
A CHRISTMAS CRACKER
A PROSPECT OF RYE
SLAUGHTER AT THE POLLS
MURDER ON THE MALLAIG EXPRESS
BURIED IN BAPTISM
THE BURNS SUPPER MURDER
FROZEN IN NICE
THE PUDDLEDUCK AFFAIR
A FUNERAL IS ARRANGED

Copies are available from:

Meadowside Publications
14 Albany Terrace,
Dundee DD3 6HR
Telephone: 01382 223510

with all good wishes at Christmas

David Shepherd.

A FUNERAL IS ARRANGED

A DETECTIVE NOVEL
BY
DAVID SHEPHERD

MEADOWSIDE PUBLICATIONS
DUNDEE
2014

Meadowside Publications
14 Albany Terrace, Dundee DD3 6HR

© *Meadowside Publications 2014*

Printed by
Robertson Printers,
Forfar

*The characters portrayed in this
novel are all imaginary and bear
no intended resemblance to any
person alive or dead.*

ISBN 978-0-9574915-2-6

Meadowside Crime
is a © imprint of
Meadowside Publications,
Dundee

Contents

The story is set in Grasshallows,
between September - November 1990

1: The Road to Nothingness

"The sooner someone murders that man, the better!"

Geoffrey Treaseman sipped his cup of rather tasteless coffee and stared down at the small rose garden in a courtyard three floors below. He was a mild, thoughtful man - liberal by nature; Amnesty International by conviction.

It was surprising for him to say such a thing, but even more surprising that none of his departmental colleagues seemed in any way shocked by his words. It was a sentiment they all shared. The departure of Timothy Shawcross, the Vice-Chancellor of Grasshallows University, by any means - fair or foul - would be a cause for universal rejoicing.

Dr Shawcross had taken up his new post on 1st August 1989. He was seen as 'a new broom' - and had been welcomed as such. But he had little experience of university life. He had been a Government statistician; an expert in time and motion studies; a non-executive director of British Leyland; a member of various, worthy Government quangos. These had carried him from commerce into the world of education. There had been some anxiety about over-spending in the universities. Expenses needed to be curbed. He was the ideal man to fill the vacancy in Grasshallows and show his political masters what could be achieved.

Almost his first public duty was to oversee the opening of a new science block by the Minister of Education. The building was grandiose, otiose and way over budget. His restraining hand had already been visible in the cheese-paring lunch and the poor selection of wines at the civic lunch which followed.

In the course of selecting the wine, Dr Shawcross had discovered the existence of the University wine cellar - a cornucopia of quality wine and vintage champagne, which had been carefully built up over the years. Dr Shawcross believed that the whole lot should be sold. What was a university doing hoarding expensive wines?

His eyes had then lighted upon the estate and building departments. The sort of people who planted small rose gardens in dreary courtyards. Surely the University did not need so many gardeners or maintenance staff? The work could be hived off to the private sector!

Early in October, he crossed swords with the student body. He had discovered that the Students' Union was paying no rent! The students claimed that the Union was part of the original buildings donated to the University. But the new Vice-Chancellor could hardly fail to notice the huge quantities of beer being sold every week. Here was precious, untapped income.

He had also developed a rather nasty habit of asking people whether they were really necessary. Did Halifax College really need twenty-four cleaners? Was medieval history really worth teaching in this modern age? Was anyone really interested in Thomas à Becket?

The University playing fields occupied many acres of valuable land. Property developers would be eager to snap them up. And, surely, the local authority could provide alternative sports facilities?

People were aghast at his suggestions. The University public relations department denied that such projects had ever been considered; but rumours persisted.

Dr Shawcross finally reached the Philosophy department just before Christmas. He had had them in his sights for quite a long time (in fact almost from his first day); but he hoped that his campaign for economy might have undermined their resistance long before he arrived.

He appeared one morning for coffee and was shown round the department, met the staff and was given a guided tour of the library, with its fine collection of books and documents illustrating the development of human thought from Socrates to Wittgenstein. Dr Treaseman was introduced as one of the leading British experts on Existentialism. He had written the highly-regarded four volume work on Jean-Paul Sartre.

Dr Shawcross had heard of Sartre. His name had been

mentioned in connection with the picket lines at Longbridge during the strikes at British Leyland.

The French philosopher had said: "Hell is other people". With hell-raisers like Red Robbo running amok, Dr Shawcross was inclined to agree.

But eventually he asked the dreaded question: "Does Grasshallows really need a philosophy department?" Surely a modern university needs to provide new industrial ideas; new scientific discoveries? It needs to train people to be wealth-creators rather than mere thinkers?

There was a shocked silence. One professor, two senior lecturers and eight ordinary lecturers could not even begin to think how to deal with such a Philistine who imagined that the search for truth, the application of reason and the exploration of the highest forms of human wisdom could ever be questioned.

But this was not just idle speculation. Dr Shawcross wanted a clear case to be made in defence of philosophy in a modern university. Otherwise, they would be the first department to face the chop. He gave them a deadline - Christmas 1990.

But that Christmas deadline was now only twelve weeks away. Furious discussions had taken place almost continuously since the ultimatum had been delivered. Everyone had produced papers, which had been argued over, amended and then torn up. Other universities, which had philosophy departments, had also been approached - and they had been having similar discussions and getting nowhere.

Morale was low in the department. There was anger, fear, distress. Close friendships had been destroyed. The situation was now coming close to breaking point. The Professor had taken sick leave. There was still no cogent defence. It looked as if the department might be axed. And, if that happened, who would ever give them another job?

Geoffrey Treaseman was very conscious of the fact that Socrates had ended his life by drinking hemlock. In the absence of a suitable defence, he asked himself whether murder was a viable option? Remove the questioner - and there is no need to answer the question! He admitted that this was a rather drastic solution but he could not think of any other way of saving his beloved department.

He was wondering whether he should invite his colleagues to put their names in a hat and decide which of them would be the murderer. It was now a question of "Who?" and "When?" Perhaps he should spare his colleagues any further agony and do the job himself? He had very little to lose. In such a situation what would Jean-Paul Sartre himself have done?

2: A Beguiling Offer

The owner of the *Grasshallows Echo* had several good reasons for supporting Miss Emily Williams in her university career.

The first was that he was a regular visitor to her family home in Wales. One of Mr Hayward's secret passions was the *Puddleduck Railway* which was operated by enthusiasts and volunteers during the summer months. For several years, he had lodged with Mrs Williams, who was an excellent cook and provided a very comfortable home. He had always been treated as part of the family. He felt that such generous hospitality should be suitably rewarded.

His second reason was that, having been divorced and having no easy access to his children, he felt a fatherly feeling towards Emily. He had watched her grow up; he had encouraged her in her ambition to go to university and he thought it might be rather nice to have her as a daughter-substitute living in Grasshallows.

He had also noticed that Emily had a marked fondness for the older man - her own father had died when she was three. And he was stupid enough to cherish the hope that one day she might become his mistress.

But, in recent months, Emily had become a little too hot to handle. She had become a rabid Welsh nationalist and her current boyfriend was still in jail for torching English-owned holiday homes. Mr Hayward knew that Emily had been involved in the arson attacks; she had been very lucky not to have been arrested. Then she had deliberately covered up the identity of the person who had killed one of his fellow railway enthusiasts. She knew who it was; but had said nothing.

She had a vicious temper and a sharp tongue. He had begun to wonder whether it had been wise to bring her to Grasshallows. She was not so much a student as a thermo-nuclear device just waiting to explode.

But there was a third reason why he wanted Emily in the University. He intended to employ her as a part-time reporter. He would pay her well for any information she managed to dig up.

The University had a very astute public relations team which lavishly promoted all the good news about the University but sat heavily on any scandal or unrest.

The students never knew what was going on. They were too bound up with their own petty, dreary squabbles; still doffing their caps to Marxism and extolling the joys of 'pot'. Their malodorous rag - *Grass* - on the rare occasions when it managed to reach the printers, was usually obscene, libellous and illiterate. (What did they teach children in those dark, satanic comprehensives?) Mr Hayward wanted someone who would home in on the real meat. He was sure that Emily would go straight for the jugular.

He briefed her over breakfast on her first morning in Grasshallows.

"The University is a closed shop as far as the Press is concerned. Even the tabloids have trouble getting in. People are very unwilling to spill the beans. Frightened of losing their jobs. Or failing to get promotion..."

Emily devoured a bowl of muesli, wondering what the food would be like in her hall of residence. It was said that the food was best in Halifax. Unfortunately, she was going to Salisbury. Perhaps student meals, lack of nutrition or health and safety issues might be a good starter?

But her host had his eyes set on a more substantial target.

"The new Vice-Chancellor is very unpopular. In the past year, he's managed to upset just about everyone. He's been very indiscreet - and vindictive. Both staff and students have suffered at his hands. I'm hoping they'll hit back."

Emily raised her eyes.

"What's a Vice-Chancellor?"

"He's the person who runs the University. A sort of managing director. He has no responsibility for what happens in the colleges; but he's responsible for the day-to-day management, the teaching facilities, the finance, the property, the awarding of degrees. He's come to Grasshallows to cut away the dead wood, to reduce staff and run the place on free market principles."

Mr Hayward stirred his cup of coffee.

"I heard a rumour last week that he intends to sell off the botanical garden. That'll cause a lot of trouble."

"Is that the story you're after?"

"Anything that sells the newspaper. People read it for the local gossip, the scandal, the gory murder - not that we have many murders in Grasshallows..." he added quickly. "People want to read about other people's tragedies. Victims of road accidents. Bodies being cut out of their cars by the fire brigade. The discovery of cannabis being grown in Henslea. A local businessman selling guns to Iraq..."

"How would I find out about such things?"

"Ask questions! Anyone you meet - ask them what they know. Even if they don't know anything about the botanical garden, they may tell you about something else. In this case, you could go along to the people who work in the glass houses and ask them what is happening. When you have a lead, follow it up.

"Phone the University Secretary. Don't let on that you are a student! Pretend that you are a national reporter for the *Guardian* or *the Times*. Ask him if the matter has been put on the agenda for the next Senate meeting? He won't tell you - but it's worth finding out when the Senate is meeting and phoning around a few of its members to ginger them up. That way you can make sure it gets on the agenda."

Emily cast an anxious glance across the table.

"I've no idea what a Senate is."

"The University's governing body. The Vice-Chancellor is accountable to them. He attends every meeting. If there's a big row, that's where it'll happen. It would be useful to have a full list of Senate members and their phone numbers. I can give you a list."

Emily had begun to see what Tom Hayward had in mind. She smiled.

"You want me to stir things up?"

"I think you could do that rather well!"

"But would people speak to me?"

"You don't have to tell them you're a reporter. You're just an inquisitive member of the Great British public asking a simple question. Nothing wrong with that. But people will talk. People love to tell you all they know. Listen carefully. Ask a few more questions to fill out the picture. Then just go to the nearest lecture room - or into the library. Write it down. Or phone me at the *Echo*. Even if you only get the merest whiff of a story, we can work on it. Put on other reporters. Call in the big boys. Dig out the dirt. And you will get your reward. We shall pay you well for anything you turn up."

Emily's eyes brightened.

"How much?"

Tom Hayward knew that he had at last caught her interest.

"A hundred pounds a week for small stuff. Five hundred pounds for a major scoop. A thousand if it gets into the national press."

He could see her mind carefully calculating the possibilities.

"I could be a very rich woman."

"You could."

Tom Hayward sounded encouraging. But he was aware that she would be receiving less than his junior reporters who were on about £8000 a year.

Perhaps Emily sensed that the offer was not all it might be. As Detective-Inspector Raynes had discovered, she struck a hard bargain.

"One thousand for a major scoop. Two thousand if it gets into the national press!"

She smiled an irresistible smile.

Tom Hayward felt that, even at that price, it was still a good bargain. If a story reached the national press, he would easily recoup his costs.

With money like that on the table, Emily Williams had every incentive to deliver a major scoop. If there was a real story to be found, she would find it. Her innate Welsh greed would sniff it out.

3: Moving In

On the Tuesday morning, Emily made her way to Salisbury College with all her luggage. Tom Hayward had arranged for a taxi - and it arrived soon after 9.00am. She gave the newspaper proprietor a big hug and received a confused peck on her left cheek. She gave him a proper kiss to show him how grateful she was for his kindness. But then reminded herself that Mr Hayward was no longer a family friend - or a sugar daddy - but a milch cow ready to be milked. And milk him, she would!

She settled back in the car and looked out at the unfamiliar streets, blocked almost solid with buses, lorries and cars.A far cry from the quiet, country lanes of Wales.

The taxi driver spoke: "Is this you just starting?"

Emily nodded.

"Yes. First year."

She didn't know whether she wanted to talk to this stranger; but they seemed to be stuck in a long row of cars - and silence might seem stand-offish.

"What part of Wales do you come from?"

"Pwddldwc."

The driver nodded.

"Mr Hayward often goes over to Wales."

"He stays with us whilst he is working on the Railway."

"Does he now?"

They advanced twenty feet and stopped again.

"Is it always like this?"

"During the rush hour. At least, this morning, we haven't got the students to contend with. They all have bicycles. Makes things much worse. You're always frightened of hitting one of them. They come at you from all angles. Have you got a bicycle yet?"

"No."

"You'll probably not need one if you're staying in hall. What are you studying?"

"Politics."

"You must be a Welsh Nationalist?"

"How did you guess?"

Emily laughed.

Already, this stranger had asked her five or six questions - and now he knew quite a bit about her. According to Mr Hayward. she should be asking the questions - if she was going to be a reporter. She decided that, from now on, she would be the interrogator - not him.

"Does anything interesting happen at the beginning of term?"

The driver shrugged his shoulders.

"People get drunk. People try to get you drunk. A few slimy locals will be out pushing drugs. Cheaply! Just to get you hooked. Don't touch them. They've probably been contaminated. But some fools will buy them."

That sounded like good advice.

"What about men?"

"Same the world over. They only want one thing from a young woman. Make sure you carry a condom - because it's certain they won't!"

Emily said: "I already have a boyfriend. But he's in jail."

"In jail? What for?"

"Burning down English holiday homes!"

"Violent fellow?"

"No. He just has principles. He should be out before Christmas."

There was silence for a few minutes as they managed to get through a green traffic light and joined another queue.

"Are there any interesting people I should meet?"

"Blessed if I know the answer to that one! If you're religious, you might want to speak to one of the chaplains. If you're interested in sport, there's a tennis club." He thought about his customer. She was Welsh. She could probably sing. "If you're musical, you could probably join the University choir or the orchestra. Do you play a musical instrument?"

"No."

There was a silence.

Emily asked: "Are the students politically active?"

"Not that I've noticed. Most of them are apathetic, I would say. There are a few African students at the university. And Pakistanis. They're probably nationalists - but they keep their heads down." He laughed. "Of course, there's always Rudy. He'll be back this term."

"Who's Rudy?"

"Everyone knows Rudy! He was rusticated last October. Sent down for attacking the animal house. He freed all the animals - and then he set the building on fire!"

He looked at his passenger in the mirror.

"They keep animals for dissection in the labs. Hamsters, mice, the occasional dog or chimp. They do experiments for the big drug companies. Rudy was dead against it. 'Animal Liberation' he called it. Caused a right stir!" He laughed. "He had principles! Bit like your boyfriend. You might get on with him!"

"Was he doing politics?"

"Bound to be. Mark you, now that he's back, he'll be kept on a very tight lead by the University authorities. The Vice-Chancellor won't tolerate a second attack. No. He'll be on his best behaviour - or he'll be out for good. But he should be an interesting classmate!"

Emily was already constructing her first article for Mr Hayward: 'Rudy Returns! The University authorities are already bracing themselves for the return of...'

She said: "What's his surname?"

"Krauss. Sounds German. His family were probably German. German Jews. Fled to Britain before the Second World War. But, if you ask me, I would say he looks more like a Balkan terrorist. He was in handcuffs when I last saw him. Didn't look as if he'd washed for a couple of months!"

Emily was feeling quite excited. Her first article! Perhaps, shortly, her first interview. And £100. All thanks to this talkative taxi man. Were there any other plums to be plucked from this particular tree?

She waited for another quiet moment and then said: "Mr Hayward told me that the new Vice-Chancellor isn't very popular."

"Complete disaster!" said the taxi driver. "He's managed to upset everyone. Of course they knew he was a political appointment; but they didn't realize he was such a fanatic. All he wants to do is cut - cut - cut!" He banged his steering wheel three times to emphasize his point. "Cleaners, maintenance men, kitchen staff, lecturers. He's got it in for all of them." He laughed bitterly. "Of course, he's keeping his own chauffeur! He's not going to give up his University car. Top of the range Jag. Beautiful piece of work. At least he's got some taste."

By now they had reached the High Street and were passing the *Green Man* - Grasshallows' premier hotel. Emily thought how nice it would be to have a meal there. But the taxi man was still going on about the Vice-Chancellor.

"I had a lecturer in my car - just the other day - and he said to me: 'The sooner someone shoots that man, the better!' And he's not the only one. Some of these people are really scared he'll axe their departments. They're worried about their families. How are they going to pay their mortgages? This week, there's rumours going about that he's going to flog off the botanical garden to property developers! What next?"

Emily asked: "Has he got a name?"

"Of course he's got a name! Shawcross. Dr Timothy Shawcross. If you ask me, someone'll pin him up on a cross one day!"

"Is he married?"

The taxi man suddenly went silent.

"Is he married?"

"Yes. But no children."

It seemed that the man knew more than he wanted to disclose.

"Do you know his wife?"

"I've taken her to a few places."

"Is she a nice person?"

"A bit hoity-toity. Swedish - or Danish. I'm not sure. Frederika. I believe her friends call her 'Freddie'."

"Has she got any friends? With a husband like that?"

"Not many. But there are one or two who suck up to her." He laughed bitterly. "Not that it'll do them much good!"

By now, their journey was almost over. They had entered the forecourt of Salisbury College. (All the residences were called after British Foreign Secretaries: Grey, Palmerston, Halifax...) The taxi driver pulled up at the front door.

"How much do I owe you?"

"Nothing. Mr Hayward paid for you."

"Well, at least I can give you a tip."

"He paid for that as well."

The taxi man grinned.

"He looks after his staff well does Mr Hayward."

"I'm not one of his staff."

The driver turned round in his seat.

"I'm sure he'll have given you a little job to do! I used to be one of his delivery men before I took early retirement. I know his ways. 'Just keep your ears open, Andy. Anything interesting, just let me know'."

Emily blushed.

She'd been rumbled already. But in the nicest possible way.

Andy smiled.

"You hang on to your money, love. But keep tabs on Rudy. I think you may get a good story there. He's bound to come a cropper sooner or later. Sooner, I would say."

He swung out of the car.

"Come on. I'll give you a hand with your luggage. I bet they've put you on the top floor."

4: Societies' Fayre

Emily saw Rudy at the Societies' Fayre later that week.

But, before that, there were two days of indoctrination into the ways of the University. Guided tours of the library, the chaplaincy, the main lecture theatres and the sports' hall. Leaflets and brochures were handed out at every stage. They would never be read. Within a matter of hours, they would be slung into the nearest waste paper bin. But, in handing out this rubbish, the University staff felt they were doing their bit to welcome the new students; to make one final bid for civilization before the rot set in - usually at the massive pre-coital binge on Saturday night when any pretence of decency and good behaviour would finally - and cheerfully - be swept away.

It was presumed that the new intake would find its own way to the Students' Union, where the beer was cheap, the discos were mobbed and - for two days only - the students could display their multi-cultural wares, hoping to gather in a fresh supply of live-bait to replenish the political and social bloodstock of the University.

Various people - mostly men - but not forgetting the occasional lesbian - were struck dumb by the beauty of a dark-haired girl, with her bobbed cut, her creamy complexion and her black button eyes. She was wearing a bright cerise jumper, a black skirt, black tights and black pointed shoes. Emily had not opted for anonymity. She was determined to make her mark in Grasshallows right from the start. When she opened her mouth, her soft Welsh lilt immediately added to her charm.

Emily lingered over the Music Society stall. She liked to hear other people sing; but was not so keen on doing it herself. Quite frankly, she preferred a male voice choir - and not just for the singing!

She was pressed to join the Green Party; but, as she said, given the amount of rain that fell in her part of the country, she felt Wales was already green enough.

A Jewish girl suggested that she might like to visit a kibbutz at Easter. The CND group invited her to campaign for a nuclear-free Wales. But since all the electric power in her valley came from Transnywdd, it seemed a little like cutting off your nose to spite your face. She also informed the bearded fanatic that it had been the policy of Plaid Cymru long before he had even been born! When he asked what Plaid Cymru was, she walked away in disgust.

The Communists were offering a glass of vodka to all new members. She drank the vodka but decided not to join. They were about to show Eisenstein's famous film: *Battleship Potemkin*; but Emily thought the Communists' moment of glory had long since passed - and the place was little more than a huge gulag.

(Little did she know that in less than three months time, the Berlin wall would fall and the peoples of Eastern Europe would walk free.)

A long-haired geek could not believe his luck when this beautiful girl spent nearly ten minutes looking at the offerings of the Railway Society. He could offer a trip to the motive power depot in Peterborough and, later in the term, the classic GPO film: *Night Mail*. When he summoned up enough courage to speak, he asked her why she was so interested in railways. She looked at him with glittering eyes.

"Because I help to run a private branch line in Wales. The Puddleduck?"

Ah, yes, he had heard of it - bless him. She gave the impression that she owned it personally and invited him to come down next Easter and do some work on the track. She also extolled the virtues of their new saddle tank, *Lady Ermintrude*. Her technical references to pistons and smoke boxes made him feel weak at the knees.

She also looked at the hearty members of the Rugby Club who were tossing a ball back and forth between them. The table was littered with empty cans of beer. She looked in vain for any reference to Cardiff Arms Park - but there was none. From their strips, she gathered that they were mostly interested in promoting the English team. They were decidedly 'the enemy'. They would never dare appear in Wales for a Six Nations Match. If they did, they would be as dead as cats' meat!

She could not avoid the Chaplaincy stall. The official Chaplain, the Rev Peter Latimer, was very much in evidence. He looked like an Aryan god - but, unfortunately, he sounded like Bertie Wooster. He put in a good word for God - and asked her if she was an Anglican? Apparently, Anglicans were to be found everywhere - even in the Church of Wales. "No," she said. "I belong to the Ebenezer Independent Chapel." With lofty disdain, the Rev Peter Latimer directed her towards the Christian Union.

The Catholic Chaplain, Father Campolini, a spherical bundle of goodwill and good food, hoped that she might be a Catholic. With her good looks, attendance at Mass would rocket.

An ardent Christian Union student asked her if she read her Bible. "In the Welsh," she said. "In the hen iaith. I am liking it for the beauty of the language." The student did not think this provided sufficient justification for Emily to get a passport to heaven. She told him that the Ebenezer Independent Chapel in Pwddldwc had been founded by John Wesley himself! The student who had only been 'born again' shortly before the summer holidays, had never heard of John Wesley. He said that she might do better coming along to the Baptists. "Lord, look you," she said. "In our village, they're no more than a bunch of headless chickens!" Obviously, the

Christian Union was not for her.

Round the corner, she found the stall promoting the Pagan Society; and with it her nemesis, Rudy Krauss.

Rudy was dressed like an Arab - in a pure white flowing robe, a corded head dress reminiscent of Lawrence of Arabia, and black sandals. His face was deeply tanned and he had grown a dark beard. In fact, in appearance, he looked very much like the average Christian's idea of Jesus. But the resemblance stopped there.

Rudy was born in Birmingham - Sutton Coldfield rather than Small Heath - but the accent remained. His theology was post-modernist Aleister Crowley and he was mounting a campaign for religion to return to its ancient roots. After three months in an open prison, atoning for his attack on the animal laboratory, Rudy had decided there was less pain and more mileage in becoming a cult figure in the University. God-like status would be conferred upon him - even though his current mantra was: "Bring back witchcraft!"

As Emily came round the corner, he was immediately struck by her dark beauty.

"Blessed Osiris!" he said. "What a divine apparition! What a gift!" To Emily, he said: "Are you a witch?"

Emily thought for a moment.

"Does it really pay?"

"Ah!" he said, "you're Welsh. You come from the land of the hobbits."

Emily was not sure whether this was a compliment or an insult.

She said: "We do have one or two in our village. But they would be mining for gold rather than sacrificing virgins at Hallowe'en."

Rudy raised his eyes heavenwards.

"Grace be to Lucifer! A chick with a sense of humour!"

Although they had not been introduced, Emily knew instinctively that this must be the infamous Rudy Krauss. His aureole had already been in mystic contact with her karma - or something like that.

In fact, if she had cast her eyes to the left - and looked at the Pagan Society stall, she would have seen badges for sale: "Satan loves Rudy." They were priced at 50p to encourage the punters. Rudy knew it would infuriate the Christian Union. Within the week, they would be praying for his soul in every college across the campus.

Rudy's elevated thoughts came down to earth.

"You new here?"

Emily nodded.

"What are you studying?"

"Politics."

"Same as me. I'm having to repeat the first year, so we'll be in the same class. That'll be great. Are you an anarchist or a nihilist?"

"Welsh nationalist, of course."

"The old spirit never dies."

Emily was thinking about her article for the newspaper.

"What happened to the animals you liberated?"

Rudy was surprised by such a sudden change of direction in their conversation.

"They were eaten!"

He smiled.

"Eaten?"

"No point in wasting good food. We made a stew. Cut off their heads and tails and put in some onions. Delivered it to the Cyrenians to feed the poor. I'm not sure they liked the furry bits."

Emily winced.

"That's a tall story."

"Tall as they come - but it's a good one. Always provokes a strong reaction. It's what you'd expect a Prince of Lucifer to say."

"What did you really do?"

"Allowed the little buggers to scarper off into the wild. We opened the cages and said: 'Off you go'. I got six months for that."

"I was also hearing that you burnt down the laboratory."

23

"That was to stop them starting up again. I'm told that their new laboratory has four security doors and two alarm systems. Bars in all the windows. So the scientists themselves are now in cages! Serve 'em right."

"Did you mind going to jail?"

"No. It was in a good cause. It should help my C.V."

The University Chaplain was heading off for lunch in the staff club. He saw the Welsh girl chatting to that creep from Birmingham. She was clearly in moral danger.

He spoke to her as he passed by.

"Be careful of the company you keep, young lady."

Rudy turned and said: "Go off and shaft your granny, you ------- hypocrite!"

He turned back to Emily and put his hand on his heart.

"It grieves me to use such explicit language in front of a beautiful young woman."

"If it's what you feel..."

"I do feel it - most strongly. He was on that committee that decided to send me down. He was the moral guidance expert whom they called in! He said: 'Mr Krauss, don't think that you will escape judgement by following in the steps of St Francis. He loved animals. You have merely exploited them for your own shameful political purposes.' He's got a real poncey voice. I'm longing to get my revenge on him. In fact, that's one of the reasons why I came back."

"Well, why don't you? If you believe in the power of the old religions, why don't you summon up the spirits of the dead to come and fight for you? Why don't you brew up poisonous potions and put them in his jam - or his HP sauce - or smear it over his chocolate biscuits?"

Rudy smiled a sly smile.

"I'm waiting for my witch to do it for me."

"Ba! Do it yourself, man! Do it the old-fashioned way - with candle grease. Melt it down and re-form it into his likeness. And then stick pins into his groin. We do it quite often in Wales. Believe me, it works a treat! Especially on the English. They are frightened of the occult."

24

Rudy looked at Emily with amazement.

She seemed to have respect for the Black Arts. For him, it was a bit of a game. For her, it was part of her spiritual heritage.

Rather lamely, he said: "I don't know where he lives."

"I will find out for you."

Emily walked back round the corner to the Chaplaincy stall.

"Where does Mr Latimer live? Is it a University house?"

The student manning the stall was most helpful.

"41 Sandringham Crescent. Were you wanting to speak to him?"

""I may have a spiritual problem."

"He has an 'at home' every Sunday evening..."

Emily's eyes twinkled.

"Does he now?"

"... and excellent coffee."

"I shall be looking forward to that."

Emily returned to Rudy.

"41 Sandringham Crescent. And he has open nights on a Sunday evening. That's your way in. But I'd start with the wax dolls. Long range attack on the enemy."

Emily was about to move on - but Rudy tried to hang on to this remarkable girl.

"Would you like a drink?"

"I would like it very much."

Rudy ran his hands down his gown.

"No pockets - sorry."

Emily shook her head.

Even Messiahs should come prepared.

He turned to the student manning the stall.

"Have we got any money?"

Emily broke in: "Come on! I'll get you a coffee. I've plenty of money."

"Well, I'd quite enjoy a beer."

Emily sighed sadly.

"If you're a Prince of Lucifer and a practitioner of the Dark

Arts, you must keep your mind clear. Avoid the corruption of strong drink. If you are going to sacrifice virgins at Hallowe'en, you must have a steady hand."

"She looked round the hall.

"Where is the coffee bar?"

"I'll show you."

5: The Apparition

As they moved through the crowds of students, Rudy was aware that they looked a striking pair. Her presence added credibility to his pose as High Priest of some outlandish cult. He felt... masterful. He found it easier to act out his part because she seemed to believe in him. She wasn't mocking him... Rather, she was urging him to use his invisible powers - and perhaps he would?

They treated themselves to cappuccino coffee and two large pieces of rich chocolate cake - Divine Decadence, as it is often called. An ideal medium for poisonous potions - as Lucretia Borgia discovered many years ago!

They found a quiet corner where they could continue their conversation.

"Are you available for October 31st?" he enquired mischievously.

Emily's black button eyes held him transfixed.

"I am no longer a virgin - so, sadly, your spells would not work. Besides, if I am to be a witch - or even the high priestess of your cult, I cannot be a helpless victim. I shall expect to share the honours of our ritual sacrifice."

"Had you anyone in mind?"

Up to that point, Emily had not been taking the Pagan thing all that seriously. It was all a bit of a tease. And she had enjoyed boosting up Rudy - knowing that she could magnify his exploits in the *Echo*. She had already got as far as 'Naked Rites in Botanical Garden'. Whether it would make the gardens more popular, she did not know. But it would certainly make her another £100. Rudy Krauss would be the goose which laid the golden eggs. He would never realize he was her benefactor - but it should certainly prove quite profitable.

But, as he asked the question, she realized that she did have someone in mind. Someone that she had never met but, quite possibly, one of those boring, dry-as-dust people who had spoken to the students at the indoctrination sessions earlier in the week. He was definitely 'an enemy of the people' and someone who was reported to be preparing a slashing attack on a whole herd of sacred cows. They wanted him stopped in his tracks - so he would be a natural target for Rudy, who already had a grudge against him. She would not have to do anything. She would simply report his progress.

In fact, it was surely the job of a proficient witch to urge on the victim to his own self-destruction? Her knowledge of the Scriptures reminded her of the Witch of Endor who had forewarned King Saul that he would die in battle at Ramoth-Gilead. He still went - stupid man - and was struck down with a spear, bleeding to death.

Emily smiled at Rudy.

"Yes, I had."

"I can't go to Wales to help you."

"No, he's here. A very unpopular person. One of your sworn enemies... He deserves to die!"

Realization dawned blissfully in Rudy's mind.

"The Vice-Chancellor!"

"Yes. I don't know what he looks like, but people do seem to have it in for him. Surely we can do something to help them?"

Rudy was almost hypnotized by her seductive Welsh voice, pouring out dreams of greatness into his willing ears.

'He's the ideal person for your dark arts. You'll be able to raise the dead souls in Hades to fight his reforms. You'll attract support right across the board. You'll be in the vanguard of public opinion."

Rudy was overjoyed.

This unknown girl had given him a cause to fight for. A

reason for living. For returning to Grasshallows University. Leading both staff and students in battle. Perhaps becoming the most popular President of the Students' Union? A political force to be reckoned with. A stepping stone to parliament... Others had done it. So could he.

Never was an apple polished so fervently before being handed to an unsuspecting male.

Emily watched him swallow her plan - hook, line and sinker. He would be the driving force in the campaign and she would record his deeds in detail for the Press. Not the 'Chanson de Roland' but the 'Chanson de Rudy.' And £2000 would be hers.

She let him think it out. More cappuccino and more chocolate cake aided their task. Rudy was set on the path to greatness - and she used the opportunity to ask him about his life, his childhood, his education and his time in prison. In gratitude, he poured out the whole story. She would have a long and busy evening writing it all down whilst it was fresh in her mind.

She smiled.

"I think I shall be more use to you as a witch than as a sacrificial virgin!"

She stood up.

"I must go. I will see you on Monday morning."

Rudy looked very upset at losing his new-found friend.

"Must you go? What about some fish and chips?"

Emily shook her head.

"No. I've got to go and write a letter to my Mam. She will be missing me."

(For everyone knows how important a 'Mam' is in Welsh family life. She is the true dynamo in every home. And, of course, a perfect excuse!)

In a second, Emily was gone - lost in the crowd.

Rudy glowed inwardly - as he asked himself: "Was she real?"

6: Chaplain's Delight

Whilst Emily was constructing her first article for the *Grasshallows Echo*, the Rev Peter Latimer was busy re-arranging the cushions on his sofa, making sure everything was in order for his dinner guest.

The velvet curtains shut out the dark autumn night. The room was pleasantly warm and the gentle strains of the 'Siegfried Idyll' were burbling through the loudspeakers. Peter was not sure whether she would like Wagner - but he couldn't think of any Danish composers. He certainly had nothing like that in his collection.

In the kitchen, the beef stroganov was close to perfection. The rice was about to be launched on its journey - with a little help from Delia; whilst an expensive bottle of Piesporter was chilling in the fridge. She loved a crisp Moselle.

Watching through the curtains, he saw her taxi draw up at the gate. He looked at his watch. Two minutes to eight. Among her many gifts, she rated punctuality most highly. She also dressed very tastefully. As she entered the hallway of 41 Sandringham Crescent, he helped her remove her expensive camel hair coat. He noted that she was wearing a pale blue jumper, a dark blue skirt and black boots. They kissed warmly with all the fervour of young lovers - which of course they were.

Freddie Shawcross was Peter's secret passion. As a bachelor - well, as a man separated from his wife and his three children - and with one or two illicit romances under his belt, it paid to be circumspect. In the eyes of the University, he tried to create the impression that he was gay. But he could not carry that message too far for fear that the Christian Union might denounce him and make his life intolerable.

Little did he know that, on Monday morning, a Miss Emily Williams would be making her first official visit to the University library to examine Crockford's Clerical Directory to discover what parishes Mr Latimer had worked in before moving to Grasshallows. She would then make a few discreet phone calls to people living in those parishes - and by lunchtime, she would have a very clear picture of the Chaplain's past sins. His charmed life was about to draw to a close.

"Freddie, darling, I hope you've had a good day?"

"Tiring. I went shopping in the morning. There was a dress I had to take back. I didn't see anything I liked. There was a lunch for the lecturers' wives. It went on till after 3.00pm. After that, I wallowed in the jacuzzi."

Tiring indeed!

"And what about you?"

"The Societies' Fayre. I had to show my face for a couple of hours. I had lunch at the Staff Club. Then I had a few words with Russell."

"Russell?"

"Russell Forrester. The University Secretary."

"Oh yes, I know him. He absolutely hates Timothy. He doesn't agree with what he's doing in the University. He causes an awful lot of trouble at the Senate meetings. He questions everything - and writes the most offensive minutes. He's Timothy's public enemy No 1."

Peter understood her feelings completely.

"I think many people have the same feelings about him. But of course, he was appointed by the previous Vice-Chancellor. Dr Bulman was a die-hard Socialist. He grabbed every penny of Government money that was going. Expansion and growth were the two things he was interested in. And Russell Forrester shared the same views. But, in the current financial circumstances, the country can't afford such largesse. The dinosaurs have to be slaughtered. Inevitably, there will be a clash of views. Your husband is right to challenge them."

"Well, Timothy is determined to get rid of him. He wants to bring in his own man."

Peter Latimer uttered a word of caution.

"I don't think it will be all that easy to uproot Russell. He has established very deep roots. There could be a long battle ahead."

He sighed - and then realized that something was missing. He hadn't offered Freddie her mandatory gin and tonic. The rice and the green beans would also need attention.

"Let's forget all these horrible people," he said. "I'll get you a G & T. Will that make life a little more bearable?"

"I thought you would never ask."

* * * *

Once dinner was on the table and the Piesporter had been served, Peter remembered another piece of bad news.

"Do you remember a student called Rudy Krauss?"

"Should I?"

"He was the one who broke into the animal testing laboratory - and then burnt it down."

"Oh. yes. I remember him. He was sent down."

"Last October. He went to jail for six months..."

"A dangerous creature!"

"Very dangerous. Well, he's back. He only served three months - and in an open prison. I saw him again this morning."

"Is he a reformed character?"

"Not a bit of it. He's now pretending to be a Druid High Priest! He's appointed himself head of the Pagan Society and he's wandering round in a white gown and an Arab head dress, trying to convert the new students to his way of thinking." Peter Latimer sighed. "He even asked me if he could become a member of the Chaplaincy Council! Of course I dismissed the idea out of hand. But the cheek of it!"

"How did he get back?"

Mr Latimer took a sip of wine.

"I think they only rusticated him for a year. We knew he was going to be charged with arson - and that he would be sent to jail. Nobody thought he would want to come back. At least, I didn't."

"So what's he doing now?"

"Provoking people. He's arranged a meeting tomorrow

night to explain the significance of Tarot cards. He's been selling them on the Pagan Society stall. He asked me if he could use the Chaplaincy library for the meeting. He must have known that the Christian Union would be holding their first meeting of term in the main room at the Chaplaincy. They would have been up in arms if I'd given him permission."

Freddie thought it might be rather fun to have her cards read. She remembered Jane Seymour in the Bond film: 'Live And Let Die'. It would be nice to see what was going to happen to Timothy. Whether she would have to endure another ten years. Perhaps the cards would give her something to look forward to?

But, of course, she couldn't say that to the University Chaplain.

She smiled.

"Peter, have you every had your cards read?"

Her host looked somewhat confused.

"Of course not! ... Well, once... It was damned embarrassing... She told me my wife was going to leave me. I wasn't expecting it... She even told me the date and the time! These things are just rubbish... The Devil's picture gallery... That's what I call them... Not the sort of thing you want to get involved in."

Freddie continued to smile sweetly.

"But it came to pass, didn't it?"

"But not the way I expected."

Freddie shook her head at Peter's weakness.

"You've done a lot of naughty things in your time, haven't you?"

Mr Latimer put a brave face on it.

"Well, what I always say is this: 'If you're going to talk about sin, you need to know something about it!'"

Freddie looked at her watch.

"I shan't be able to stay with you too long tonight. Timothy's due back at half-past ten. He's been at a meeting in Oxford." She looked at Peter meaningfully. "With his secretary..."

"The delectable Mrs Hobbs!"

"She's not delectable! She's fat! She's a witch! She's getting her claws into Timothy. Distracting him from his work. I can't imagine what he sees in her."

"Sex?"

Freddie laughed.

"I shouldn't think so. He's not very good at that!" She put her hand on Peter's arm. "Not like you, darling! You're wonderful. You are God's gift to a woman. How you learnt all that at an all-male boarding school, I shall never know."

"I was married for ten years."

Peter was embarrassed about his past. Some people thought that clergymen should be completely asexual. Not talk about it. Not do it. Be as pure as driven snow. But Freddie was irresistible. The first day he met her... he knew. Love at first sight! They had both felt the same way. And now he was swimming in very dangerous waters. An affair with the Vice-Chancellor's wife!

Freddie said: "We've still got over an hour. Shall we take the bottle and glasses upstairs?"

How could the Rev Peter Latimer say "No"?

7: The University Secretary

It was only the second day of term, but already the problems were beginning to roll in.

The students at Halifax College had flooded the senior common room, which was now unusable. A new ceiling might be required.

There had been complaints about the new French lecturer. She talked far too fast - and had some strange Breton accent which could not be understood.

The cleaners in Grey College had gone on strike. A first year student had brought his dog with him. It had been making messes in various public places. The dog must go.

An electrician had fallen off a ladder in the science block.

Whether it was his fault - or not - was unclear. The man was now in hospital. A claim might be made against the University.

The auditors had been very slow in getting the accounts done. They were asking for an extra week. They had done the same thing last year. It had caused a lot of problems further down the line. Should he now crack the whip?

The University Secretary regarded himself as the Clapham Junction of Grasshallows University. All the problems ultimately landed on his desk. It was up to him to phone people, to write letters, to delegate junior staff to sort out problems, to supervise meetings and sub-committees, to draw up agendas, to call people in to be reprimanded or to seek further information.

Russell Forrester had been doing this job superbly for the past fifteen years. He was believed to be omniscient and omnicompetent. He had a wealth of experience of everything that could go wrong in a university and knew exactly what levers to pull to put things right. Everything was handled with efficiency and complete discretion. His small department of twelve people functioned like a well-oiled machine. Russell was widely respected throughout the University; he was trusted with many secrets; and he was regarded as a friend by everyone who went to seek his help.

The Vice-Chancellor himself had become the biggest source of problems. Everything he said - or did - raised a barrage of questions. Every visit he made - to any department - produced complaints. He was forever making policy on the hoof - threatening cuts, raising fears and leaving people deeply worried or extremely angry. People demanded to know if this was University policy. When had it been agreed? Would it affect them? Should they now start making plans? Arranging cuts? There was total confusion.

Even when you told people that the Senate had not even discussed such things, people felt there was a hidden plan. Such things then had to be put on the agenda for the next meeting - and this produced very heated meetings.

When the University Secretary urged him to be more cautious in his public statements, Dr Shawcross had replied that he was 'an ideas man'. It was his job to think the unthinkable; to do the impossible and to make everyone realize that no one was indispensable. He seemed to think he had a divine right to ride roughshod over everyone. And that others were there to pick up the bits.

It was very tiresome - and very annoying. One full year of this irresponsible behaviour had brought most of the University staff up to boiling point - which he, Russell Forrester was trying to cool down. He conceded - sadly - that he was not succeeding in his task.

This morning, two secret reports were giving him fresh cause for anxiety.

The Press had picked up that Mrs Shawcross was saying harsh things about the University and its personnel. She had also described the people of Grasshallows as 'peasants' - and the city itself as 'a boring provincial dump'. Even though Mrs Shawcross had lived almost all her life in England, she was regarded as a foreigner - and people were quick to take offence. Mr Forrester was aware that she deeply resented being torn away from the bright lights in London; but she could go back there whenever she wanted. Her diary appointments could easily be reduced.

However, he had also received an alarming report that she was having an affair with someone in Sandringham Crescent. Quite a few lecturers lived in that street - and one of their wives had said that she had been seen arriving in a taxi - and not going home till the following morning. Names had not yet been mentioned; but it could soon prove embarrassing.

On the other side of the fence, it was being said that the Vice-Chancellor was having an affair with his personal secretary, Linda Hobbs. Russell found this almost impossible to believe. Mrs Hobbs was an excellent woman. She had been part of his department for several years; which was why he had recommended her to Dr Bulman.

But there were stories about the two of them going away to

conferences together; little intimacies being exchanged and the report of an electrician at the University House, that she had been seen there with Dr Shawcross when Mrs Shawcross was away. It was all idle tittle-tattle; but it came from several sources and might contain an element of truth. He wondered whether the electrician was the same one who had fallen off his ladder? He noted that Linda's husband worked in the maintenance department.

He put these worries to one side. Dr Treaseman was due to see him at 11.00am. He knew what it was about.

It was now 10.55am. He arranged for coffee to be brought to his room in five minutes time.

"Dr Treaseman."

"Thank you so much for taking the time to see me. I'm afraid things are beginning to get a bit desperate in our department."

"How long is Professor Hampton expected to be away?"

"It could be the whole term."

"Surely not?"

"Well, I think he's trying to avoid making any decisions involving his colleagues. As you know, we are a very close-knit department."

"Indeed."

"And people have been getting very worried... Ah! Coffee. Most welcome."

The coffee smelt delicious. Russell poured it into deep china cups. This ritual always brought comfort to his visitors. Soothing their savage breasts. Perhaps he should try it on Mrs Shawcross? Perhaps not!

"You were saying..."

"Oh, yes. The department has been getting increasingly restless. There's only one thing on their minds. The 'defence paper'. As you know we're expected to get this in to the Vice-Chancellor before Christmas. There's no way we can do it. I think there are about four papers circulating - there were at the last count. But that's the trouble with philosophy; there are so many different viewpoints. They simply can't be reconciled."

Russell tried to help Dr Treaseman.

"But apart from the Vice-Chancellor, no one else has put a gun to your head. No one is wanting a defence document. We're all perfectly happy to have a Philosophy department. In fact, I can't imagine a civilized university without one. I've always regarded it as an excellent department - well run and brimming with talent. Your own books on Sartre have brought great distinction to the University. I don't think you should let the Vice-Chancellor's adumbrations disturb your peace of mind. Really, I don't. Remember! It won't be him who makes the decisions. It'll be us."

That should have been enough for anyone; but Dr Treaseman still felt the sword of Damocles hanging over his head.

"I tell you, Russell, people are finding quite violent thoughts coming into their minds. One of my colleagues has bought a gun - well, an air pistol. Another is planning to poison him. A third has threatened to batter him with a spade. The atmosphere's deteriorating - and I'm just wondering where it'll all end."

Russell Forrester could see that a quite irrational fear had gripped members of the department - even its Professor. The work of the Philosophy Department would suffer if this were to continue.

He smiled pleasantly.

"I often think such thoughts myself. And I see him more often than you do. I manage to control myself..." He paused. "... most of the time! But I agree it is all most worrying. I would beg members of your department not to blow up the University House! It is, after all, a Grade A listed building."

After the brief touch of humour, a tiny shaft of ice entered the conversation.

"I think you, Dr Treaseman, as the most senior lecturer, should do your best to calm these quite irrational fears; and help your colleagues to concentrate on more important things - such as teaching the students. Perhaps, if you concentrate on them, you'll have your answer?"

Dr Treaseman said: "Well, I'll do my best. But we've got

to get rid of this man as soon as possible. He's doing so much damage to the University. I felt I had to tell you what ordinary people are thinking. And if anyone does kill him, then at least I've done the decent thing and warned you."

The University Secretary felt that he had alloted sufficient time, listening to Dr Treaseman, who might - like his hero, Jean-Paul Sartre - soon see large crabs pursuing him down the street. He smiled graciously.

"Thank you for your advice. I do hope the dogs of war will be kept safely under lock and key."

8: Another Nutter

As if one nutter was not enough for one morning, Russell Forrester had another difficult encounter in the Staff Club at lunchtime.

Peter Latimer - his least favourite chaplain - came up to him whilst he was selecting an aperitif to go with his lunch.

Rather aggressively, he said: "Have you thought about what I said to you on Thursday?"

Russell put on his most world-weary expression.

"I expect so. But I can't remember what it was. So many things have happened since Thursday."

Mr Latimer hissed: "That Rudy Krauss!"

"Oh, yes!" He did remember. "You thought we should get rid of him - for being a pagan."

"Oh, it's worse than that! He's practising the Dark Arts. Do you know what happened on Friday night?"

"No."

"He was giving a lecture on how to use Tarot cards. He was doing it in the Students' Union. I wouldn't let him do it in the Chaplaincy."

"Of course not. The Students' Union is a much more appropriate place for that sort of thing."

"But he was influencing the minds of many impressionable students."

"I'm sure they won't be taken in." He looked at Mr Latimer, whose aristocratic good looks always annoyed him. He should really have become a private detective. Harriet Vane would have adored him. "Any more than your Christian Union students will believe in Predestination in five years time! They'll take it in their stride."

Peter Latimer thought it was outrageous that the University Secretary should compare a fine, upright body of Christian students with a convicted jailbird who was clearly embarking on a career in sorcery.

He said: "Our students are taking it pretty badly."

"I'm sure they are."

"He's on all their prayer lists."

"Let us hope their prayers will prove effective."

Peter Latimer felt that the University Secretary was mocking him.

"But where's it all going to end? I hear that he's thinking of holding a spirualist meeting in Palmerston. Ouija boards and spirit writing. Do you really want such things to happen in our University?"

"There are a lot of unpleasant things that happen in a university."

"I'm sure there are. But we have to fight against them."

Mr Forrester smiled broadly.

"Perhaps Rudy should invite the Vice-Chancellor to come along to one of his meetings? Then we might get rid of both of them at the same time?"

He laughed.

Peter Latimer did not laugh.

"What you don't know is that Rudy is encouraging students to make wax dolls of the Vice-Chancellor. He's telling them that if enough people do it - sticking pins into his heart or his groin - they'll be able to get rid of him."

The University Secretary looked piously heavenwards.

"Let us hope Rudy succeeds. Then perhaps we can award him with an honorary doctorate - for services to the University!"

Peter Latimer's face flushed angrily.

This conversation was not going the way he wanted. The University Secretary was condoning the Dark Arts, rather than condemning them. Praising Rudy when he should be sacking him.

"You've always been against the Vice-Chancellor."

Russell poked the Chaplain in the stomach.

"And so have you!"

In the past hour, his spies - or rather, one of his most trusted sources of information - had told him that the man Mrs Shawcross had been seeing was the University Chaplain. This was valuable information.

Russell paid for his aperitif and sniffed at the rich aromatic herbs which gave the drink its special flavour. Then he looked at the Chaplain with a cold, hard stare. This was the killer moment.

"I believe you've been seeing Mrs Shawcross. She's been coming to you for spiritual advice. Your neighbours have been telling me how much you have been helping her cope with the breakdown in her marriage. Spending half the night in deep spiritual counselling..."

Mr Latimer's face lost some of its deep tan.

The University Secretary smiled grimly.

"Perhaps, if Mr Krauss succeeds with his wax dolls - and manages to kill off the Vice-Chancellor, you may also find the way is open for your future happiness. I do hope so."

He lifted his glass of Dubonnet.

"Cheers! And may the best man win!"

9: At The Green Man

On the following day, Mr Hayward took Emily out to lunch. He took her to the *Green Man* which made the meal doubly special. She ordered roast duck whilst her host chose filet steak. This was accompanied by a bottle of Nuits St George. Emily assumed that her first article must have found favour with the proprietor of the *Grasshallows Echo*. She could not imagine that other young reporters were treated quite so lavishly.

And, indeed, whilst they were waiting for the starters to arrive, Tom produced the first proof of her article for the Friday paper: "Rudy's Return".

"I was very impressed with this," he said. "Not just the article itself - but also the background material on Mr Krauss. Thanks to you, we now know a great deal more about this young man. Last year, he seemed to be no more than a mindless thug, burning down a laboratory; but you've made him much more interesting. A colourful rogue with whom our readers can identify.

"You have also referred to the faceless mass of new students coming to Grasshallows this autumn. You've taken the trouble to get the correct figure from a quoted source. I checked with the University to see if you were right. Amongst this immense crowd, Rudy stands out.

"I wonder if we might get a photograph of him in his flowing robes? Our readers would like to know what he looks like. Does he wear these garments all the time?"

Emily laughed.

"They're getting a bit grubby now. But he's got a lot of mileage out of them so far. Everyone knows who he is."

"Are you keeping in touch with him?"

"He's in my politics class."

"He's not yet your lover?"

Emily raised her eyebrows.

"I'm not sure that he's all that clean. He may be harbouring some unpleasant diseases." She laughed. "No. I'm remaining faithful to my boyfriend. I'm still hoping he may be out by Christmas."

At this point, the scallops *au gratin* arrived. They were beautifully presented in a shell, garnished with herbs and cream.

The wine waiter discreetly poured out her wine.

"And where is Rudy going next?"

"I am thinking he will be championing the old religions. He

claims to be a Druid - but I don't think he believes in anything."

"Does that mean he'll be going to Stonehenge?"

"Not till next June. He's hoping to organize an overnight bus. But whether the students will be able to afford it - is doubtful, to say the least."

"Most of them will have gone down by then."

"I am thinking so."

Mr Hayward rather enjoyed Emily's quaint accent. In Wales, it seemed perfectly natural. But, in Grasshallows, it made you stop in your tracks to listen to her - even though the city was inhabited by students from many nations.

The starters were cleared away and the roast duck and the filet steak took their place.

"She asked: "Do you come here often?"

"Perhaps once a week. One gets tired of eating at home. And if I stay in the office, its usually just a coffee and a sandwich. Is the food all right at Salisbury?"

"Not very exciting. But as my mother would say: 'It is nutritious'. Their coffee is foul. I make my own."

"Are you thinking about your next article?"

She smiled.

"Yes, I am. There is a Chaplain who is arousing my suspicions. He is not very nice to Rudy. In fact, I am told that he has been to the University Secretary to get him sacked. I am investigating his past life. It will shock your readers."

"Why does he want to get rid of Rudy?"

"Because Rudy upsets his flock. They are all very enthusiastic young Christians. They believe - everything! Even Jonah, look you! But he is angry with Rudy for promoting paganism; telling people how to read Tarot cards and experimenting with spiritualism. I am thinking the students are finding his religion more attractive than theirs."

Emily's eyes twinkled with mischief.

"I have been encouraging him to hold a Hallowe'en party in the botanical gardens. Young ladies with no clothes dancing in the moonlight." She looked serious for a moment. "I have checked. There will be a full moon at Hallowe'en. It will bring out the beast in Rudy! It will certainly make the botanical gardens more interesting."

"So what about the Chaplain?"

"Well, I have discovered the places where he worked before he came to the University. I have spoken to the people in those places. He has deserted his wife and children. I am thinking it will be difficult for him when the truth is known. If anyone is to go, it may be him."

Mr Hayward looked at her plate.

"Is the duck all right?"

"It is gorgeous. What is it they put on it? Orange? Honey? Curacao?"

"Probably all three."

Mr Hayward wished that he too had chosen the duck.

Emily asked: "Is it very expensive?"

"Very."

The wine waiter returned to pour her more wine.

"I am hoping you will not be deducting this from my fee?"

"No. I shall treat you to a good lunch now and again. I'm hoping you'll become one of my star reporters. So what about the Vice-Chancellor? What's happening to him?"

"Rudy is organizing the opposition. The students are very angry with the wretched man. He is now charging the students for their Union building. And their electricity - which has not happened before. They use a lot of electricity. I have the figures. So - the beer - it has gone up by 10p a pint. Everyone knows who is to blame. If the Vice-Chancellor were to enter the building, he would be roasted alive!"

(She did not mention the wax dolls.)

Emily looked the publisher straight in the eye.

"So what will I be getting for my article - and for the picture which I shall arrange?"

Mr Hayward gave a guarded smile.

"Well, Rudy's not yet national news. Perhaps when the Vice-Chancellor is tarred and feathered - or even roasted alive - he will achieve national prominence.

"But it's still page three stuff. It will attract attention. It will make him a local celebrity. It will make our readers yearn for more information about his doings. I think it's worth more than £100. Should we say £250?"

"A lot of work went into it."

"I could see that. You've laid strong foundations for further articles. But we must have the picture. Could you get Rudy - in all his gear - outside the University's main entrance at 4.30pm?"

"If I'm not too drunk! We have our first tutorial this afternoon at 3.00pm. Rudy is gunning for the Fascists!"

Whilst they were talking, Tom had been keeping an eye on two other diners. Now he saw them getting up and coming his way.

"I think we're about to meet some old friends."

Emily, who had just finished her last piece of duck, turned round to see who they were. There was the unpleasant sight of Detective-Inspector Raynes and some other policeman she did not know.

Mr Hayward stood up.

"I thought it was you." He indicated his guest. "I think you will remember this young lady..."

Raynes did not shake hands.

"I don't think I shall ever forget her."

He looked down at the small dark-haired girl - so beautiful, so beguiling, so utterly treacherous.

"What are you doing here?"

"I'm a student at the University..."

"... and working for Tom? I hope he's paying you well?"

There was a sarcastic edge to his voice. From past experience, he knew that Miss Williams would do anything to boost her savings. Blackmail was her chosen method.

Tom Hayward produced the proof article from his inner pocket.

"Do you remember this gentleman?"

Raynes nodded.

"Arson. He got six months. He should have got more."

Emily instantly flared up.

"No, he shouldn't! He did what he believed was right."

Raynes raised his eyebrows.

"He destroyed a building worth about half a million pounds... a lot of valuable equipment... The University lost income... and there was the cost of the trial... I would say he was lucky to only get six months."

Emily was now on her feet.

Raynes remembered the violence of her anger. It was no use provoking her. It would only lead to an unpleasant scene in the hotel dining room. His own reputation would suffer.

Raynes adopted a softer tone of voice.

"So where is Rudy now?"

"He's back in the University - studying politics."

Tom Hayward said: "Emily tells me that he's leading the student campaign against the Vice-Chancellor. A most worthy objective. The man has upset a large number of people. When the students lynch him, Emily'll phone and let you know."

Raynes said: "Much as it may surprise you, I do not revel in violence. I do not like mob rule. I would like people to live peaceably with their neighbours." He looked at Emily. " I hope you will use all your charm and female guile to keep him out of trouble. It's no use arranging a murder just to get a good story!" Then he looked at Tom Hayward. "And you're rich enough as you are. Don't stir up the fires of hell. You know what students can be like once they get out of control..."

There was an embarrassed silence.

"Well," said Raynes, "we must get back to our work. Keep busy. That's what the public expects. Nice to see you again, Tom."

The two policemen departed.

Tom looked at Emily"

"I hope that didn't spoil your meal?"

"No," she said. "It was lovely. But that man really hates me."

"Time is a great healer" said Tom.

His gentle words fell on deaf ears.

Outside the *Green Man*, Raynes said to Detective-

Constable Carlisle: " Well, it's nice to know Rudy is back in town. But we had better keep an eye on her as well. She's malice personified. If there's any murder in the University, she's bound to be involved - if only as a reporter."

Back inside the hotel, over coffee, Miss Williams was contemplating revenge.

10: Impending Divorce

Bill Hobbs sat in the *Kirby Arms* having a pint with his friend, Andy. They often went for a pint on the way home. It gave Linda a chance to get the supper ready and Andy a break from his taxi work.

Bill worked in the maintenance department at the University. He had worked there for almost twenty years. The two men had known each other for most of that time. In fact, Andy had been best man at Bill's wedding. He always asked after his friend's wife in a kindly fashion:

"Is Linda all right?"

"She's doing a lot of overtime."

Bill looked thoughtfully at his friend.

How much did he know?

"I would imagine he keeps her busy."

"Never stops. He's forever writing letters, visiting departments, calling meetings. All that generates a lot of work."

Andy sniffed contemptuously.

"It doesn't make him any more popular."

"I should think he's the most hated man in Grasshallows. Certainly the most hated man in the University."

"If he gets too unpopular, perhaps he'll leave?"

Bill shook his head sadly.

"He'll never leave. Now he's got his teeth into real meat, he'll never let go. He's determined to push his plans through - whatever the cost."

Andy cast his mind back.

"Wasn't it this time last year when he said the maintenance department must go? 'Private firms can do the job more cheaply'."

Bill nodded.

"I'm sure he still believes it. But, last winter, he had a leak in his roof. Did quite a bit of damage in the attic. I was there - right away. Replaced the rotten timber; got the slater to replace about one hundred and fifty slates. We also put in new cast-iron gutters. They had to be specially made. Grade A listed building. You've got to replace like with like so that it'll last another hundred years. No plastic stuff allowed. We did a pretty good job. I think that, after that, he gave us a stay of execution. But, when it suits him, he'll come back with all guns blazing."

"Not a nice man?"

"No."

"I sometimes give his wife a lift in the taxi."

"Queen Freddie!"

"She doesn't like him either. When she gets into the car, she really lets fly!"

Bill wasn't surprised.

"Why doesn't she leave him? He's such a shit."

"I think she enjoys the high life - and the money - and the free house. They've got quite a cushy number."

"Far too cushy if you ask me."

Bill fell silent.

Andy said: "There's quite a few people who would like to bump him off."

"Such as?"

"Dr Cooper. She's one of the Philosophy department. She was sitting in my car one day and she said: 'I've got a pistol. I'm going to kill him. After what he's done to Professor Hampton, he deserves to die'."

"What did he do to Professor Hampton?"

"Gave him a nervous breakdown last June. He won't be back till after Christmas - if then."

"She hasn't killed him yet."

"She's waiting."

"They're always waiting. These academics! They talk but they're too frightened to act. Philosophers have always been cowards."

Andy agreed.

"And Mrs Shawcross - Queen Freddie - tells me that Peter Latimer is also going to get the chop. He's the official chaplain. Apparently, he's already been told on the grapevine: 'Once the Philosophy department goes, you're next! There's no place for God in a modern university'."

"I still don't think these people will do anything."

"Well, perhaps the students will shift him? They're fairly buzzing with anger. Ever since he made them pay a rent for the Students' Union and they had to put up the price of their beer."

But Bill didn't have much faith in students either.

"Students come; students go. But they haven't the power to get rid of him. It needs someone like the University Secretary, Mr Forrester. If he lifted his little finger, people would take the hint. What they need is a palace revolution." He took a swig of his beer. "But it'll never happen."

Andy was worried about his friend. He'd never seen him so depressed. He said: "It's not like you - being so negative and pessimistic. Why should you get so upset about him?"

There was a long silence - lasting perhaps three or four minutes. Bill stared out of the window, seeing nothing. Eventually, he turned to his friend.

"It's because of Linda."

"What's he done to her? Sacked her?"

"No."

Bill's eyes filled with tears.

He looked at his friend.

"You don't know?"

"Nobody's told me anything."

"Well," said Bill. "They're saying Linda's having an affair - with him."

"Who's saying it?"

"People in the maintenance department. I just broke down this afternoon. They sent me home - early. But, of course, she wasn't there. She's doing overtime!"

Andy found it difficult to say anything to his friend. He too was thunderstruck. Linda was such a sensible person. She was devoted to Bill. He had always thought the two of them were a perfect couple. They'd never had any children; but that seemed to bring them even closer together. It was impossible to believe that she would have been so stupid as to have an affair with that creep.

"Have you spoken to Linda?"

"I've tried to. But not today. We've had quite a few rows about all the extra work she's been doing... if it is work..."

Andy felt out of his depth.

He knew what he would say to anyone else in the same circumstances. But Bill and Linda were probably his best friends. It was difficult to take a strong line with either of them.

"What are they saying - these people?"

"They say she's been going back to the University House and drinking with him. One of the tradesmen said she'd been seen in her underwear running into the bathroom. I've noticed she's been drinking - it's on her breath when she gets home. But if I say anything about him, she blows up. We have a row. Then she sends me to Coventry for the rest of the evening.

"'She's protecting him,' they say. Helping him to carry out his diabolical policies. They'll soon be saying she should go - as well as him. It's a hopeless situation."

Andy asked anxiously: "What are you going to do? You're not going to get a divorce - or anything like that?"

"I did think of suicide - this afternoon..." He looked at Andy's face. "... but only for about five minutes... No," he said grimly. "I've decided - for everyone's sake - not just Linda's - to get rid of him myself. Now I know the pressures everyone else is under."

Andy admired his friend's courage; but the solution was foolhardy. Bill was not the sort of person to commit murder. He needed to be disabused of the idea immediately.

"You're bound to get caught. That detective - Raynes - he's got a terrific reputation for solving murders. He'd get on to you very quickly. Murderers always leave clues - even when they think they've committed the perfect crime. Even if you did kill him, that wouldn't help Linda much; not if you go to jail."

"Well," said Bill slowly, " the way I look at it is this. If I've lost Linda - and perhaps I have - what else is there in my life? We have no children. My only brother lives in Australia and I don't see much of him. If I did get put in jail, it'd only be for a few years. It wouldn't be the end of the world." He smiled. "I might even become a bit of a hero - getting rid of him!"

He looked happier and more confident.

"Linda might even be proud of me…"

"She might."

"And anyway, I don't intend to get caught. I intend to make everyone think it was an accident. I've been thinking about it for some time. Ever since I was working on his roof. I said to myself: 'Bill Hobbs, what would you do to get rid of this bastard?' And the answer's quite simple. Electrocute him. Send 10,000 volts through his body when he touches a metal object that's wired up to a plug. They still haven't re-wired the University House. The electrics are dreadful. They're frightened of changing the character of the house. Digging into ancient walls. They've been arguing about it for years. I had a look at the circuits when I was in the building. They were positively lethal.

"Once you've electrocuted him, you remove the cable, pull out the plug. There's no evidence to connect me with the murder. He'll be lying on the floor. Someone'll find him. I don't think even your precious Inspector Raynes would be able to solve that one. Providing I leave no fingerprints and I go twenty miles down the road to get rid of the cable and plug. If no one sees me going into the house - or leaving it - I should be all right."

"You're thinking of doing it in the University House?"

"I know my way around. I've got a plan of all the circuits. I've got a key to the house - at work. I've made a copy and brought it home. I've put it in a tin box on a shelf in the garage. I've labelled it 'Tool Box'. Linda won't throw it out.

"I'll probably need to do a recce beforehand. I can easily arrange some excuse: I've come back to check the woodwork in the attic' - or something like that. All I need to do is to make sure the equipment will work. I'm not going to do it on the spur of the moment. This needs careful planning.

"I'll look up his appointments' diary. Linda carries it around with her. I'll choose an evening when he'll be on his own; when he comes back late from some meeting. And that's it. The perfect crime - and one less rat polluting the earth."

Andy did not know what to say. He had never thought Bill would do anything so drastic. He was not a bloodthirsty man. In fact, he was extremely placid. If he had worked all this out - and was prepared to do it - he must be pretty desperate. It seemed a good plan. A simple plan. It had a good chance of working - and of Bill not being caught.

All Andy could say was: "Your secret is safe with me. I hope you don't have to take such action. I hope Linda comes to her senses. Indeed, I hope it's a nasty rumour about her having an affair. I'm sure it is. All I can say is: I think you are being very brave. But if you do do it - as your oldest friend - I'll stand by you. Whatever happens, Inspector Raynes won't get a word out of me."

11: Saving Linda

The University Secretary chose his moment carefully. He knew the Vice-Chancellor was away in London seeing some of his cost-cutting cronies. Linda Hobbs would not have too much work to do. More importantly, she would be alone.

He arrived at the Vice-Chancellor's office at about 11.00am - his favourite time for seeing people. He had cleared all his correspondence and dealt with the latest batch of problems. Mrs Hobbs would have dealt with all her correspondence. He knew she was an ultra-efficient person.

He told his secretary where he was going and said that he was not to be disturbed for the next hour. His secretary knew why he was going to see Linda. She knew it might be difficult. She whispered: "Good luck!"

So there was a knock at the door.

"Come in."

Russell Forrester put his head round the door.

"Are you busy? Could I have a word with you?"

Linda knew immediately why he had called.

In fact, she had expected some such visit.

But not quite so soon.

"Please come in."

Russell wandered over to the window and looked down at the large rose garden beside the main entrance to the University. He looked - but did not see.

He turned back - and sat down on a chair beside her desk.

"Linda, are you really happy working for Timothy?"

"Not really! Who is? But one just gets on with it."

"I know. I know. I have the same problem."

He swallowed.

"Now, Linda, people tell me that you've been doing a great deal of overtime. But it doesn't seem to appear on the wage sheets."

"I wouldn't put in for overtime. Dr Shawcross wouldn't approve."

"No. Of course he wouldn't! But how much extra work are you doing?"

"A couple of hours most evenings."

"It mounts up. I also hear you've been going to meetings outwith the University - with Timothy. That must have added to your duties?"

She knew what he wanted to ask.

"You think I've been seeing too much of Dr Shawcross just lately? Time spent beyond the call of duty?"

"Well, yes."

"He has asked me to do a lot of extra work - much of it highly confidential - because it involves cuts in budgets and personnel. He also likes me to take notes at some of the meetings he goes to."

"Are these meetings essential?"

"Perhaps not. But he has asked me to go with him and I don't like to refuse."

"So, when you go, it is for work purposes - not personal pleasure?"

Linda chose her words carefully:

"I feel - as his Personal Secretary - that I have to support him. No one else seems to like him. I think he feels very isolated. He trusts me. I don't share his views… I've made that perfectly clear to him… on an almost daily basis… but my duty is to do my best to help him in his work - whatever my personal feelings may be."

"Quite! Quite!"

Mr Forrester now came to the difficult bit.

"A report has come to my ears that for some of these overtime sessions, you have been going to the University House."

Linda nodded.

"Is that true?"

"Yes."

"You will perhaps be aware that there is a rumour going about that you have been having an affair with Dr Shawcross."

"Yes. My husband told me last night. He works in the Maintenance department."

"It was a member of the Maintenance department that reported this. It was said that you had been seen - in your underwear - going into a bathroom at the University House. Is that true?"

Linda Hobbs smiled.

"It is true."

"Ah."

"But it's not what you think. On one occasion, I did spill milk over my skirt in the kitchen. I was pouring out a pan of milk into a flask. I did take off my skirt to scrub it down in the bathroom. The report you received was perfectly true."

Mr Forrester looked greatly relieved.

"I'm very glad it was nothing more serious. We can easily deal with this rumour - and say that there has been no inappropriate behaviour."

Mrs Hobbs did not smile.

She looked anxious.

"But there has been inappropriate behaviour. Not on that occasion - but at other times. It has been troubling me greatly. I should have come and spoken to you long before now.

"Dr Shawcross has come to depend on me - not just for the work I do - but also for emotional support. There are times when he completely breaks down and weeps in my arms.

"He derives absolutely no help from his wife. No help at all - and no love. She hates him - and he knows she is having an affair with... Peter Latimer..."

"I know about that. I have spoken to him."

"Well, I'm glad you know. But it doesn't help things here - or at home.

"Dr Shawcross works hard but he does need some human warmth and encouragement. Over the past year, I have felt really sorry for him. He is so unhappy. Always reviled. At first, I thought he had a thick skin. That he could take it. But as time went on, I found myself comforting him... putting an arm round him... saying kind words... I didn't intend it to go any further. But he has kissed me; hugged me; thanked me. He has made it quite clear that he would like the relationship to go a lot further..."

Linda sighed deeply.

"There have been many intimate moments - but I have prevented things going too far. There is no doubt about what he would like to happen. He has asked me many times to have sex with him. I have refused. But he has pressurised me; threatened me. I didn't report it because I didn't want anyone else to know. He is my boss - and I have tried to protect his reputation. I thought I could handle it; but the last few weeks have been quite unbearable."

Linda broke into tears. She wept bitterly. Mr Forrester did

not make any move to comfort her. But he was deeply upset. This was a clear case of sexual harassment. Dr Shawcross would have to be dealt with. Linda would have to be moved. There would be a major crisis. Harsh words. If this got out into the public domain, the reputation of the University would suffer. The Press would go for Linda. Her life would be made completely intolerable. It would probably break up her marriage. The matter must be handled with great delicacy.

When she stopped crying, Russell Forrester said: "How is your husband coping with this?"

She clasped her handkerchief tightly in her right hand.

"He says he has suspected it for some time. He has accused me of having an affair and when I say I haven't, he accuses me of being a liar. I know he loves me very much and this has hurt him. Especially when the rumours have come from his own department."

She wiped her eyes carefully.

"We had a terrible row last night. He said he had been thinking of committing suicide. He said he couldn't bear it any more. I said that he was blackmailing me. I walked out of the house and went back to my mother's. It's all a complete mess. I'm so sorry for causing all this trouble."

Mr Forrester himself was very fond of Linda. He had watched her develop - and grow - in confidence and skill. It was he who had recommended her to Dr Bulman and he had reckoned her to be strong enough to guide the new Vice-Chancellor. But Dr Shawcross' problems, which no doubt had been bubbling under the surface for many years, had come to a head with his move to Grasshallows. Linda had mishandled the situation - but the fault was not entirely hers. In a more peaceful era, she would still make an excellent Personal Secretary for a Vice-Chancellor. She must be preserved for that role.

Whilst she had been weeping, he determined what he must do.

"Now, Linda, listen to me very carefully. This is what we are going to do… I am going to move you from this post as Personal Secretary on health grounds. You will immediately take four weeks holiday - and use it to put your marriage right. If you choose to go abroad, I will also grant your husband four weeks paid leave. In your place, Mrs Gordon will be employed as a temporary secretary for Dr Shawcross.

"The moment Timothy comes back from London, I shall speak to him. I shall tell him that his behaviour has been quite unacceptable and must not be repeated. If there is the slightest recurrence, the matter will be brought to the attention of the police and the Senate. This would almost certainly lead to his enforced resignation.

"I shall ask him - in view of his deep unpopularity, the unhappy state of his marriage and the sheer impossibility of carrying through his plans for the University - whether he wishes to continue in his post. If not, I shall press for an early resignation.

"Until he departs, you will continue to work in my office in a temporary capacity. When - and if - he departs, then I will restore you to your present job to prepare the way for a new Vice-Chancellor.

"In the meantime, you must say absolutely nothing to the Press. And this applies to your husband as well. If Dr Shawcross phones you at home, you must put down the phone. You must not meet him. The relationship has ended."

He looked at Linda.

"Do you understand?"

Linda nodded.

"My plans must not be mentioned to anyone. Should there be any leak, the University public relations department will clamp down on it immediately. I am sure it is in everyone's best interests - especially yours and Timothy's - to resolve this matter as quickly as possible. If you could put all your current business in this office in order - for Mrs Gordon to take over - your holiday should start no later than 3.30pm this afternoon."

Detective-Inspector Raynes was leafing through the pages of the latest copy of the *Grasshallows Echo*, when he came across Rudy's photograph on page five of the newspaper; and, beside it, the article "Rudy's Return" - from "our University correspondent."

He snorted.

"What's Tom Hayward doing - promoting an ex-jailbird?"

Detective-Constable Carlisle came over to see what was annoying his colleague.

"Bit different from the Rudy we knew."

"I never thought we would see him again."

"He's got religion," said Raynes. "We're led to believe that Rudy has given up his violent past and is now providing leadership for those seeking to follow the ancient religions."

"Did that young lady write it? The one we saw in the *Green Man*?"

"Emily? Yes, I expect she did." He shook his head. "Leopards don't change their spots that quickly."

"Perhaps she's become his lover?"

"Yes. Perhaps she has… Her mother would have hoped for better…" He put down the newspaper. "Actually, I did wonder if Tom Hayward was lining her up to be his mistress. He might be feeling a bit jealous."

"Presumably he must approve? Or he wouldn't be paying for the article? She must be making a few quid out of this."

"Every woman has her price!" said Raynes.

He had a very low opinion of Miss Williams.

Carlisle looked out of the window.

"Shall we go and see Rudy…?"

"Why not! At least we can find out where he is living. Just in case we have to make an arrest." Raynes threw aside a consultation document he had been reading: 'The Misuse of Invalid Vehicles'. "Anything would be more interesting than that! What are you doing?"

"Our expenses for September. We're about £300 down on

August. Mark you, nothing much has been happening."

Raynes smiled and rubbed his hands together.

"We need someone like Rudy to fire us up."

* * * *

Carlisle phoned the University Accommodation office and asked where Mr Krauss was staying this year.

"Palmerston College. Second floor. Room 59."

"I hope he's in," said Raynes.

"Perhaps the concierge will give us a key and let us have a look round?"

"Let us hope he's not spending the afternoon with Miss Williams!"

Carlisle suspected that Tom Hayward might not be the only one suffering from a tinge of jealousy.

"Where is Palmerston?"

"On the outskirts of the city, near the Botanical Gardens."

Being early afternoon, the roads were clear.

Raynes walked into the building and showed his police identity card.

"Is Mr Krauss in? I believe he's in Room 59."

The concierge looked at the key board.

"He's in. But he could be anywhere in the College."

Rudy was in. He was writing his first essay of the term: "The political consequences of Fascism in Italy." His viewpoint was predictable - he was against Fascism - but he needed facts to support his prejudices.

He was rather annoyed at being disturbed.

"Mr Krauss? Good afternoon... You will remember me."

God! It was the fuzz.

"Come in - if you must."

There were two of them. Rudy recognised the second man. That was Raynes' sidekick - the one who took the notes.

Detective-Constable Carlisle sat down whilst Raynes wandered round the room and looked at the large gravestone sitting in the far corner. It must have been a fairly recent arrival. It still had live moss on it.

"Is there a problem?"

"No."

"Well, why are you here?"

Raynes said politely: "We've just been reading the article in the *Echo*. Did Emily write it?"

"Yep. She's a bright chick."

"Nice photograph."

"Not bad."

"She suggests that your days as an Animal Liberator are over."

"Yep. You have to move with the times."

"So it's religion this year?"

"Paganism. It's greatly under-rated. Our forbears had the benefits of Paganism for over five hundred years. They built massive structures like Stonehenge. It was an observatory, you know. They watched the movement of the stars; predicted eclipses; where and when the sun would rise. They worked it all out. They were quite brainy people."

Raynes looked at the gravestone.

"Is this part of the Pagan cult?"

Rudy put on his most professional manner: "It's part of the Symposium I'm giving this evening. Contact with distant relatives... Renewing our relationships with the departed... Discovering our rich heritage with the hereafter..."

"Is Mr Jeremy Dawkins one of your relations?"

"No. But he's exhibit No 1 in my talk."

"Do you know a great deal about Mr Dawkins?"

"We hope to discover more tonight. Why don't you come along? There'll be a few spare seats."

Raynes ignored the invitation.

"Where did the gravestone come from?"

"I'm not sure. Somebody brought it along. I believe it was found in a stone-mason's yard."

Raynes said to himself: 'That sounds like a lie.'

"Will it be returned after your... Symposium?"

"Of course."

"We'll give you till Monday evening to get it back."

"I'll make sure the people who brought it - return it."

"Thank you. Is there anything political you're doing in the University this term?"

"Not really. We're fighting the University authorities over their decision - their sudden decision - to make us pay rent for the Students' Union. It's been rent free for the past fifty years. But that... bastard... if I may use such a strong word in your presence... has really stitched us up. We've had to raise the price of a pint by 10p. The students - all of them - are really kicking up."

"Capitalism in action!" said Raynes.

"You don't like it either?"

"If I were a student, I should react violently."

Rudy Krauss felt that the Inspector had some redeeming features. Not many - but perhaps one or two."

Raynes continued: "I hope, Mr Krauss, that your activities this year will be non-violent?"

"Well," said Rudy, "we pagans pursue a path of peace. We believe in a return to nature, to the soil, to the water, to the heavenly bodies which move constantly around us. Our ceremonies are dedicated to love and fertility."

Raynes smiled.

"I know Miss Williams' mother. I don't think she would welcome too much fertility, if you know what I mean?"

"Got it! But she's not up for grabs. She's got a boyfriend. Coming out at Christmas, I'm told."

"He's another man of violence. I'd watch out if I were you."

Raynes stood up.

"You weren't planning any violence against the Vice-Chancellor?"

"Not me. But I can't answer for the other guys. Some of them are really gunning for him in a big way. If they could tar and feather him, they would. But, as for me, I'm a reformed character. A man of peace."

"I don't believe it," said Raynes.

Rudy looked towards a small brown cardboard box near the door.

"Would you like to buy a set of Tarot cards? They're only £10 a pack."

"No," said Raynes. "I can think of better things to do with my money!"

And found himself wondering what Mrs May might be doing that evening...

13: A Time of Trial

"And how did you get on with the Vice-Chancellor?"

Russell Forrester was speaking to Mrs Gordon on Friday afternoon after her first full day working with Dr Shawcross.

"He wasn't very pleased to see me. Of course, he'd received your note. I don't think he could believe that Linda had been spirited away so swiftly. He tried to phone her several times; but obviously he didn't get an answer. I suggested that she might already be abroad."

Mr Forrester nodded happily.

Mrs Gordon continued: "He asked me if I knew where she was going. I said 'No' - but I thought it would be somewhere warm where she could recover."

"'Recover?' he said.

"'Yes,' I said, 'she's had a very serious breakdown.'

"He was silent after that. I didn't say: 'It was your fault'. But it left him thinking.

"Then he came back.

"'Are you able to type out this report?'

"'Of course,' I said. 'But the correspondence has to be dealt with first. I came in early, but there's still a lot to be done. I've left the first part on your desk'.

'Oh, yes.'

"He hadn't looked at it. Too full of his own ideas. He seemed quite lost without her. I got stuck in. Typed his report. He said very little. I kept adding things to the pile on his desk. I said that I'd wait till he dealt with them."

"Did he deal with them?"

"Eventually. But then he went off to the Chaplaincy at 4.00pm. I believe he was intending to have a showdown with the chaplains."

Russell Forrester looked pleased.

"You've done a good job. Keep his nose to the grindstone. Give him no comfort. No comfort whatsoever!"

* * * *

Dr Shawcross did not arrive at the Chaplaincy in a very good mood. His first question - as he crossed the threshold - was: "How much does this Chaplaincy cost us each year?"

Peter Latimer looked surprised.

"I've no idea. We don't deal with the finances. We just get on with the job."

"The job?"

"Caring for the students."

The Vice-Chancellor looked round the empty coffee bar.

"I don't see any students."

"They're still at lectures. They'll be here this evening. Every room is used. The Christian Union are in the main hall and this coffee bar. There's about a hundred of them. The Students' Welfare Committee meet in the library and the Ba'his use my office."

"What about the Jews?"

"They meet tomorrow - on the Sabbath."

A small, smiling little man was waiting to be introduced.

"This is Father Campolini, our new Catholic Chaplain…"

There was a brief touch of hands.

"And how much do we pay you?"

Father Campolini looked surprised.

"Pay? I receive nothing. I am sponsored by my Diocese."

"No expenses? Travelling expenses?"

Father Campolini shook his head.

Dr Shawcross dug deeper.

"Who pays for your candles? Your communion wine? Your laundry?"

Peter Latimer intervened.

"The Chaplaincy pays for those things."

"And who gets the collections? I presume you do take collections?"

"They go to my church."

"You have a church in the city?"

"St Joseph's. A very fine Church. You must come and see it…"

Dr Shawcross pursed his lips.

"I am a humanist. I have no time for religion. I really do not see why the churches themselves cannot fund the Chaplaincy, pay for the heating, lighting and a reasonable rent for the use of the premises. Why it should all fall on the University, I do not know."

He looked at Peter Latimer with a chilling stare.

"I believe you are costing us £40,000 a year - plus a free house. Very generous holidays. Are you the only person being paid?"

The official Chaplain was very annoyed to have his salary details made public. Father Campolini would tell everyone what he was being paid. It could be most embarrassing.

"I have a secretary," he said defensively. "She works part-time. Mornings during term time. We also have two University cleaners who are here for a couple of hours each morning. That's all."

"No other chaplains? Rabbis? Imams? Any high priests?"

"None."

Dr Shawcross smiled contemptuously.

"You are not yet employing Mr Rudy Krauss?"

"Certainly not!"

"I believe he is providing very effective leadership for the Pagan Society."

Peter Latimer sneered.

"Selling badges - and tarot cards. We don't encourage such things."

The Vice-Chancellor continued to twist the Chaplain's tail.

"I believe he's holding a Symposium in Palmerston College this evening. 'Understanding the Dark Arts: Our

Contact with the Departed'. I've seen his posters around the University. Were you thinking of going to the lecture?"

"Certainly not."

"It might be interesting?"

"I think many of our Christian students would find it deeply offensive."

Peter Latimer began to feel the conversation was moving his way.

"Would you like to sit down, Dr Shawcross? Would you like some coffee? We would like to talk to you about that young man. We're finding him a very disruptive influence."

Whilst Father Campolini was pouring out the coffee, Peter Latimer laid into his current *bête noire*.

"We were very surprised that he was allowed back into the University after all the damage he did to the Animal Laboratory last year. We thought the University Court had rusticated him - permanently. But then he re-appeared last month, posing as a religious leader, dressing up in that ridiculous costume and uttering all sorts of religious nonsense. I've spoken to Russell Forrester about him; but he won't do anything. I think he's enjoying the embarrassment he's causing."

Mention of the University Secretary reminded Dr Shawcross of the sudden departure of Linda Hobbs. Russell Forrester could move pawns round the board as and when it suited him. He was subject to no controls.

The Vice-Chancellor listened more attentively to Mr Latimer's complaints.

"He's the person leading the campaign in the Students' Union against the higher price of beer. I believe he is also urging the students to use black magic against you."

"Against me?"

"Father Blazer - he's the curate at St Benedict's - he tells me that the students have been pinching his votive candles to make effigies of you and then pierce them with pins."

Dr Shawcross laughed.

"I haven't felt them yet. I'm still perfectly healthy."

Peter Latimer shrugged his shoulders.

"But this is not something which should be happening in a modern university. This is taking us back to the dark ages."

The Vice-Chancellor drained the final dregs of a particularly tasteless cup of coffee.

"Well," he said, "I regard this as a spiritual problem. If you can't deal with Rudy, what does that tell us about the power of your faith? Useless! If you can't even perform a decent exorcism, what justification is there for us spending this vast amount of money to maintain the Chaplaincy? We'd be better turning this building into a squash court! Prove that your prayers can work - on Rudy - and I might have a change of heart. Otherwise…"

He drew a line with his finger across his throat.

The message was painfully clear.

Time was not on Mr Latimer's side.

14: Sacking The Chauffeur

Peter Latimer may have felt the scourge of the Vice-Chancellor's tongue; but Dr Shawcross reserved his full venom for Mr Clifford Brown. For some time, he had been wondering whether his Jamaican-born chauffeur had been reporting on his movements to the University Secretary.

Clifford was a man who kept himself very much to himself. He said: 'Yes, sir' and 'Right away'. He was an excellent driver and never spoke unless he was directly spoken to. He never intervened in any conversation and never cracked any jokes. The Vice-Chancellor regarded him as a complete cipher.

But perhaps, behind this outer wall of discretion, he was listening - and taking note? He had driven Linda and himself to many meetings. He had waited in the lobbies of many hotels whilst they dined. They had chatted away to each other in the back of the car. They had joked and laughed. Some of the jokes had been quite risqué. Perhaps, all the time, Clifford had been reporting back?

How else would Russell Forrester have known so much about them? She would never have said a word. She was utterly loyal. He knew that he could trust Linda not to say anything. There were no other witnesses of their time together. So it must be him.

As the car returned to University House, he decided to have it out with Clifford.

"I should like a few words with you - before you put the car away."

"Fine."

Dr Shawcross watched his face in the mirror. Clifford did not look particularly perturbed.

"I should like to know whether you have been speaking to anyone about myself and Mrs Hobbs?"

"No, sir."

He sounded flippant.

"I'm told she's had a nervous breakdown."

"Nothing to do with me, sir. She looked perfectly fine when I last saw her."

"Well, I thought so too. But she's been sent away for a holiday."

"Some people have all the luck."

Dr Shawcros felt there was a distinct lack of sincerity in the man's voice.

"I think you may be responsible…"

"Not me, sir."

"You've been present on all our journeys. You've heard all our conversations. I think you have been indiscreet. You have reported things to the University Secretary!"

Clifford Brown took off his peaked hat and turned round in his seat to face his accuser.

"That is a lie… sir!"

"Who else has been present? I have never spoken to anyone. Mrs Hobbs would never have said a word. But Mr Forrester, the University Secretary, has accused me of having an inappropriate relationship with my secretary."

"Well, he probably knows more than me."

"How can he? There must have been information passed about our conversations together. You are the only person who has been with us. How much have you been paid to spy on us?"

Clifford Brown was becoming extremely angry at the accusations being made against him.

"I ain't said nothing!"

He opened the front door of the car and put on his peaked hat. He opened the rear door of the Jaguar.

"I know my place," he said.

Dr Shawcross leapt out of the car - his face contorted with anger.

"You have betrayed my trust. I shall see that you are dismissed. I expect the utmost loyalty and discretion from my staff. You have been told. At the end of this month, you will collect your P45. I shall find a more trustworthy successor."

He turned on his heel and walked into the University House.

Clifford Brown was almost in tears. He flung his driving keys at the departing figure - but he never noticed. They lay on the gravel.

With tears in his eyes, he turned back to his car. He loved the Jaguar. It was a beautiful car. Such a joy to drive. He would never be behind the wheel of such a superb limousine again. It was his pride and joy. And Dr Shawcross had falsely accused him.

Of course he had noticed their goings-on in the back of the car; but there had never been anything sordid or immoral. A bit of flirting perhaps; but mostly they had talked about business matters and Clifford wasn't interested in that.

All he was interested in was the car. The gentle touch on the accelerator. The sudden burst of power. The silent brush of the tyres. The glow of the dashboard lights on a dark night. The powerful headlights showing a clear road ahead.

And all this was going to be taken away from him! Just because Dr Shawcross refused to believe him. What could he say to his wife? How could he tell her he was losing his job?

Would he ever be able to get another decent job if the University gave him a lousy reference?

Sad and humiliated, he went back and picked up the keys. He returned to the front seat of the car and drove the car slowly round the north side of the house to the old stables, where it was locked away. He did not go back to the house with the keys - as he normally did - and hang them on their special hook in the kitchen. He locked the car and the stable door; and took away all the keys with him. He was so angry.

As he got into his own car - a battered old Vauxhall Cavalier - he decided that the only thing to do was to speak to Mr Forrester. He knew he was one of the high-ups in the University. He was a very important man; but he no idea what he looked like. Clifford believed that he was the only person who would listen to him - who would protect him. Anyone who was an enemy of Dr Shawcross must be a friend.

* * * *

When Dr Shawcross entered the University House, he was still in a raging temper. He flung his brief case down on the chaise longue in the hallway and headed straight for his cocktail cabinet; and poured himself a very strong gin and tonic.

Freddie Shawcross heard the slam of the front door and read the signs immediately. She stayed in the kitchen putting the final touches to their evening meal. She looked at the bottle of wine that she had chosen - and immediately went to get a more expensive wine. At least he would not be able to complain about the food.

She carried the tray through to the dining room and said nothing. She knew that any fatuous comment - such as 'Have you had a nice day?' - would only make things worse. She made sure that everything looked fresh, tasty and sparkling - including herself.

Dr Shawcross came into the dining room with his tumbler of gin, looking like thunder. He headed for the table and made an appreciative grunt when he saw the wine.

Freddie took her napkin out of its silver ring. In silence, they devoured the salmon and fresh lobster. By the time they had got to the second course, Timothy had calmed down and was at least willing to speak.

"Russell's taken away my secretary."

"Mrs Hobbs?"

"He's given me a complete cow. A Mrs Gordon."

Freddie knew how to be diplomatic.

"What's happened to Mrs Hobbs?"

"Russell says she's had some sort of nervous breakdown. He's sent her away on holiday." He downed the rest of his gin and tonic before turning to the wine. "And he blames me!"

Freddie felt like saying: 'I'm not surprised.' She had heard far too much about the 'delectable Mrs Hobbs' - the perfect secretary. She had known the relationship could not last much longer. Something had to give. The sheer intensity of coping with Timothy professionally - and emotionally - would prove too much. But she could not express her true feelings…

"Did she speak to Russell?"

"No. I don't think she did. I think someone reported us."

"Who would do that?"

Timothy's brow darkened.

"I think it was Clifford."

Freddie was surprised.

"Why would he do that?"

Dr Shawcross shrugged his shoulders.

"When we go anywhere, he's always there. He was perfectly capable of listening to our conversation. Putting two and two together and making five." Timothy looked at his wife. "There was nothing scandalous to report. No kissing or cuddling. Most of the time we were discussing business matters. But he might have got the wrong idea."

Knowing her husband's selfish nature, Freddie knew that Timothy would not hesitate to kiss and cuddle any available female; but surely he would not be so stupid as to do it in front of the chauffeur?

She waited to be told more.

In the meantime, she ate her peppered steak and wondered if Linda Hobbs was pregnant. That would prove embarrassing. But she reckoned the 'delectable Mrs Hobbs' must be in her late forties - too old for that sort of thing. But it would certainly be bad publicity for Timothy. She wondered how much longer the University would put up with him.

Her husband clearly enjoyed his meal. As he drank his second glass of wine, his confidence returned.

"Anyway, I sacked him."

"Who?"

"The chauffeur."

Freddie was worried.

"They'll accuse you of being racist!"

"Why?"

"Well, he's Jamaican. You can't sack coloured people. He'll take you to a tribunal. It'll be all over the papers. He'll receive the sympathy vote - not you. It could be most unpleasant." She paused. "Are you allowed to sack him?"

"If you can't sack your own chauffeur, who can you sack? I've told him he'll be leaving at the end of the month. The University will have to find someone else. I won't have him."

Freddie said nothing. She was sure that her husband had made another major blunder. She liked Clifford. She didn't think he would report anyone. He seemed to live in his own little world. He wasn't interested in University affairs. He was only interested in the car. That was how she saw it.

But she wasn't going to say any more.

Timothy would have to answer for his own mistakes.

Freddie looked at the clock.

"Remember, we're going to the theatre."

"I don't really want to go anywhere."

His wife shrugged her shoulders.

"We'll have to take my car."

"Why?"

"Clifford hasn't returned the keys."

* * * *

Mr Russell Forrester had only been at his desk for half an hour, when he was told that a man called Clifford Brown was at reception trying to arrange an appointment to see him.

Did he want to see him?

"Who is Clifford Brown?" he asked. "Is he one of our employees?"

"He's Dr Shawcross' chauffeur."

She gave Russell a knowing look.

"Of course I know who he is! I didn't know he was called Clifford. Send him in."

"You don't want to arrange a later appointment?"

The University Secretary looked thoughtful.

"No. I think if Mr Brown is pressing for an urgent appointment, I should see him right away."

"Would you like coffee brought in?"

"No. But we might need a box of tissues."

The chauffeur was amazed that Mr Forrester was willing to see him so swiftly. Had Dr Shawcross already spoken to him? Told him of his suspicions? He had certainly said nothing when he was being driven into work that morning.

"Mr Brown?"

Russell rose to his feet to greet his visitor. "Please sit down - and tell me what's troubling you."

Clifford sat down at the other side of the large desk. He felt very small and insignificant. He was nervous and his voice sounded husky.

"Well, sir. Mr Forrester, sir. I'm here because Dr Shawcross has sacked me. He told me to collect my P45 at the end of the month."

"Well, that's a bit drastic, Mr Brown. What have you done?"

"Nothing, sir. But he's accused me of speaking to you about himself and Mrs Hobbs. He says that I've been reporting their conversations to you. He says I've been indiscreet and disloyal. But I never have, sir. As God is my witness…"

Russell looked at him with some surprise.

"No, Mr Brown. You haven't said a word to me. In fact,

we've never met before. But I've seen you driving the University car."

Clifford broke into tears.

"I love that car, sir. It's the most beautiful car I've ever driven. And now he's taking it away. For no good reason. He's lying, sir. I've never said anything about him to anyone. Not even my wife. I'd never sneak on anyone."

"Of course you wouldn't."

Russell Forrester pushed the box of tissues closer. Clifford wiped his eyes and his nose.

"There's nothing to tell you, sir. They mostly discussed business matters. I never listened to them…"

"You were busy driving the car…"

"… but he's accusing me of causing Mrs Hobbs to have a nervous breakdown. He says she's been sent on holiday and he's extremely angry."

Russell thought to himself:

'Another victim! How many more?'

He pulled his papers together.

"Mr Brown," he said, "there is no reason for you to be dismissed. You will not be collecting your P45 at the end of the month. I would like you to continue driving the University car. I'm sure it is safe in your hands."

He wondered how much more he should say.

"Dr Shawcross is naturally distressed about the departure of his secretary - but it is no fault of yours. And there is no justification for him taking out his anger on you. Dr Shawcross has no power to sack you."

He paused - to give some weight to his words. "You are a valued member of the University and you have an important job to do. I would ask you to ignore what Dr Shawcross has said. There may be more abuse but I would be personally grateful if you could hide your feelings and say nothing. If Dr Shawcross should speak to me, I will tell him that I have spoken to you; and you will remain the chauffeur of the University car."

Clifford looked deeply relieved.

"Thank you, sir. I knew as how you'd listen to me."

Russell Forrester smiled.

"I'm very glad to meet you, Mr Brown. You're doing a splendid job. Make sure you look after that car."

As Clifford left the room, he muttered under his breath: "Poor sod!"

15: Sunday Evening with the Chaplain

Sunday had already been pencilled in to Emily's diary. She felt it was now time to attend one of the Chaplain's 'open nights' in Sandringham Crescent.

As she had told Mr Hayward, during their lunch at the Green Man, she had been busy doing her homework on Peter Latimer.

First of all, she had gone to Crockford's Clerical Directory in the Reference department of the University Library. That listed the Chaplain's past appointments. Then she phoned up members of the parishes where he had served before coming to Grasshallows. She had posed as a friend of a fellow student who was going out with the Chaplain and was hoping to get engaged to him. She said that there were some things that worried her about Mr Latimer. Could her friend be making a great mistake?

The unanimous opinion of the locals was that, where women were concerned, Mr Latimer could not be trusted one inch. Whilst he had been their vicar, there had been one of two scandals which only came to light after he had left.

What was perhaps more worrying was that, no sooner had he been appointed the official Chaplain at Grasshallows, than he deserted his wife and three children. Yes, three! One of them had learning difficulties. He had tried to hide that fact from his congregation.

His wife was living in a nearby village. Peter had rented a nice house - and it was thought that he might still be supporting her. But the separation had caused the family a lot of grief.

No one questioned Emily's credentials. They were quite willing to tell her all they knew. Mr Hayward had been proved right. People were only too willing to report on the sins of others. They would of course have been much more guarded if they had known that their stories would appear in print. But Emily's expressed desire to help her friend proved to be ideal bait.

It was all so gruesome that Emily had no hesitation in phoning up one of her older sisters, Ruth, to ask for a helping hand.

Ruth also had a passion for rooting out scandal. She knew that Emily was working for Mr Hayward. She was only too happy to drive over to the village where Mrs Latimer now lived, which was only twenty miles away from her own home. She had taken photographs of the house and spoken to the lady herself. Mrs Latimer's bitterness was ripe for revenge.

Ruth had changed the storyline just a little. She implied that the person going out with Mr Latimer was someone she had known at university. She was told the full story. She had been introduced to the children and stayed for tea. She dictated the main facts to Emily on Saturday afternoon.

So, with all her homework done, Emily drafted out the text for her next article in the *Grasshallows Echo*: "The Hidden Years of a University Chaplain." That should be enough to scupper him. Rudy would be pleased and, with a little bit of luck, it would soon be in the *News of the World*. She hoped that Mr Hayward would reward her with a larger cheque.

* * * *

Ten days had passed since Emily had seen Mr Latimer at the Societies' Fayre. She hoped that he would not recognise her.

So she dressed in a grey jumper and a grey pair of jeans. She could not change her looks or her voice, but she looked as demure as possible - no make up, no lipstick. Carrying her Welsh Bible, she joined a group of five or six students as they arrived at the Chaplain's house. She did not want to go in alone. She sat down on a royal blue pouffe beside the window. Mr Latimer was busy in the kitchen, preparing the coffee.

By the time everyone had arrived, the sitting room was full. People were sitting on the floor or propped up against the bookcase. Most of them seemed to know each other; but she did not recognise anyone. Mugs of coffee were handed round - followed by milk, sugar and chocolate biscuits. First impressions were good.

Peter Latimer eventually came in with his mug and sat down in the vacant armchair beside the fire. He would not be looking in her direction. She tried to blend into the background. The person sitting next to her turned out to be the student on the Chaplaincy stall who had told her about the 'open night'. "Glad you were able to come," he said.

The general pattern of the evening was that people talked about things that were worrying them. Problems they had encountered during the summer vacation; work and food; the price of beer - and the return of Rudy Krauss.

Emily was interested to see what a large impact Rudy had already made on the student community. Two of them had been to the Symposium in Palmerston College - and found it quite thought-provoking. Rudy's main point had been that since the other world was so close to our own, we should not hesitate to get in touch with the departed to seek their help and advice.

One of the students, a girl from Halifax College called Anne, said that many of the Catholic students prayed to the Virgin Mary as if it was the most natural thing in the world. And even the traditional 1662 Book of Common Prayer spoke of the dead praying for us. Why then did the Church discourage spiritualism? Would it be wrong to go to a spiritualist meeting?

Mr Latimer did not answer the question. He let the students voice their own feelings - putting in a comment here and there; and asking people who seemed a little confused to explain themselves more clearly.

From spiritualism, the discussion moved on to whether the dead could actually help us. The Chaplain said they could. "But would they help us to get rid of people?" "Such as who?" Inevitably, a few of the students said: "The Vice-Chancellor!"

Mr Latimer feigned surprise.

"Why should they want to get rid of him?"

"He's not very popular at this moment…"

"He's forced us to put up the price of our beer…"

"He wants to destroy our department!"

"Are you a Philosophy student, Anne?"

"Yes, I am. And we're all very angry about what's been happening. He bullied Professor Hampton - and now he's off sick. No one knows whether he'll be coming back. One of our lecturers said Dr Shawcross should be shot! But what happens if our department is closed down before we do our finals? Would we have to go to another university?"

Having been on the receiving end of Dr Shawcross' bullying tactics as recently as Friday afternoon, Mr Latimer knew exactly the problems the Philosophy department was facing. But he said nothing.

Anne continued: "Dr Treaseman's been to see Russell Forrester."

"Has he?" The Chaplain smiled. "Well, at least he went to the right person. If anyone can solve the problem, Russell can."

From the problems of the Philosophy department, it was only a hop, skip and a jump to wax dolls. This was being discussed widely in the student community. Mostly it was treated as a joke; but some people were taking it seriously.

One of the students - Stephen - wanted to know if it would be right to employ the dark arts to get rid of the Vice-Chancellor?

The Chaplain appeared amused.

"Are people actually doing this?"

"Rudy is."

Everyone laughed.

"But has anyone actually seen him sticking pins into these wax dolls?"

Various people said: "No…"

"But he's told people how to do it. There's a poster in the Students' Union showing exactly where you should stick in your pins."

"I think he said you had to use thirteen…"

"Through the brain, the heart, the eyes, ears and mouth - as well as his stomach and groin…"

"That's only seven."

"Well, I can't remember all the others. But you've got to get a piece of the victim's hair - or   cuttings from his fingernails - to make it really effective."

"Or an article of his clothing…"

"Then you take it to his house and bury it in the garden…"

Peter Latimer allowed the discussion to flow on before adding his own news.

"I believe there's been quite a demand for candles in the past two weeks. Apparently, someone has pinched a whole box-load of large candles from St Benedict's. Their curate, Father Blazer was quite distressed." He laughed. "Father Campolini has already perceived the danger. He's been issuing very small votive candles for the time being."

"But do you think it will work?"

"Rudy thinks it will."

Peter Latimer was quite irritated by the constant references to that wretched jailbird; especially when he was trying so hard to get rid of him. The students had obviously taken him to their hearts; but the Chaplain was sure that Mr Krauss would be the architect of his own doom. He would go too far… and that would be the end of him. The higher he flew, the further he would fall. Mr Latimer tried to raise the conversation to a higher plane.

"There's a great deal of psychological pressure in these things. Fear can dominate people's minds quite irrationally. President Roosevelt once said: 'We have nothing to fear; but fear itself.'   And to add a religious dimension to proceedings... "I think it was St Paul who said: 'Perfect love casts out fear...'."

Emily was pleased to see that Rudy had made such a strong impact on even the Christian students. Her suggestion of using psychic powers to attack the Vice-Chancellor had set people talking. They were discussing things that had never been discussed before in the university. There would be plenty more she could write about Mr Krauss.

But Peter Latimer had had enough.

He proposed a final cup of coffee before people went back to finish off their essays or have a decent night's rest. But he knew that most of them would be heading back to the Union bar.

He stood up and looked around the sitting room to see if there was anyone who had not spoken. His eyes immediately lighted upon Emily.

Her face was familiar. Her black-button eyes were familiar. He remembered where he had last seen her. She had been talking to Rudy Krauss beside the Pagan Society stall. He had warned her to keep away from Rudy. But he had heard on the grapevine that she was seeing quite a lot of him. They were sitting together in lectures. He was calling her his 'Vestal Virgin'. By now, they were probably lovers. A great pity - because she was such a beautiful girl...

Whilst the students were heading into the kitchen to make more coffee - or going home to write their essays, Peter Latimer cornered Emily beside the window.

He asked politely: "Did you go to Mr Krauss' speech in Palmerston on Friday night?"

"I did."

"And what did you think?"

"I thought it was a very good turn-out for a young man giving his first symposium in the University."

Like many people hearing her for the first time, Peter Latimer was very taken by her Welsh accent and the precise way in which she spoke.

"Were you sitting in the front row?"

(Adoring groupie?)

Emily smiled.

"No. I was at the back of the hall, selling Tarot cards!" She knew that would annoy him - and it did. "I'm afraid they have all gone; but if you wanted a pack, I'm sure Rudy could get a few more."

"That will not be necessary."

"You have a pack already?"

(She was mocking him.)

Peter Latimer paused.

"As a matter of fact, I do. I bought them when I was a student. But I have never used them."

In her lilting Welsh voice, she said: "I am thinking that would be a pity. They might help you see the future more clearly."

Although he did not know it, his future was very much in her hands. His Nemesis was close at hand.

He looked at this devil-woman.

"And what happened to Mr Dawkins? I believe his gravestone had a prominent part in your proceedings."

"It has been returned to its final resting place. I believe Inspector Raynes insisted it should be back in its place by Monday."

As he was about to turn away, Peter Latimer said: "Did you agree with Mr Krauss' speech?"

Emily shrugged her shoulders.

"I suppose the answer has to be 'yes' - for, you see, I wrote most of it myself!"

16: The Reporter

On the Monday morning, before she went to her first lecture at 10.00am, Emily made her way to the office of the *Grasshallows Echo* with her latest contribution. It seemed quite a peaceful place at that hour of day; but she knew that, by Friday, things would become more hectic.

Mr Hayward was pleased to see her bringing in her copy in good time. Her first article had excited a lot of comment: "Not him again!". "They should have given him a longer sentence." Others wondered who this new University correspondent might be. It was in Emily's best interests to remain anonymous.

Tom was expecting more of the same. So, even though Emily had warned him at their lunch, that she was now pursuing the Chaplain, the publisher's first reaction was one of disappointment.

His second reaction was that this was almost too hot to handle! The article was again well written and accompanied by a very handsome photograph of Peter Latimer which Emily had removed from the 'Meet the Team' noticeboard in the Chaplaincy. But the allegations which she made could land the newspaper in court with a libel case. For although she had used phrases like: "Mrs Latimer told a neighbour…" and "It is said in the village…" there were still several strong accusations.

There were also references to the child with learning difficulties. They would have to come out. It was said quite categorically that "he" had deserted "her". All this was undoubtedly true, but it might cost the newspaper an arm and a leg to prove it. Mr Hayward was not sure that the University Chaplain was worth all the effort.

"I take it that you have back-up to prove all these statements?" he said.

Emily opened up her file and handed over the notes she had received from her sister, Ruth.

Mr Hayward looked surprised.

"You got your sister to go round and see her?"

"She only lives twenty minutes away. She enjoyed the visit. She had tea with Mrs Latimer and the children. She was only too glad to think that her husband would be publicly exposed. She has given Ruth a copy of a legal letter he sent to her, threatening to prosecute if ever she set foot in Grasshallows. It should be here by Wednesday."

There was no doubt that Emily had quickly adapted to the demands of her trade. Ecomony of language. Hard hitting blows. The expectation of more to come. Her investigations would have a devastating impact on Mr Latimer's career. He would probably be suspended. The University expected better things from its spiritual leaders.

Tom Hayward noticed that Emily had not mentioned the Chaplain's current affair with the Vice-Chancellor's wife. He had heard about it from the taxi man who ferried her to and from Sandringham Crescent. He didn't think the secret could last much longer. People were beginning to talk. But Emily didn't seem to know anything about it. He did not enlighten her.

He knew the story would go higher and further when it broke. It was just the sort of thing the Sunday tabloids were looking for. But it was a question of timing. Emily's article would have to appear on the Friday; *but it would be the News of the World* which would bring him down.

He explained his reasoning to Emily. She disagreed. A lot of work had gone into the article. Both she and her sister had done a superb demolition job. She expected at least £500.

But Tom said: "I'm only suggesting a short delay. I need time to sell it to the Sunday shockers."

What he did not say was that he would send one of his most experienced reporters to see if he came up with the same facts. If he confirmed the story, it could go out on Friday October 26. But he still needed something for the coming week.

"Have you got anything else about Rudy?"

"Plenty!"

Emily smiled.

"He is an unending source of excellent copy! He gave a talk to the students and staff on Friday night. It was entitled: 'Understanding the Dark Arts. Our contact with the Departed'. Very statesmanlike, it was. He made it sound like a proper University lecture - with time for questions at the end." She paused. "I was very proud of him. A lot of work went into it. I think people felt that it was a subject which should be seriously addressed. Most people stayed till the end."

"What did you do?"

"Me? I sold Tarot cards. He had bought about twenty packs. He's been trying to sell them at £10 a time. I sold them for £8 - and got rid of the lot."

"Your mother wouldn't approve."

"What the eye don't see, the heart won't grieve over!"

Tom Hayward returned to the possibility of an alternative article.

"Is there anything else he's doing?"

"Well, there's the Hallowe'en celebrations in the Botanical garden."

"Is that still on?"

"It's attracting a lot of interest. A great excuse for everyone have a party." She looked at the publisher. "I may have to bare my breasts to encourage the others! But it's all in a good cause."

Mr Hayward felt vaguely aroused.

"You mustn't put that in the article!"

Emily laughed.

"Don't worry! I'm trying to present Rudy as a spiritual leader. I hope that the people who turn up won't spoil it for him. That Inspector Raynes is watching him closely. He has to behave. But it would be helpful for us if the Echo could send along a photographer on the Wednesday night. I've hired a very fine head-dress from a theatrical costume shop in London - and a fancy crook, all decorated in stars and cabalistic symbols. It will be very impressive." She smiled happily.

"Perhaps when Mr Latimer crashes to earth, a new star will arise!"

"So you could do another article?"

"I'll have it to you by tonight."

Later that Monday morning, Dr Treaseman reported back to his colleagues:

"I'm afraid I got very little help from Russell. He said that he had every confidence in the work of this department. There were no plans to abolish it. And the Senate would oppose any such suggestion were it ever to be made. Russell said that the only person who held the contrary view was the Vice-Chancellor. Rather than getting worked up about it, he felt we should concentrate on our teaching. 'Il faut cultiver les enfants'."

Dr Barnes disagreed.

"A threat has been made. Until it is withdrawn, we cannot sleep peacefully in our beds. I am sure Russell means well - in fact, I know he does - but the Vice-Chancellor could get rid of him tomorrow and the situation would change very quickly."

Miss Rabstead nodded.

"We have been asked to justify our existence - and I still think we should; so that we may be ready for any future attack."

Dr Charlotte Cooper said: "Think of all the people we have consulted - and all those who have offered us their support. We cannot let them down. They will expect us to fight."

Dr Treaseman said patiently: "But Russell's point is that there is nothing to fight about!"

"Well, I don't believe that. We are always under threat from unseen forces. We never expected Dr Shawcross to appear, did we? Where did he come from? Certainly not through the usual channels."

"Good point, Charlie! The man himself is a positive danger to any civilised university. It's not just us he's after. He's attacked the students, the gardeners, the maintenance men. He's trying to sell off the playing fields... the botanical garden... None of us is safe."

"Think what we've gone through since last Christmas," said Miss Rabstead. "Remember what happened to Professor Hampton. Dr Shawcross causes people acute psychological distress. I never had headaches till he came along. I still say that he should be got rid of as quickly as possible. Our students would expect us to fight."

Dr Coomaraswamy smiled.

"I would prefer them to fight our battles. Perhaps the spirit of Paris 1968 could be invoked?"

Dr Cooper who had been studying at the Sorbonne when the student battles were being fought in the streets of Paris, nodded her head in approval. In those days, she had been a feisty Marxist. At heart, she still was. In that era of revolution, she had been known as 'Burn your bra, Charlie'. She had burnt most of them.

She had also met Jean-Paul Sartre in the heady days of the Paris Spring. They had danced together in a cafe - with or without her bra, it was never said. This made her memories very precious to Dr Treaseman. Charlie always said that Sartre was a very small man, incredibly ugly, invariably smoking a cigarette, urging the students on to smash up the State. She claimed that he had been a coarse but demanding lover.

Dr Treaseman wondered if Charlie would still be capable of fighting battles in the street. He hoped it would never come to that.

Dr Coomaraswamy said: "I am thinking that Mr Rudy Krauss would be a very good person to run a revolutionary movement. He has real leadership skills. He is not frightened of taking violent action when it is required. He has certainly done more than the other students to fight this man. I went to a symposium he gave the other night in Palmerston. I did not agree with him; but he made a very good case for the Dark Arts."

Dr Treaseman was conscious that, as usual, they were getting nowhere.

"I'm sure Mr Krauss may have many fine qualities; but what are we going to do about the Vice-Chancellor?"

"I shall use my gun!" said Charlie.

"I told Russell it was an air pistol."

Charlie looked affronted.

"It certainly is not. It's a Beretta 4.62. It belonged to my uncle. It is small but deadly."

"Rather like yourself!" said Miss Rabstead. "Have you got a licence for it?"

"I keep it in a lockfast place."

"But are you prepared to use it?"

"Only on Dr Shawcross - but nobody else."

"Well, that's a blessing!"

Dr Treaseman said: "I did wonder if we should draw lots and see which one of us…"

Several people said: "No."

Dr Treaseman back-tracked immediately.

"I rejected it myself. I think it is much better that each of us should continue to pursue our own individual plan; and when we see an opportunity to strike, we should do so." He smiled. "Of course, if we all maintain our customary discretion, no one will ever know who it was."

Miss Rabstead said: "I make no pretensions to secrecy. I have been following an ancient herbal recipe which is reported to be fatal. It is, I am told, tasteless. I am thinking of using it at the reception after the Bradbury Lectures in November. You will recall that Dr Shawcross prefers a fruit cordial to wine or spirits. I shall make sure his glass is well and truly spiked."

Dr Barnes laughed.

"You may beat me to it. I am waiting for the dark winter nights. Ice and snow. The Vice-Chancellor returning home after a Senate meeting. A hefty blow on the back of his head - and all our troubles will be over."

Dr Treaseman summed up their feelings.

"I think we have to accept personal responsibility for getting rid of this man. We can see the dangers to the University more clearly than other people. Instead of waiting for others to act, we should be proud to take up arms against a tyrant…"

"To justify our beliefs?"

"Precisely."

He looked at round at his eager colleagues.

"And may the best man - or woman - win!"

18: Tarot Cards

Freddie Shawcross had her cards read on Wednesday 17 October at 11.00am. She had sent a message to the President of the Students' Union asking him to get a message to Mr Krauss. Together, they had arranged a time when she knew that Timothy would be extremely busy.

Rudy arrived at the University House wearing his white robe and his Arab head-dress. He had brought with him a de-luxe set of Tarot cards which he had bought in a souk in Morocco. (Most probably, they had been been printed in South Korea - but who cared?)

Rudy was ushered into Dr Shawcross' library and given a cup of coffee.

"I normally charge £20 for a reading…"

"Oh?"

Freddie hadn't thought about payment. Her handbag was in the kitchen.

"… but I shall do it for free because you have such beautiful eyes!"

Which she did.

(And a little flattery does no harm!)

Freddie looked down at the pack of cards rather nervously.

"Do you believe that what they say is true?"

"Usually," said Rudy confidently. "But there are occasionally rogue readings. And sometimes, they don't seem to make sense. But people tell me later that, strange though the reading was, these things do happen."

He picked up the cards and placed four of them uppermost on the green leather surface of the desk.He looked at the cards. They spoke to him quite clearly.

"You are a wealthy woman… You come from a rich family…. You were brought to England as a child… You went to a school frequented by royalty… You have two sisters and one brother…"

Everyone knew that Mrs Shawcross was Danish. When she and her husband had come to Grasshallows, a personal profile on both of them had been published in the University Gazette. Rudy had read through the Gazette before he visited Freddie. The cards simply confirmed what he already knew.

But there was more.

He looked up.

"Your mother also had twins, who died… This made a lasting impression on you and your family… It is because they died, that your family moved to England…"

He turned back to the cards.

"Both your parents are dead… Your mother died of poison in her leg…"

He looked up.

"Gangrene," said Mrs Shawcross. "She had diabetes. They had to cut her leg off."

Rudy said: "I see a four."

"She died four days after the operation."

Rudy had not expected the cards to tell him more - but they did. And it surprised him. Unknown facts suddenly sprang into his mind. Perhaps he did have the gift after all…?

"I see a bicycle… a blue and green bicycle… She is picking it up. Your father is laughing…"

Mrs Shawcross was impressed. There was no way this student could know any of this. Even she had forgotten such details. Very quickly, she became convinced that he was genuine.

"My mother was always falling off her bike. We used to tease her about it. When I got older, it was my bike."

There seemed little more to say.

Rudy scooped up the four cards and put them at the bottom of the pack and dealt four more.

The card with lovers entwined was the first of the four. Rudy smiled to himself. This would be more interesting.

"You are lucky in love… You always will be… You have had many lovers… I see a horseman… You loved him very much… but he died in an accident… I see a grey car…"

Mrs Shawcross nodded sadly.

Graham Page. She would not forget Graham.

"And a black man… with a trumpet… That did not last very long…" Rudy paused. "One night…"

He looked up.

"But he was a great trumpet player."

"He was."

"… And a man with an awful lot of money… Too much…. He bought you a ring… A large diamond… Twelve carats…" Rudy corrected himself. "No. 1.2 carats…"

Mrs Shawcross nodded.

It had been a lovely ring.

"But you didn't really like him. You didn't trust him… You gave it back… And he was angry…"

Rudy felt an invisible blow.

"… He hit you… He marked your face… You had to have stitches…"

Mrs Shawcross was not sure that she really wanted this student to be sifting through her list of lovers. He clearly had the gift of reading the cards - she could see that - but it was uncomfortable not knowing what would turn up next. However, she let him proceed.

Eventually, he looked at the last card.

He said quietly: You do not love your husband… Not at all… In fact, you hate him… You would like him to die…"

He looked up.

Freddie's face was showing pain.

"Is it that clear?" she asked.

"Absolutely. But I promise you that I shall say nothing about what I see."

He turned back to the final card. There was nothing outwardly to tell him - but he could see the Rev Peter Latimer, naked, lifting a glass and smiling a very insincere smile.

Rudy said: "The man who is your current lover is not good for you. He is deceitful and treacherous. He will desert you in your hour of need… He has a wife - and three children… He has told you he only has two… but that is untrue… There is something wrong with the third child… He rejects it… One day, he will return to his wife… She will forgive him for some

88

great crime… But he will be punished…"

He kept his head down.

"I'm sorry - but that's what I see."

"You see who it is?"

"Yes. I am sorry it is such bad news."

Mrs Shawcross sighed.

"I wanted to know the truth."

Rudy said: "Your secret is safe with me. I promise."

There was a long silence.

Did she really want to know any more?

Almost reluctantly, she said: "What about my husband?"

Rudy put away the second set of four cards and dealt out seven more. Why he chose seven, he did not know. It seemed the right thing to do.

But as he laid them out, he immediately regretted it. He felt a sense of panic. It was an awful combination. Terrifying. He wanted to gather them up and stuff them in his pocket - out of sight, out of mind - but he couldn't do it. He just couldn't.

Nor could he be frank about the contents of these cards.

He began slowly: "Your husband is a clever man… He has achieved a great deal in his life… It has made him selfish and insensitive to the feelings of others…

"He thinks about nothing but work… He is very proud to be the Vice-Chancellor of this University… He believes it is the most important job he will ever do… He will ruthlessly pursue his objective… even though it will hurt other people… He will be hated by many people… They will want to kill him…"

Rudy found himself breathing heavily - as if those who wanted to kill Dr Shawcross were breathing out their hatred through him.

"And will they succeed?"

"They will."

He said the two words quietly. He hoped they could leave it there. The rest was too dreadful to contemplate.

"Will it be an unpleasant death?"

Rudy continued to stare at the cards.

"It will be quick… And totally unexpected…"

As he said these words, Rudy saw a blinding flash like lightning cutting across the card. But it was not just lightning. He felt the heat boring into his right hand. God, it hurt! He looked at his hand.

"What was it?"

"Something to do with his right hand. Pain in his right hand."

"You cannot see any more?"

"No. It has gone."

What a lie!

"And will I be free?"

Freedom seemed very important to her.

He remembered something from the previous cards which had escaped him up till now.

"You will return to Denmark… You will be very happy… There is someone you will love very much… I see a farm… Two children…"

"Never!"

"No. They are not your children. They are his. You will love them very much. You will forget all this."

He waved his hand at the final seven cards.

He found himself shaking. He had never felt this feeling before. He also felt quite drained. His face had gone white despite the artificial tan.

Mrs Shawcross noticed.

She thought he was going to faint.

"Shall I get you another cup of coffee?"

"Please."

As she rushed out of the room, Rudy looked again at the cards. They seemed to dance before his eyes. Faces full of hatred came and went. There was the University car. A rope. A rough piece of metal crashing into a skull. Sand blowing in the desert… A brown curly wig… He could not understand it at all.

But, quite clearly, Timothy Shawcross was going to die in the near future - and most violently. A calendar date flashed past but he could not take it in.

Suddenly, he saw himself being escorted in handcuffs by the police. And a glaring headline: "Rudy Arrested!" It too flashed away. And then he saw Mrs Shawcross laughing. She was raising a glass of champagne, saying: "Well done!" She had escaped. Behind him, he heard the crackle of breaking glass. He felt small shards of glass pricking into his neck. He was struggling to get out of a dark room. There was smoke and a feeling of panic.

He did not know what to make of it. He had never expected such a terrifying outcome. Trembling, he gathered up the cards - wondering if he could burn them.

Mrs Shawcross returned with a large mug of coffee.

"I've put in three sugars," she said. "I hope it'll bring some colour back into your cheeks."

Rudy gratefully drank the coffee.

"So Timothy… my husband… is going to die?"

"Yes."

"Soon?"

"Before Christmas."

"Is there anything else you can tell me?"

Rudy didn't really want to say another word. But he found himself saying: "The person who will kill your husband is someone close to you - someone you know.

"Did you see his face?"

"I saw a lot of faces. But there wasn't anyone I recognized." He paused. "There could have been - but they flashed by so quickly."

"A man?"

"No. There were women's faces as well."

He picked up the cards. He hoped they would not burn his hands. He would dispose of them in the nearest litter bin.

Mrs Shawcross said: "We shall have to wait and see."

"Yes."

"Have you finished your coffee?"

He nodded.

Clearly, she now wanted him to go. He had served his

purpose. Told her what she wanted to hear. She handed him a £20 note - but he refused to take it.

He left the house as quickly as possible. He hurried back to the University. He had missed a lecture; but he hoped Emily would have taken full notes which he could copy up. She would doubtless question him about his visit. But the less said, the better.

19: Rudy Discovers His Gift

Later that day, he told Emily some of what had happened.

"Mrs Shawcross was very welcoming. She gave me a nice cup of coffee. And I gave her a reading in his study. Very posh. Green leather top to his desk…"

"What did you see?"

"A lot about her. And a few things about her husband."

"Did you make them up?"

"No. It was very strange. Once I laid out the cards, I could actually see things."

Emily's eyes sparkled.

"So you do have the gift?"

Rudy shook his head.

"I never expected it. It suddenly came to me…"

He still looked shell-shocked by the experience.

"So what did you see?"

"Scenes from her childhood. She had a blue and green bike. Once I told her that, she knew I was genuine. I saw her father and mother. I found out that they had had twins. They died. That's why they came to England.

"I also saw some of her past lovers. One who played the trumpet in a night club. Another one riding a horse. A man who bought her a huge ring. I saw the ring."

Rudy looked at Emily.

"I promised her not to speak about all the things I saw. It was too embarrassing. I could see everything."

He dared not mention Peter Latimer.

92

"And what about Dr Shawcross?"

Rudy put his head in his hands.

"Was it that bad?"

"Awful. In fact, it was frightening. I saw lots of faces. All the people who hated him. There were hundreds of faces. I could feel their anger pouring through me."

Tears rolled down his cheeks.

"Is he going to die?"

Rudy was silent for several minutes. Then he said simply: "Yes. But don't ask me any more. I just couldn't go through all that again. It's something you want to forget."

Emily did not ask any more questions. But she was quite amazed to think that Rudy had seen anything.

She smiled at him.

"So you're no longer a con man," she said. "You're the real thing. *A bona fide* prophet. I'm proud of you."

Rudy still did not look happy.

"I'm not sure it's a gift I want. There are some things you just don't want to know." He paused. "One of the things I saw was newspaper headline: 'Rudy Arrested!' and I was in handcuffs."

"Are you going to murder Dr Shawcross?"

"I don't know." He looked at Emily. He was once again crying. "I actually felt sorry for him. It must be dreadful having so many people hating you…"

Emily dismissed his sympathy.

"He deserves everything he gets. He's a cruel, vindictive man. He's hurt so many people. You were right to campaign against him. Don't let this experience stop you. A lot of people have put their faith in you. Don't let them down!"

Rudy sighed deeply.

"I'm not going to read the cards ever again. I've thrown them away!"

Emily was horrified.

"You said they were a really good set."

"They were."

"What have you done with them?"

"I've put them in the litter bin at the bus stop outside the University house."

Emily stood up.

"I shall go and get them. Immediately. You can't throw them away. They're part of your gift. You'll need them. They're part of your aura. Throwing them away won't save you. You cannot escape your destiny."

Emily genuinely believed what she was saying. When she had first met Rudy, she had thought - like most people - that he was a complete 'poser'. That was why she had challenged him to do something - to be what he claimed to be. And it had worked. The student campaign against the Vice-Chancellor was blindingly successful. The 'wax doll treatment' had captured people's imaginations. There was something they could to do to fight back. All they needed was a couple of votive candles and a few pins. Simple but highly effective.

She had urged Rudy to give the Symposium at Palmerston College. She had helped him dig up the gravestone. She had helped him write his speech. People had said how good it was - even if they didn't agree with him. She was proud of him; but she had never dreamt that he had second sight. This was an added bonus. If he was now genuinely 'a seer', it was very important that he should be true to his vocation. She would not let him chicken out.

So she left the Union coffee bar right away. The bus would only take three or four minutes. She hoped no one would have pinched the cards before she got there. Fortunately, the University House was in a respectable area of the city where most people would not be stuffing their pot noodles and their tandoori chicken into litter bins.

She descended from the bus.

There were two litter bins.. The first one was empty. She crossed the road. As she got closer, she saw the top of the red box sticking out. She breathed a deep sigh of relief - and was almost hit by a passing car.

She was concentrating too much to notice. She plucked the box out of the litter bin and made sure no card was left behind.

It seemed to be intact. She put the precious box into her handbag and waited at the nearby bus stop for the next bus back into town.

She felt like Moses bearing the precious tablets of the Law down Mount Sinai. Rudy would be fully equipped to do his work as a high priest and she would provide the ark of the covenant to keep his treasures safe.

Putting it more simply:

Now that she knew Rudy's true value, she would milk him for every penny she could get.

20: Hallowe'en

Emily's article in the *Echo* drew immediate attention to the Hallowe'en celebrations being planned in the Botanical Gardens.

Whilst Rudy was thinking of a quasi-religious event, the leaders of the Students' Union saw this as a heaven-sent opportunity to mount a defence of the Gardens - and a public protest against the Vice-Chancellor's stated aim of selling them off to property developers.

The University staff were mostly on the side of the students. "Let them fight our battle" was their attitude. "Give him a bloody nose!"

By contrast, the Marxist firebrands and the Anarchist group regarded it as a useful cover to launch a vicious attack on Dr Shawcross. They had thought of storming the University House and smashing all his windows; but the greenhouses in the Botanical Gardens offered a greater acreage of glass which might produce more spectacular results.

This more violent protest was immediately picked up by the police. Detective-Inspector Raynes had not forgotten the violent scenes outside the City Hall during the Miles Hart by-election. He realised that he faced a serious threat to public order.

So Emily's article provided everyone with a twelve-day warning.

* * * *

Rudy and Emily made several visits to the Botanical Gardens to choose the best possible location for their pagan rites.

Rudy was still concentrating on the spiritual aspects of the service. He had accumulated quite a bundle of notes telling him how Hallowe'en should be celebrated. Animal and human sacrifice were obviously ruled out; but nudity would be permitted. Worship of earth and sky - sun, moon and stars - would be encouraged. Candles, torches and lanterns would provide a colourful background. Perhaps Chinese lanterns could be hung from the trees? Olympic-style torches, filled with sand and petrol, could be stuck into the flower beds.

Rudy knew that the students liked dressing up. Angels, devils, witches and warlocks would add to the fun. If they couldn't afford a costume, they could always wear masks. There would have to be free booze. Rudy had already decided to blow the Student Union grant to the Pagan Society on a barrel of cider. Perhaps two? They would also need plastic cups.

Emily felt that the rose garden would provide a secluded area. The layout of the flower beds ensured there would be just one entrance; and, in the corner, there was a cream-coloured folly, with Doric pillars, surrounded by a small flight of steps.

Prayers would be simple and repetitive. People would be encouraged to bring guitars and other musical instruments. There would be banners and cabalistic signs mounted on poles. These could also be thrust into the flower beds.

There would be a procession of worshippers from Palmerston College with tambourines and bells. Rudy was thinking of bringing the large dinner gong. He would be preceded by a company of semi-Vestal Virgins and an incense bearer. She would be swinging a censer which had been stolen from St Benedict's Church. Vast quantities of Jerusalem incense would be dispensed over the faithful. Sight, smell and sound would all contribute to the magnificence of the occasion.

* * * *

The Students' Union had no particular interest in the Pagan Society's plans. They intended to surround the glasshouses with several rings of students. Posters were being printed to go on every available window denouncing the Vice-Chancellor: "Save our Uni!" "Down with the V-C!" and, more bluntly: "Shawcross must go!"

Speeches would be delivered by the Union President and Dr Charlotte Cooper, who was always willing to deliver some violent oratory, steeped in vitriol. Several megaphones were dug out of old cupboards and their batteries replaced.

The Union was hoping that at least five hundred students would turn up. That would show the University their depth of feeling. It would also look good on television. The fact that it was intended to be a peaceful protest would impress the viewers.

Unfortunately, the Marxists and the Anarchists were planning a violent confrontation. They were expecting violence. Because of the imminent approach of Bonfire Night, the shops were full of fireworks. Everyone was asked to buy bangers to throw at the police and rockets that could be launched horizontally from wine bottles. When they had gone, they would be followed by the bottles themselves.

A mischievous old sailor had given them a dozen distress rockets which could blast into the sky with a brilliant flare and a colossal bang. They would waken up the citizens of Grasshallows! The Left-wing groups also infiltrated the grounds of the Botanic Gardens to collect caches of stones and bricks, which would soon deal with the glasshouses.

They too dismissed the presence of the Pagan Society. Their aim was to disrupt the Union protest and set student against student, creating a violent mêlée which would lead to hand-to-hand combat with the police.

* * * *

When the Vice-Chancellor heard about the Pagan Society's celebrations and the official Union protest, he demanded that the University Secretary should ban the march and take steps to prevent any student from entering the Botanical Gardens.

With his usual diplomatic finesse, Russell Forrester refused. He explained that the grounds were open to the general public at all times. It was part of the original bequest under which the land had been gifted to the University. The local bye-laws prevented the University from acting unilaterally.

What he did not say was that the President of the Union had come to him to ask permission for the students to mount a peaceful protest on Wednesday October 31. Russell Forrester had given him his tacit approval and invited the President to use the University's official stamp on his letter.

He had signed nothing. If anything went wrong, he would deny all knowledge of how the student could possibly have used the official stamp. There was to be a Senate meeting on the Thursday night. All blame for the protest could be laid at the Vice-Chancellor's door.

On the following day, Emily Williams arrived at the University Secretary's office with a similar request for the Pagan Society to use the Gardens on the same night.

Russell Forrester had not met Emily before - and he was much taken by her dark beauty and her lilting voice. His spies had already told him that this friend of Rudy Krauss was the *Echo's* University correspondent. He presumed that she would have the backing of the proprietor, Tom Hayward.

With a generous sense of complete irresponsibility, he also gave the Pagan Society his tacit approval and invited Emily to use the official stamp. His fingerprints would not appear on stamp or letter.

He smiled at her.

"I believe the motto of the Pagan Society is 'Make love - not war'?"

Emily's eyes twinkled.

"I believe the Welsh people have been doing precisely that for the past 700 years. It is one way of keeping the *saesneg* - the English people - in their place!"

* * * *

Detective-Inspector Raynes had never been to the Botanical Gardens. On his map, they were just a large, green oblong on the outskirts of the city. He noted that the river ran along the eastern side of the gardens; and on the western side, there a single approach road which led to a small car park in front of the main gates. From a defensive point of view, the site looked promising.

Raynes and Carlisle drove out to the Gardens on the Friday afternoon, immediately after they had read Emily's article in the newspaper. On their right, they passed Palmerston College. On their left, there were several research laboratories belonging to the University. They all faced the river and the final block - the Geo-physics department - was effectively the north wall of the Gardens. No one could get in from that direction. From that point, there was a continuous high wall all the way to the car park.

Carlisle parked their car - and the two men stood facing the main gates. The walls here were slightly lower - but could not be scaled without a sixteen foot ladder. The gates looked quite strong. With a couple of chains, they would withstand attack. They walked through the gates. The first building was the café; then a bookshop and ticket office; thirdly, the toilets. There was then an internal car park with small tractors and lorries. Beyond that were six huge glass houses, containing thousands of exotic plants and trees. Raynes looked back at the main gates. No stones would reach them.

Their observations were interrupted by an officious looking lady.

"Have you got your tickets?"

"No," said Raynes, "We're police."

Carlisle flashed his identity card.

"Has there been some trouble?"

"Not yet."

They decided to leave before any more questions were asked.

* * * *

Back in the office, Raynes drew up the first draft of his plan to protect the Gardens.

All police leave would be cancelled. Every officer would be on duty that night. There would be a small police presence outside the main gates. His main force would occupy the car park. They would control the main approach road. But along that road, there would be several groups of police - with vans and dogs - who would monitor the progress of students. Plain clothes officers would be placed beyond Palmerston - on the route to the city centre and the Students' Union - to report on numbers and judge the mood of the crowd.

As the students got closer, they would be broken up into smaller groups. The Pagan worshippers would be let through the police cordon - on the grounds that they were relatively harmless. The *bona fide* student protestors would be checked in a friendly fashion to make sure they were carrying no offensive weapons. They would then be divided into four groups. They would presumably be carrying placards - but the presence of quite a large number of police officers between each group and a few fierce-looking dogs would probably prevent any trouble.

Raynes expected that most of the trouble would come from the Left-wing militants. First of all, they must be identified and kept well away from the other students. As they came down the approach road, they must be split up into four groups and kept about a hundred yards apart. That would reduce their effectiveness. Once again, police with dogs would occupy the gaps. The dog handlers must look as if they were having great difficulty in restraining their dogs.

If possible, each group would be stopped and searched. Fireworks would be permitted. But possessing Molotov cocktails would be grounds for immediate arrest. Ladders and ropes would be confiscated. The police vans on the approach road would be ready for immediate action. If the students tried to rush through the police cordon, then the police on the approach road would immediately follow them so that when they reached the car park, they would be surrounded. Under no circumstances should they be able to get anywhere near the other students. Thus it would appear that the police were protecting the *bona fide* student protestors and the Pagan worshippers. If there was to be any battle, it would be contained on the approach road.

Raynes arranged for officers to join him from neighbouring forces. With quiet satisfaction, he felt that every possibility had been considered. He would fight them on his chosen ground - not theirs. He would break their hearts, but not their bones.

* * * *

On the Wednesday morning, the inspector received a personal phone call from Dr Shawcross. His voice was cold and uncompromising.

"I shall be present at the Botanical Gardens this evening. I shall arrive at 7.00pm."

Raynes was politeness itself.

"I would not advise it, sir."

"You think there will be violence?"

"Not if we can prevent it. But your presence may aggravate the situation. The students have nothing against the police. You being there might be seen as a deliberate provocation. A red rag to a bull…"

There was a brief pause at the other end of the line.

"I feel it is my duty to make sure University property is protected. I am told it will cost thousands to repair the glass houses if they are damaged."

Raynes was tempted to ask why Dr Shawcross should

worry about that when his principal object was to sell off the grounds.

"Many flowers and plants will die if they have a sudden change of temperature."

Raynes agreed.

"That is probably true; but we are hoping to prevent any attack. If you are there, the students may decide to attack you rather than the glass houses. You will require a number of officers to protect you. That would upset all our carefully-arranged plans."

"I will not come in my official car. I shall come in my wife's Mercedes…"

The Inspector marvelled at the stupidity of the man.

"And what colour is that?"

"Light blue."

"If you come in anything, sir, I would suggest a taxi. A dark coat and a thick scarf. That way you would be less conspicuous…"

"Are there going to be any lights?"

"There will be a few street lights around the gardens; but there will be fireworks. And I believe one group want to have a bonfire on some waste ground just across from the main gates. That will require a fire engine - perhaps two."

The voice sounded a little less certain.

"If I do come, what time would you recommend?"

Raynes did not want to recommend anything. But, standing beside a set of locked iron gates, facing a line of grim-faced policemen, and being kept as far away from the glasshouses as possible, on a damp, misty October night, was not his idea of fun.

He said: "I think 8.00pm would be the best time to arrive. I think the Hallowe'en party will probably appear at about 8.30pm. The main student body shortly after 9pm and the Red Brigade some time later. They may all want to go back to the Union bar afterwards to lick their wounds."

"Are you expecting many injuries?"

"I hope not."

"Have you spoken to the ambulance people?"

"I have notified Grasshallows Royal Infirmary that they may have a sudden influx of students. Mostly burns, bruises and black eyes…"

"Nothing worse than that?"

"I think the students may draw the line at murder. But Dr Stewart, the police surgeon, will be glad to welcome visitors at any time."

The Vice-Chancellor had no sense of humour.

"Well, it wouldn't be a very good advertisement for the University if a student got killed."

"Or a policeman… "

The man was only thinking of his own reputation.

"…We shall do our best to avoid it."

Raynes longed for the wretched man to get off the phone and let him get on with his work. He didn't seem to realize it was all his fault."

* * * *

Dr Shawcross arrived at 7.30pm - in a taxi. Raynes saw him getting out of the car. He said to Carlisle: "Keep him away from me. I need to concentrate on the students - not on him."

"Sergeant Evans? He'll keep an eye on him."

"Perfect."

Raynes chatted to the officers already lined up in front of the gates.

"Not very many here so far, sir."

"No. But I'm told they're quite well-organised - and I believe the first ones are on their way. Make sure you break them up into small groups."

Raynes was expecting the Hallowe'en party to be the first to arrive, but about 8.00pm the advance party of the Union protestors could be seen coming down the approach road. There were about fifty of them, all carrying placards: "V-C must go!", "Save the Gardens", "Axe Shawcross!."

Raynes watched how the police dealt with the students.

They had been told to be friendly and respectful - but very firm. The dogs were being held further back; but everyone was conscious they were there. They didn't bark but their eyes were fierce and menacing. The students were directed to stand about twenty yards away from the gates.

Half an hour later, the main body of protestors arrived. Raynes reckoned that there were about 250 of them. They were not as well-organised as the advanced guard. In fact, they appeared to be something of a rabble. The Inspector suspected that most of them had had a few drinks before they set out. If they had been equipped with placards, they seemed to have lost them.

At this stage, they seemed to be quite a cheerful crowd. Like students all over the world, they were singing the protest songs of the 60s - or at least what they could remember of them. To keep their spirits up, they shouted abuse at their unseen persecutor: "Kill the V-C!" Raynes hoped that Dr Shawcross would keep out of sight; but he could not fail to hear the repeated calls for his death.

Among the students, there were quite a number of older people, who were probably lecturers with their wives or mistresses. They were more experienced in marches and demonstrations. They would be likely to stir up the students.

The police worked their way through the noisy crowd, making sure that none of them was carrying offensive weapons. And then sent them down to join the other students, who looked rather lost standing in front of a row of burly policemen.

The sheer number of police came as a surprise to everyone. And the delay in processing the students gave each group time to look at the dogs waiting in the background. The whole area was under strict control.

One of the lecturers had a large knapsack, full of posters for the glasshouses.

Raynes shook his head.

"No one's going into the Gardens."

"But we've had 2000 printed."

Raynes said politely: "I'm sure you can use them elsewhere."

The lecturer became more aggressive.

"You can't stop us!"

"I'm afraid we can."

Raynes quickly proved his point. As the lecturer wandered off towards the gates, he was quickly stopped and escorted back to the students. They were having a fight over who should hold the placards. One of them hit the lecturer on the head. As he went down, his knapsack fell open and the posters began to pour out on to the ground where they were trodden under foot.

The President of the Student's Union was having a hard time, bringing the crowd into some sort of order. He manoeuvred the cheerleaders and the musicians into position - whilst the police calmly occupied the space between the four groups.

Raynes could tell that the veterans did not like the lay-out. They also protested at the presence of the dogs. And the dogs obviously didn't like them. They had been brought a little closer, but they were still fifty yards behind the crowd. They were a chilling reminder of what might happen if things got out of control.

Once some sort of order had been achieved, the students were harangued by a succession of speakers. Certain words were repeated again and again: Revolution... Human rights... The fight against the capitalists... Liberty... Freedom... And the more violent the speakers became, the more they were cheered.

An older woman was perhaps the most virulent. She had a strong, clear voice but her message was one long attack on the Government, the Education Department, the University authorities - and of course, the Vice-Chancellor. She laid particular emphasis on the "Vice...". She accused him of corruption and greed. He was hand-in-glove with the housing developers. He had received large backhanders. He might pose as a cost-cutter, but he had been bribed by the

Government to privatize the University assets and oppress the students. They would seize all their money and grind their faces into the dust. If they protested too strongly, they would send in the tanks. She levelled a torrent of abuse at the police, who were just mindless Fascist thugs. She was rewarded with countless cheers and frequent shouts of "Kill the Fascists!"

Within twenty minutes, the crowd was fired up; but their anger did not lead to any violence.

Many of the students had only just come to the University. They were not used to fighting or hitting a policemen over the head with a placard. They would learn soon - but for the moment, they were content to shout and jeer. And there were always those dogs in the background - just waiting...

* * * *

At about 9.15pm, the Hallowe'en students emerged from Palmerston. They were carrying a large dinner gong and various students took their turn in beating it. There were people with tambourines and maracas. Behind them came the torches and lanterns - but no placards. They were dressed in a variety of costumes and some were wearing animal masks. Quite a few of the girls were wearing very skimpy dresses. Raynes reckoned that they would soon be complaining about the cold. But they seemed a very cheerful bunch.

A large barrel of cider was being carried on a porter's trolley. A policeman looked at it.

"Is that for us?"

"No, it's for the party."

"They won't let you in."

The students looked very disappointed.

"You'll have to drink it outside. There'll be plenty of people needing a drink before the night is over."

The policeman turned to his colleague.

"Quite harmless."

The other one shook his head.

"He had a butcher's knife tucked in behind his waistband."

106

"What was that for?"

"Animal sacrifice! He'll use it on the Vice-Chancellor if he gets a chance."

"Do they know he's here?"

"The first group of students didn't recognize him."

The policemen looked further down the road.

"Here comes the next lot!"

He pointed at the main party - a collection of beautiful young women in black cat suits and tall black boots - all carrying whips. They strode purposefully towards the police - obviously with no intention of giving way. These were Rudy's semi-Vestal Virgins on their way to the sacrifice. It looked as if Dr Shawcross would be flayed alive before he was put to death.

The policeman tried to stop them.

"Come on, girls! Hand over those whips."

But the procession swept through the police cordon. Emily was part of their number. She waved the University Secretary's official letter in the policeman's face.

"We have permission to be here," she said.

"We're friends of Inspector Raynes," said another.

"Well, you won't get in. No one's getting in."

But they were already through the first cordon and moving rapidly towards the police and the dogs.

Pepper was liberally sprayed.

The dogs retreated quickly.

The first two lines of defence had been broken. But police attention was now focussed on the final member of the procession. A tall, bearded patriarch in fine golden robes - with a small blonde girl twirling a brass incense censer to purify his path. The patriarch had a massive - but lightweight - headdress containing several hundred glass stones which twinkled magnificently under the street lights. In his right hand, he held an elaborate staff with all sorts of weird, cabalistic signs. With his left hand, he offered blessings - left, right and centre.

The policeman's first impression was that a Greek Orthodox archbishop had lost his way and gatecrashed the

107

party. This impression was reinforced by him speaking in a foreign tongue: "Pax vobiscum!" and "May the spirit of Aleister Crowley bless you!"

The policeman suddenly found Inspector Raynes standing beside him.

"Who is Aleister Crowley?" he asked.

"The Archbishop of Canterbury's private secretary."

"So he's all right then?"

Raynes said nothing.

Rudy said: "We shall not cause any trouble."

The Inspector looked at the pastoral staff.

"That looks like an offensive weapon!"

"Might be useful against the Marxists…?"

"You have a point. But one step out of line…" It was an unmistakable threat. "… I wouldn't like to see that lovely outfit get messed up."

Emily suddenly appeared on the other side of the Inspector.

"And neither should I. I paid for it!"

Rudy said: "We just want to get into the Gardens and enjoy our party. We won't cause you any trouble."

Raynes was firm.

"No one is going through those gates."

He looked at the small blonde student carrying the smoking censer. It was quite a pleasant smell.

"Jerusalem incense," said Rudy helpfully.

"And what about the censer?" asked Raynes. "St Benedict's had one stolen last week."

Emily reacted quickly.

"Father Blazer spoke to me. We've promised to get it back to them before ten o' clock tomorrow morning. They need it for the High Mass of All Saints."

Raynes smiled.

"Will they know where it's been?"

"I hope not."

Raynes looked further down the road. Dark figures were moving in the shadows. The real enemy was on its way.

He followed the Hallowe'en party down towards the gates

of the Botanical Gardens. In his wake, police reinforcements moved to block the approach road.

Raynes spoke to the President of the Students' Union, who was holding a large megaphone.

"Tell Rudy's lot to stand on the right hand side of the gates, in one group. Tell the rest to stay exactly where they are - and not to move. There must be absolutely no violence. If there's any trouble, they'll all be arrested."

"That's a very provocative statement!"

Raynes looked at him.

"The Anarchists are on their way. About a hundred of them. They're spoiling for a fight. With you - and with us. If you retaliate, a lot of people will get hurt. We have to contain the trouble-makers. If everyone here sticks together, you'll be safe."

The President lifted the megaphone.

But before he could speak, a distress rocket blasted off - only about two hundred yards away.

Everyone looked up.

Raynes grabbed the megaphone.

"All companies on red alert!"

A second distress rocket screamed over their heads.

Raynes said calmly: "Keep your heads down. We are all of us under attack. The police will deal with these people. Do not join in any fighting. Do not try to get into the Botanical Gardens. Please extinguish any fires which may be created." He looked towards Rudy and his friends. "And no more pepper, girls! Save it for the Red Brigade!"

As he lowered the megaphone, he found the Vice-Chancellor, with a very anxious face, tugging at his sleeve.

"We are all in great danger," he said. "You must stop this demonstration - immediately! People are going to get hurt. You must think of the University's reputation…"

Raynes looked at him with cold contempt.

"You should have thought of that when you announced you were going to sell the Gardens. It's all your fault. And if the students discover you're here, they'll kill you. Several of them have knives."

He turned to Sergeant Evans: "I thought I told you to keep him out of my way. Lock him in the car - and when we've dealt with the students, take him home - and lock him in his own garage!"

He turned back to see how the battle was progressing.

Several more distress rockets blasted off.

He wondered where they had got such things. He hoped none of them would land in the crowd.They could cause quite a lot of damage.

But people had accepted his orders. The Hallowe'en party were ignoring the fracas and were pouring out glasses of cider. The police at the gates were holding firm. The Union students were no longer protesting. They were confused - rather like sheep - not knowing what to do or where to go. None of them had any intention of taking on the police. Nor did they show any sign of joining the Anarchists. Police and dogs were steadily moving forward to confront the main opposition.

They were now firing ordinary rockets horizontally at the police. Fireworks had been bundled together and were now being hurled at the police. They caused multiple small explosions which went off at irregular intervals.

The dogs were still under the control of their handlers but were straining on their leashes, anxious to get their teeth into this gang of hooligans. If they were released, there would be a lot of injuries. They were his ultimate weapon.

Raynes looked over his shoulder to see if the Vice-Chancellor was locked safely in a car. He was still arguing with the police, refusing to get into the car. If the students recognised him, they would certainly attack him.

Raynes sighed - and looked at the dark outline of the glasshouses. They were still intact. But someone had dropped the posters which were to have been stuck on the windows. They were floating around in the wind - like autumn leaves.

He returned to the battle which was being fought out at the corner of the approach road. There were screams, flames, a tremendous amount of noise and still there was an occasional distress rocket. But there was a new sound - breaking glass.

Fortunately, there had been no sign of Molotov cocktails, but the students who had used empty bottles as launchers for their horizontal rockets were now hurling the bottles at the police. Some of the broken bottles had been thrown back - with unexpected success. Some of the attackers had cuts and were bleeding from their injuries. The battle was by no means one-sided; but once the bottles had gone, it would be hand-to-hand combat.

Some of Anarchists broke away from the battle and swooped down on the non-protestors and seized their placards to use them against the police. But this brought the police reserve into action - with their dogs joining in the fight and trying to bite the more violent students. They could smell blood; they could see blood and they wanted more.

Raynes decided that this was the moment to try and stop the battle. He went over to the President of the Union, who was standing beside Rudy. He said: "I think this is the moment for you to intervene. They've used up all their ammunition. I think you should call a halt - for everyone's sake."

The Student President looked shocked.

"Me?"

Raynes shrugged his shoulders.

"You organised this protest. Now's the moment to calm things down."

He looked at Rudy.

"And if you have any spiritual powers, Mr Krauss, this is the time to use them." He looked at Rudy's headdress. "And if you have any magic rabbits in your top hat, this would be a good moment to produce them."

Rudy said nothing. But he took off his headdress and handed his robes to one of his Vestal Virgins. He handed his staff to Emily.

He said to the President: "We'll go together."

Raynes admired him for his courage.

Emily passed the staff to someone else.

"I'll come too."

Whilst they were getting ready for peace negotiations, the

police directly facing the mob, decided that the enemy were far too close for comfort. Three canisters of CS gas were thrown into the middle of the jeering crowd of hardliners. As the cans burst open, the gas drifted slowly down the approach road.

The students retreated rapidly - but the more moderate students protested loudly about the use of gas. "That was not playing the game! It was police violence!" The next thing would be the police using their batons.

In his mind, Raynes was already concocting his defence. "The police had to protect themselves." But, in fact, they were handling the confrontation rather well.

The police advanced over the broken glass as the Anarchists moved back. The dogs could move more freely on a road which had no broken glass. In the confusion of the CS gas, the police with their dogs surrounded the Marxist mob - but left a good safety margin - a no man's land between them.

The President, Rudy and Inspector Raynes went through the new cordon to speak directly to the men of violence. Emily followed.

The President had recovered his nerve.

"Enough!" he said. "You mustn't take this any further!"

The Anarchists sneered at him.

"Bugger off!"

"Leave us alone!"

"Who are you anyway?"

"I'm the President of the Students' Union…"

"Bloody Trotskyite!"

Rudy stepped in: "This is a protest against the Vice-Chancellor - not against the police. Nobody minds if you kill the Vice-Chancellor; but, at this moment, it is the students you are hurting."

He looked round at the tense and desperate faces. All the milder students were now standing behind him. He continued: "You've obviously run out of ammunition. The police have surrounded you. If you fight any more, the police will certainly let loose their dogs. And they could bite anyone."

112

One of the students shouted: "Fascists!" and spat at Raynes.

Rudy recognised him as one of his Politics class.

The Student President said: "You're not attacking Dr Shawcross. You're attacking the student body. You're achieving nothing. It is up to the Senate to sack him."

Several students raised their fists and shouted: "Kill the Vice-Chancellor!"

Raynes said: "If you had come earlier, you could have spoken to him."

"Was he here?"

"At 7.00."

"Where is he now?"

Raynes lied forcibly - knowing full well that Dr Shawcross was only two hundred yards away. "Four officers have taken him home. And don't even think of attacking the University House. He has full police protection."

At that moment, a heavy champagne bottle, aimed at Rudy, hit the leader of the Anarchists on the back of his head. He collapsed in a heap in front of them.

"Stop!" said Rudy. "In the name of Satan! Revolutions always devour their children."

Raynes moved forward.

"Rudy's right," he said, "and so is the President of the Students' Union. You've made your protest. The Gardens will never be sold off. The Vice-Chancellor will not get his way. The battle is over!"

There was a sound of more crunching glass behind them. The Hallowe'en crowd had come to see what was going on. They were still drinking their cider out of plastic cups.

In desperation, one of the Marxists, still anxious to leave his mark, said: "What about the glasshouses?"

Rudy said: "If you smash them up, the University will make us pay for the damage. It will be added to our bills."

The President of the Union said: "They might even close the Union."

Emily said: "The rest of the students will blame us."

There was an unhappy silence.

Then the older woman, who had delivered the fiery speech earlier in the protest, came forward. Raynes did not know who she was - but she seemed to be someone the students respected. He guessed she might be one of the lecturers in the Philosophy department.

"Well done, you guys!"

Tensions relaxed. This was one of their own.

"It reminded me of Paris in May '68. You've made your point. The University will take note of your views. The V-C is our enemy - as well as yours. We shall all continue to fight him - to the death! Cut off his head and the Bastille will fall!"

Dr Charlotte Cooper was cheered. Other staff members came forward to offer their congratulations:

"Splendid!"

"Inspirational!"

"The department is proud of you."

Raynes said firmly: "The battle is over!"

"Back to the Union!" said Rudy.

"Free drinks all round!" said the President of the Union.

It was kiss-and-make-up time. But their hatred of the Vice-Chancellor had not diminished. There was still a simmering anger on all sides. Raynes hoped that Sergeant Evans would not let Dr Shawcross loose at this moment. It could prove fatal.

Two of the students were trying to revive the fallen martyr.

"I think he needs an ambulance."

"We'll get one in a couple of minutes."

Carlisle said: "It's already on its way."

Raynes quickly summed up in his mind what still had to be done.

In a fairly relaxed manner, the police would move the students back down the approach road and see them on their way. The police guard would stay at the gates all night. Patrol cars would cover the area till dawn. The road sweepers would arrive at first light and clear up all the glass and remove the debris. Once the students were out of the way, Dr Shawcross would be taken home. There would be a police presence at the

University House. He looked forward to writing his report.

He turned to Carlisle.

"Have you got full notes on all that's happened?"

"Everything!"

Raynes was grateful for such stalwart support.

But his thoughts were interrupted. A photographer had arrived.

"*Grasshallows Echo*", he said. "What about a few photographs to go in Friday's paper? The battle of Waterloo all over again!"

Raynes turned on his heel. Emily would be writing two thousand words about the confrontation - having helped to provoke it. And she would be getting paid for it! The whole thing would be turned into a media circus. It sickened him.

But perhaps it was the CS gas, still lingering in the air?

Raynes vented his anger on the Vice-Chancellor:

"Stay in this car - and do not move. If you try to escape, they'll kill you. Several of them are carrying knives."

Dr Shawcross was white-faced. Sitting in the back seat, surrounded by four policemen, he was unlikely to escape.

* * * *

It took another hour and a half to clear the approaches to the Botanical Gardens. The students showed a distinct unwillingness to leave. They stood arguing with each other. Rudy's followers had the brass neck to ask if they could use the rough grass beyond the car park to celebrate Hallowe'en.

Raynes said "No" very firmly. There could not be a rule for one set of students and one for another. That would cause real trouble. He suggested - politely - that they should make their way back to Palmerston and use the College grounds for their Saturnalia.

He observed tartly that when the worshippers collapsed - as some of them looked like doing after several glasses of cider - their beds would not be far away. With some reluctance, Rudy and Emily agreed.

So for a further ninety minutes, the Vice-Chancellor was kept in the police car. He protested at regular intervals; but his complaints were ignored. Raynes was adamant that all the students must be clear of the area, before he was driven home.

As the students drifted away, the Inspector reduced the police presence. Their cars and vans began to leave the cul-de-sac where they had been parked. A final squad of twenty men were left to guard the gates. Finally, Raynes gave Dr Shawcross permission to leave. He felt relieved to see him go. He turned to Carlisle who was noting down the time of his departure and said: "He may not have enjoyed himself; but at least he survived!"

21: The Body

Detective-Inspector Raynes was awakened by a call from the control room at 7.15am on Saturday morning.

"There's been a suicide outside the golf club at Skipper's Hill."

(Well, it made a change from road accidents!)

The entrance to the golf club had always been extremely dangerous. A sharp right-handed turn across a dual carriageway close to the brow of a hill. Cars approaching from the other side of the road - up the hill - could not see what was ahead of them until the last moment - and often that was too late. There had been some spectacular crashes and a series of dead bodies - many of them golfers. The local authority had been urged many times to instal warning lights or speed humps; but, characteristically, nothing had been done.

Inspector Raynes turned carefully into the central gap between the two carriageways and then accelerated into the car park. in the far corner, he could see a police patrol car waiting beside a claret-coloured Jaguar. There were several other cars parked nearer to the club house.

Raynes coasted slowly up to the patrol car.

Two officers came forward to meet him.

"Morning, Sergeant. A beautiful morning."

"A very fine day, sir."

Raynes got out of his car.

"So what have you got for me?"

"A suicide. Bit of an oddball…"

"… dressed up in women's clothes."

"Really?"

Raynes noticed the green garden hose running from the exhaust pipe through the top of the rear window. Some air would have got in.

He turned to Sergeant Evans:

"Did you switch off the engine?"

"No, sir. But I did open the door - with gloves," he added.

"Who did switch off the engine?"

"Probably the man who reported the incident."

"And who was that?"

Sergeant Evans took out his notebook.

"A Dr Geoffrey Treaseman."

The name meant nothing to him.

"And where is Dr Treaseman now?"

"Playing a round of golf - or perhaps seeking a little refreshment at the nineteenth hole…"

Raynes smiled.

"A bit early for that. Perhaps he's having a coffee?"

"Could be, sir."

Raynes turned his attention to the car.

"Would you be kind enough to open the door again?"

A strange figure was sitting in the driving seat. Obviously a man wearing a brown pair of men's shoes, old-fashioned brown lisle stockings, a beige skirt, a pink blouse, a thick brown woolly cardigan - and a wig with brown curls. He had bright pink lipstick on his lips, powder on his cheeks and some pink make-up around his eyes. The effect was garish.

Raynes had expected his complexion - or at least what he could see of it - to be cherry red in colour. But it was not.

Raynes looked at the man's hands. Slim, elegant, white. A writer's hands. Which suggested a desk-bound job. There was a wedding ring of his left hand. And on the palm of his right hand - a savage brown mark - blackened deep into his skin.

"Interesting," he said.

He put his hand on the man's wrist.

Cold, dry, hard. No pulse.

(Well, he hadn't expected one.)

He looked into the body of the car, with its rich leatherwork and mahogany finish. An expensive piece of work. He looked for more clues.

He noticed that the driver's seat had been adjusted to make the victim more comfortable. A nice touch.

Raynes reckoned that the car must have been in the car park for several hours. Rigor mortis would by now have set in. He looked again at the crumpled figure in the driving seat.

Helpfully, Sergeant Evans said: "You'll probably have noticed it's the University car, sir. GU 1."

Raynes looked at the little sticker on the right hand side of the windscreen. 'Grasshallows University Car Park' - and a crest.

He straightened up.

"So this is the much-loved Vice-Chancellor?"

"But what would he be doing in women's clothes?"

Raynes raised his eyebrows.

"I haven't the vaguest."

"Not exactly the height of fashion!"

"No. It looks like an Oxfam job to me."

Sergeant Evans felt obliged to air his knowledge:

"He has a very beautiful wife, sir. Tall, blonde, Danish, I believe."

Raynes looked down.

"Well, he certainly wasn't wearing her clothes. And she certainly didn't do his make up."

He asked the Sergeant to close the door.

"Has Dr Stewart been contacted?"

"I would imagine so."

Raynes laughed.

"Bit early in the morning for him! But I daresay he'll rally round pretty quickly when he sees that lot. Our bride from hell!"

Raynes looked down the length of the car park. Many other cars were beginning to arrive. Saturday morning - they could soon be mobbed.

"I think we need to close off this end of the car park. About fifty or sixty yards, I should think. We don't want anyone getting too close. Certainly not the Press."

Whilst the incident tapes were being unrolled and the first cars turned back, Raynes phoned up headquarters to ask if Dr Stewart was on his way.

"He'll be there shortly after 8.30am."

Raynes looked at his watch.

Five past eight.

There would be time to go and speak to Dr Treaseman.

"We shall also need screens. The scene of the incident is extremely public."

He walked over to Sergeant Evans.

"Make sure these people keep well away. Dr Stewart will be here in about half an hour. I'm going over to the club house…" He caught the Sergeant's eye. "… to see Dr Treaseman!"

22: The Witness

Dr Treaseman had not gone out on the course. He knew the police would want to see him. Running away - going back home - would look suspicious. So he stood near the front door of the club house, waiting and watching, till he had seen the Inspector arrive. After that, he went in to the bar and ordered a much-needed cup of black coffee.

So Raynes did not have far to look.

He sat down at the other side of the table.

"I think I'll have a coffee as well." He turned to the woman behind the bar. "Another black coffee, please. Two sugars."

119

He returned to the golfer.

"Dr Treaseman… Are you a medical man?"

"No. I'm a philosophy lecturer at the University."

"I see. And you recognised the car?"

"Immediately. And I thought: 'What's that car doing up here?' I know the Vice-Chancellor's not interested in sport of any kind. I thought for a moment that it might have been stolen."

"But then you saw the green hose?"

"Yes. It was then that I realised something nasty must have happened."

"And you felt you had to go and look?"

"Yes. But it was most odd. I was expecting to see the Vice-Chancellor - but it looked like an old woman."

"You opened the door?"

"Yes."

"You turned off the engine?"

"I did."

"And was there a smell of gas?"

"Carbon monoxide is odourless. You can't smell it."

"No. But I'm wondering whether the fumes penetrated he car. The back window was partially open. And the hose was attached to only one exhaust pipe. This particular model of the Jaguar has two."

"Well, I wasn't really thinking about the gas. I was trying to work out how Dr Shawcross came to be wearing such extraordinary clothes."

"But you recognized it was him?"

"I recognized his shoes."

"His shoes! Why should you recognize them?"

Dr Treaseman looked mildly embarrassed.

"Well, whenever I've had to deal with him, I try not to look into his eyes. I find them very harsh and unfeeling. So I tend to look at his feet. He always wears the same style. Whether he's wearing black or brown. But it was definitely him. I can't imagine why he'd want to die in that way."

"Perhaps he had no choice?"

Dr Treaseman looked surprised.

"You mean - it wasn't suicide? That someone dressed him up? To kill him - and humiliate him - at the same time?"

Raynes was careful how he replied.

"At this moment, we are treating the incident as suicide. But, like you, I cannot imagine that the University's Vice-Chancellor would want to be seen looking like that. I imagine he is a very fastidious sort of person. Very precise about what he says. Very particular about how he looks."

"That's right."

The Inspector looked sharply at Dr Treaseman.

"But you don't like him?"

"I can't bear him! He's caused all of us so much trouble and misery during this past year. He's been really cruel to the people in our department... You've probably heard..."

"I haven't heard anything."

"Well, he wants to abolish our department. He doesn't think philosophy is a subject worth teaching in a modern university. He asked us to justify our existence. In fact, he set a deadline - the end of this term - for us to come up with an answer."

"And have you?"

"No. Everyone's come up with an answer. But none of us can agree. We all think the other people's answers will be shot down in flames. And we're all so frightened about what may happen that we daren't let other people's suggestions go forward. So we're in a complete log-jam." He sighed. "It's pathetic really..."

Raynes did not know much about philosophy. But what little he did know - repelled him. It was the same with religion. The Inspector thought the Vice-Chancellor had probably been right to ask the question. The resulting confusion merely proved his point.

However, he tried to sound sympathetic: "How many people are there in your department?"

"At the moment, there are eleven of us. The Professor is on sick leave. That puts us in a very difficult position."

"Does everyone in your department feel the same way as you?"

"Yes. But…" He looked at the Inspector anxiously. "… But I have expressed my views more forcibly than the others. … and more publicly. If you interview the other people in my department, they will tell you that I have said - on several occasions: 'The sooner someone murders that man, the better.' I can't take it back. I have said it - and I believed it. Whether it is murder or suicide, I don't know. But I have wished for him to die - and now he has."

Raynes tried to sound comforting: "But not necessarily at your hand. Remember, we do not yet know the facts. When he died… or how he died. The police surgeon will tell us in a couple of days - and then we shall know. At the moment, we can only speculate." He looked at Dr Treaseman. "But your fingerprints will be on the door handle and on the keys…"

"Of course! I didn't think. My first reaction was to stop the gas coming into the car."

Raynes nodded.

"A perfectly reasonable explanation. But it also makes you a suspect. I shall have to see you again - once we know all the facts. If he was as unpopular as you say, I would imagine that we shall have a very large number of suspects."

"Most of the university I should think. Including his wife!"

"Did she hate him as well?"

"You'll have to ask her."

23: Dr Stewart Examines The Body

When Raynes returned to the claret-coloured Jaguar, Dr Stewart had completed his preliminary examination of the body.

"Bizarre!" he said. "Quite bizarre! Never seen anything like it."

Raynes raised his eyebrows.

"It's not suicide?"

"Never in a month of Sundays!"

Dr Stewart peeled off his gloves and flung them into a yellow plastic bag.

He looked at Raynes.

"How far did you go when you looked at the corpse? Not very far, I should think."

He drew the Inspector to one side so that no one could hear what he was saying.

"There's a massive blow on the back of his skull. A hammer or a chunk of lead, I would say. That's hidden under the wig. Then he's had a ligature tied round his neck. There's no sign of the cord or rope. He may have been gassed - we're being encouraged to think so. But none of the gas would have got into his lungs."

Raynes thought he knew the answer to that one.

"The open window? The faulty hose?"

"More than that!" said Dr Stewart. with a sour grin. "Someone's taken a leaf out of your book."

"My book?"

"Yes. The scouts. Remember Allan Foster?"

"They've put sand down his throat?"

"I'll have to see how much. But it could have blocked his windpipe."

"What about the burn mark on his hand?"

"I was coming to that. Electrocution. Someone's sent a couple of thousand volts down the line. But whether it was before or after, I just don't know. I'll have to think about it. A lot of analysis, measurement, timing, temperature. This one's not easy."

"How long's he been dead?"

"At least twenty four hours."

"And during that time, someone dressed him up in all those clothes - a sort of ritual humiliation?"

"It's a queer business."

"They didn't like him."

"No one liked him! If I'd had the chance, I'd have shoved a couple of thousand grams of warfarin into his stomach - rat that he was! Indeed, I might still do it - just for the hell of it!"

He looked at the Inspector's face. "Don't worry! It won't be in the report." He smiled. "But he was quite the wrong person to be put in charge of a university. He had no idea how such a thing works. I was even beginning to worry about my own job. He might have tried to pension me off."

"That would have been a sad loss."

"Kind of you to say so. Now, if you don't mind, I must get back to the lab. I know it's Saturday, but this one requires immediate attention. I'll try and get you the full report by Tuesday."

Raynes looked thoughtful.

"In the meantime, would you mind if I put the emphasis on suicide? Despair... defeat... drove him to take his own life?"

"You can say what you like. But the comedian who did this will know what really happened."

"Comedian?"

"Well, he's obviously pulling your leg, isn't he? When most people commit a murder, they strike just one blow. This chap's given you a selection. A veritable smörgasbord of options! This is murder *à la carte*. It's rather nice to see a murderer with a sense of humour. I wish you luck!"

Dr Stewart stomped away to his car. The ambulance closed its doors. Raynes was left with the two patrolmen and a beautiful car.

"This'll have to go back to the garage for tests."

But Sergeant Evans was looking further ahead.

"I don't suppose the University will be wanting it back now. Probably go for a song. Might be quite a nice car for some aspiring officer. Don't you think so, sir?"

Raynes laughed.

"I'm sure Inspector Morse is still quite happy with his 3.4 model. I have no intention of replacing my Rover. But if you have a few quid to spare, you might enhance your social standing!"

"The wife will never let me drive a thing like that!"

"Ah," said Raynes. "The curse of wives!"

Speaking of wives made Raynes think of the Vice-Chancellor's wife. She must be seen - and spoken to - before the news of her husband's death was made public. He wasn't sure of her name - he had meant to ask Dr Stewart - but he would find out soon enough. He drove directly to the Vice-Chancellor's residence, one the finest houses in the city, which had often caught his eye but - unlike the car - would not be up for sale.

There was a pale blue Mercedes parked beside the front steps. Raynes drew up beside it.

Mrs Shawcross had been about to set off for London when she saw the Inspector getting out of his car. Damn! What a nuisance! She took off her coat and scarf and headed for the front door.

"Yes?"

"Good morning. I am Detective-Inspector Raynes of Grasshallows police. I would like to ask you a few questions."

"About what?"

"About your husband."

"Come in."

It was a good excuse to look at the interior of the house. The building was Georgian. The rooms were perfectly proportioned and the decoration was all in pastel shades. The furnishings were tasteful but minimalist. He noticed the coat and scarf lying over the back of a sofa.

"You were just leaving?"

"I was going down to London."

"To meet your husband?"

"No.To do my Christmas shopping."

Raynes detected a lie.

Without being asked, he sat down in the nearest chair.

"Is your husband at home at this moment?"

"No."

"When are you expecting him back?"

"On Sunday night."

No sign of a lie there.

"And where is he at this moment?"

"At a conference on cutting University spending." (Did he ever think of anything else?) She added: "It was organised by the Government."

"Are you sure about that?"

"As sure as I am about anything he does!" she snapped. "Sometimes, the only way I know what he is doing is by looking at his Appointments Diary. If his personal secretary bothers to fill it in!"

Clearly no love lost there.

"When did you last see him?"

Mrs Shawcross paused to think.

"Thursday, I think it was. We had an early meal on Thursday night because he had a Senate meeting at 7.00pm. I think he was planning to leave on Friday morning; but by the time I got back to the house, he'd gone."

"Have you any idea where this conference is being held?"

"No. But I'm sure if you contact Mrs Gordon, his new secretary, she will give you all the information you need."

"Have you got her number?"

"No."

"She wouldn't be away with him?"

"No. The last one went everywhere with him. But this one won't. He said she was a complete cow."

"Who was his last secretary?"

"A Mrs Linda Hobbs. She had a nervous breakdown a few weeks ago. She was given sick leave."

"Was your husband responsible for her having a nervous breakdown?"

"Probably."

Mrs Shawcross crossed her beautiful legs and adjusted her hemline by a fraction. Yes, he could tell that it was expensive…

She looked up.

"So what has Timothy done? Has he committed some crime? Broken a speed limit? Assaulted a member of the

Philosophy department…?"

"No," said Raynes. "He's dead."

For a second, there was a glint of triumph in her eyes; but she recovered her poise almost immediately.

"Dead?"

"His body was found this morning in the University car - a dark red Jaguar."

"Had he had an accident?"

"If you call suicide an accident?"

The Inspector had been watching Mrs Shawcross very carefully for any sign that she might know her husband was dead. Clearly, she was glad to hear that he had died, but the news seemed to hit her like a bolt from the blue. There was no acting. If anything, there was suppressed anger.

"Suicide?"

"Yes."

"But why?"

"You tell me."

Mrs Shawcross shook her head in disbelief.

"It's not the sort of thing Timothy would do. He was enjoying himself. He had so much to live for."

"No sign of depression?"

"None whatsoever. He loved being Vice-Chancellor. It was the most challenging job he'd ever done. I didn't enjoy it; but he did. Of course, a lot of people hated him - but he seemed to thrive on their hostility."

She looked at the Inspector with appealing eyes.

"How did he do it?"

"Gassed himself in the car."

Mrs Shawcross began to cry. Her hands were soon covered with tears. Her distress seemed to be entirely genuine.

Raynes waited till she could bear a little more.

"His car was found at Skipper's Hill. It's a golf course on the outskirts of the city. It was at the far end of the car park. It was seen at about 7.00 this morning. The engine had probably been running all night."

"Was he on his own?"

Raynes nodded.

"There was no sign of anyone having been with him."

Mrs Shawcross tried to control her feelings. At one point, she seemed to be choking. Raynes offered her his handkerchief; but she went over to her coat and drew out a concoction in pink lace. She stood in the middle of the room, staring out of the window for several minutes.

"Poor Timothy," she said. "Fancy dying like that!"

Raynes thought that when she knew the full story, she would be completely shattered. At least, she would no longer blame her husband. He could imagine her fury against the person - or persons - who had killed him. Her rage would be uncontrollable.

She looked at the Inspector.

"Where is he now?"

"His body has been taken to the pathology department at the hospital. The police surgeon will be examining him."

"A post-mortem? Timothy wouldn't like that."

"It's not very nice; but it has to be done."

Talking about practical things, she seemed to re-gather her strength.

"When will I be able to see him?"

"Monday - or Tuesday."

At least she wouldn't see the make-up or the lipstick. That would raise even more questions. His main injuries would not be visible. With a bit of luck, the suicide story might last for two or three days.

"And what do we do now?"

"First of all, we need to inform the University public relations department. They will need to know - and they will issue a statement on your behalf. The Press will pester you for information about your husband. But the University will look after you," The Inspector looked at his watch. "It will be too late to get more than a paragraph in the Sunday papers; but it'll be all over the front pages by Monday morning." He paused. "You will also need an undertaker. I should go to Ferguson's. They're a family firm. I've always found them helpful and discreet."

Mrs Shawcross looked glum.

"Could I go and stay with friends?"

"If you want. But I would need to know where you were. I shall probably need to see you again. Especially when I come to write my report. I shall need facts and dates."

"I'm sure the University would supply all the information you need."

Mrs Shawcross had recovered her nerve. She was once again the Vice-Chancellor's wife. The Vice-Chancellor's widow. Whatever failings Timothy may have had - whatever sordid deeds he may have committed, she would handle the whole thing with dignity. No one would reproach her.

Raynes looked at her thoughtfully.

"I would prefer to do it now."

* * * *

Detective-Inspector Raynes spent another half hour with Mrs Shawcross, taking notes about her husband's life and work, his interests and his friends. Then he contacted the University and, after some difficulty, he reached a junior member of the public relations department. She promised to speak to one of her superiors and agreed that a statement would be released at 12.00pm.

Mrs Shawcross was glad to see the back of Inspector Raynes. He was a common little man - with a horrid British car. He had no taste - no finesse. She was glad to see him driving away from the University House.

Once he had gone, she put away her coat and scarf; took her weekend suitcase out of the car and put all the clothes back in the wardrobe. She looked at the slinky black nightdress with some regret. She placed her wedding photograph in a prominent position in the drawing room. (It had been languishing in a back bedroom.) Then she went through to the study and picked up the phone.

"Peter, darling…"

"Where've you been? You said you would be here at ten o' clock. I was going to phone you."

"It's a good job you didn't. I've just had a visit from the police."

"Oh, my God, Freddie! What have you done?"

"Nothing, darling. They just wanted to tell me about Tim."

"What's he done? Embezzled the student Care Fund? Been caught with his trousers down in a public car park with the delectable Mrs Hobbs?"

Freddie was a bit annoyed about the reference to 'the delectable Mrs Hobbs' - and how did he know about the car park?

"Neither of those. Haven't you heard? Timothy's dead!"

There was a terrible silence at the other end of the phone.

"Peter, are you still there?"

"Yes, of course I'm still here. What happened? Has someone killed him? Was he in a car crash?"

"No. He committed suicide. Last night - or early this morning…"

"That doesn't sound like Tim! I can't imagine him doing a thing like that." A guilty thought crept into Mr Latimer's mind. "It wasn't because of us, was it?"

"He doesn't know anything about us."

"I'm sure he did. In fact, you told me he did. You said it didn't matter because he was happy getting his noggins from.. you know who."

A second reference to Mrs Hobbs - and a suggestion of blame. This conversation was not going well. There was a caustic tone in Freddie's reply.

"Take it from me. He didn't know! I told him you were my spiritual adviser! And so you are."

She thought about the slinky black nightdress she would have been wearing that night.

"Did he leave a suicide note?"

"How should I know? The police have got his body."

"It might have been in one of his pockets. You should have looked before you phoned the police."

By this time, Freddie was getting quite exasperated.

"He didn't commit suicide in the house! He did it in his car. At a place called Skipper's Hill."

"That's the golf club."

"So I believe."

Mr Latimer was clearly rattled.

"You know, this could be damned awkward, Freddie. The police might find a letter. If it leaked out - about us - it might do us a lot of damage…"

There was an icy silence.

Freddie was very disappointed with his reaction to Timothy's death. When she had picked up the phone, she had wanted to say: "Good news! I'm free. Now I shall be a rich woman. In a few weeks' time, we shall be able to move in together and do all the things we've been longing to do!" And she had expected an equal outburst of joy at the other end of the line. The sound of champagne corks popping in celebration. But all he was doing was moaning about his reputation.

She said coldly: "I can always speak to the Inspector. He told me to phone if I needed any further help."

Peter realised that he had blotted his copy book badly. He adopted a more humble tone:

"Would you like me to come over and comfort you?"

"No," said Freddie firmly. "I can manage. The undertakers will be arriving shortly. And we have to think of your reputation!"

She put down the phone.

What a prick!

Well, even if they couldn't drink champagne together, she would have a very large gin and tonic. She could manage perfectly well on her own. Bloody men! Cowards - or creeps! All of them!

But, as she poured out her gin and put in two lumps of ice, she again burst into tears. And it was a long time before she added the tonic. Her hands kept shaking. Suddenly, she felt very lonely and vulnerable.

Why had Timothy committed suicide?

And was it her fault?

Perhaps there was a note in his pocket? If there was, that Inspector Raynes would be the first to read it.

25: So It Must Be Murder?

Detective-Constable Carlisle was summoned to Grasshallows police station shortly after 11.00am. He was still wondering why he had been called out on a Saturday morning.

"We have another murder!"

"You must be a very happy man."

"I am. This one was a complete Philistine."

"A foreigner?"

Raynes shook his head sadly. Some people's education never took them any further than David and Goliath.

"No. It was the University Vice-Chancellor."

"Was it Rudy who killed him?"

"I have no idea who killed him. All we have at the moment is a body. He was found in the official car - a rather nice claret-coloured Jaguar - GU 1."

"How did he die?"

Raynes smiled happily.

"We are supposed to think he committed suicide. Topped himself in the car. There is a nice piece of green hose attached to the exhaust, running into the car. But Dr Stewart doesn't think he was gassed - and neither do I. There was a rope round his neck. Sand down his throat and a rather savage blow to the back of his skull. But we think he was electrocuted."

Carlisle's jaw dropped.

"All that?"

"Yes. Which makes me think it was highly unlikely that he drove himself out to the golf club at Skipper's Hill, parked at the far end of the car park - and gassed himself."

"So it must be murder?"

"Yes. But I would prefer people to think it was suicide. I've drafted a statement for the Press. The University public relations office is putting out a similar statement in about forty minutes time. I should like to buy ourselves some time before we release the full facts."

The Inspector looked grim.

"It may be that the murderer's friends know more than we do. They may leak the details before we do. That would save us a lot of trouble. All we would have to do then, is follow up their leads."

"Do you think Emily will get there before us?"

"Very probably. She's closer to the action than we are. She will have access to two or three thousand students. I'm sure she would be delighted to get a real scoop; but her first opportunity to appear in print is next Friday. A lot of things can happen in six days. From her point of view, the murder was badly timed. If we catch the murderer first, we shall release the news and spike her guns."

Carlisle laughed.

"Do I detect a sense of rivalry?"

"Most certainly. We can't let that bitch win!"

"But if it was Rudy, she'll probably know by now."

"That's true. But there are one or two aspects of this case which worry me." An anxious look came over the Inspector's face. "The Vice-Chancellor was not found in a Pentagram or a Double Seal of Solomon. He was not dressed in his normal clothes - except for his shoes."

"Was he naked?"

"No. But he was dressed up as an old woman. With a skirt, stockings, a pink blouse and a cardigan. There was a brown curly wig to cover up the blow on the back of his head…"

Carlisle looked amazed.

"… He was made up - badly. This was not just murder. It was deliberate humiliation. Normally, murders are committed on the spur of the moment. A shooting. The stab of a knife. A bash on the head. But this man had been killed, stripped, given a change of clothes and then transported out of the city. We don't know where he died. I've been to see his wife at the

University House; but there's no sign of any violence. Not that I could see. This thing had been very carefully planned."

"Do you think it was someone at the University?"

"That's where most of his enemies were. I had a chat with a Dr Treaseman. He's a lecturer in the Philosophy department. He says the whole department were gunning for him. So that's about twelve suspects for a starter. I think we can take it for granted that the students hated him. You saw the posters on Wednesday night. 'Kill the V-C'. They would have attacked him if they had got half a chance. The fact that he died just after that protest demonstration does suggest that students might be involved."

Raynes handed over the notes he had made whilst he was talking to Mrs Shawcross. "She says that she thought he was in London attending a conference. That's a rough outline of his life, work, habits and interests. Not very interesting. A typical civil servant. Dr Stewart has promised us his report by Tuesday. But we had better open up a file right away."

He turned back to his desk.

"And that's the note we're putting out to the Press. It needs to be typed and run off. Ten copies should be enough."

"Are you going out to see anyone?"

"No. The University seems to have shut down for the weekend. Nobody's answering their phones. We'll just have to wait."

26: Russell Forrester Reveals All

On Monday morning, the Inspector's first port of call was the University Secretary. He had been trying to trying to get in touch with him all weekend, but either he was not answering his phone or he was away.

Raynes and Carlisle arrived at his office at 9.15am. There was little ceremony and no offer of coffee.

"You will have heard that Dr Shawcross has died."

"Most distressing."

Raynes looked at him.

"Do you actually mean that?"

Russell Forrester looked a little taken aback.

"Well, no. Actually, it's a great relief. But when you hold a position of authority, you are expected to say such things."

"I would like you to be completely honest with me."

The University Secretary quickly realised that he was not speaking to some recalcitrant lecturer but to the full force of the law. He had heard about Inspector Raynes; but this was the first time he had met him in person. He quickly changed his tune.

"The Vice-Chancellor was the most detestable man I have ever had to deal with. He's only been in Grasshallows for fifteen months; but in that time, he has caused the University endless trouble. There have been constant rows and disagreements which I have tried to sort out. He has bullied people, threatened people and tried to change the whole character of the University - all in pursuit of some economic theory which requires everything to have a purpose and a price. He felt there was virtue in cutting - for the sake of cutting. No section of the University was spared."

"Who chose him?"

"The Government."

"Did they know what they were doing?"

"I think it was a deliberate decision. They seem to think these older foundations need root and branch reform. They want to shake us up. It was a horrible experience."

"Dr Treaseman has told me that his department was directly under threat."

Russell was surprised that the Inspector had already spoken to the Philosophy lecturer.

"Yes. All of them. The stress has caused Dr Hampton to have a nervous breakdown. He's been on sick leave for the past six months."

"He should be able to return?"

"I would hope so."

"Do you think his department could have had any part in his death?"

Russell looked at the Inspector.

"I thought it was suicide. That's what the press release said."

"It was murder."

"Oh, I see. Well…" Russell paused. "Well, if I'm to be honest with you, the whole department has been thinking of how to get rid of him. They've been discussing methods for several weeks. One was going to shoot him; another was going to poison him. And a third was going to hit him with a blunt instrument on a dark night."

Carlisle looked at Raynes.

Noticing the look, the University Secretary asked: "Has Dr Treaseman been arrested?"

"No. But he was the person who found the body. He realised it wasn't suicide."

"I believe Dr Shawcross was found in the University car?"

Raynes nodded.

"Has it been damaged?"

"Not at all."

Russell looked thoughtful.

"Are you aware that the car was stolen?"

Raynes was surprised.

"It went missing on the Thursday night. Or rather, the chauffeur found it had gone when he went round to clean it on Friday morning."

Raynes said: "No one mentioned that to us."

Russell continued: "We didn't report it, because we thought it was an internal matter. We thought the Vice-Chancellor had driven it away himself. He was due to go to a conference in London on the Friday afternoon. We thought he'd deliberately left the chauffeur behind. They had a big fall-out about a fortnight ago and Dr Shawcross sacked him. For no good reason. We reinstated him. But there was some very bad feeling between the two men."

Carlisle underlined 'Chauffeur'.

Mr Forrester smiled.

"I'm glad the car's been found."

Raynes asked: "When was Dr Shawcross last seen? His wife says that the last time she saw him was at an early meal on Thursday night. At about 6.00pm... She said he had to attend some sort of meeting..."

Mr Forrester sighed.

"There was a meeting of the Senate on Thursday night at 7.00pm. It finished at about 9.30pm. The Vice-Chancellor was there the whole time. It was a very difficult meeting. There were a wide variety of issues. The Philosophy department, the Chaplaincy, the Student Union, the Botanical Gardens, the University playing fields - all of them problems caused by Dr Shawcross. He refused to accept any responsibility - or take any advice. And then, of course, there was that article in the local paper making allegations against the University Chaplain. You probably saw it...?"

Raynes nodded.

He always read the *Echo* to see what was going on. Especially now that Emily was writing her weekly article. He had been expecting more about Rudy - but the attack on Peter Latimer was quite devastating.

"Is he going to be suspended?"

"Not because of the article in the press. No..."

The University Secretary hesitated. Should he tell the Inspector more? Well, the man had asked for honesty - so he would get it.

"... We are consulting our lawyers about the article in the *Echo*; but we are worried about the University Chaplain on other grounds. We have good reason to believe that he is having an affair with Dr Shawcross' wife."

There! That did surprise him.

"Have you met Mrs Shawcross, Inspector?"

"I met her on Saturday morningwhen she was about to set off for London to do her Christmas shopping. I told her that her husband had committed suicide"

Russell Forrester shook his head.

"Not true, I'm afraid. We had advised Peter Latimer to take a couple of weeks off. She was intending to spend the weekend with him."

Carlisle underlined Mrs S and Peter L.

The suspects were beginning to mount up.

The University Secretary continued: "I did try to warn Dr Shawcross; but he refused to listen. In fact, he accused me of scandal-mongering. But we have reliable proof that she spends the night with Mr Latimer when her husband is away. She was with the Chaplain last Thursday night. She didn't return home till 1.00am.

"It was she who noticed the car keys had gone. The chauffeur says that he returned them to the kitchen when he brought the Vice-Chancellor home. But Timothy must have gone off immediately after the Senate meeting. Whether he went to that conference, I don't know."

"We shall find out," said Raynes.

He was already beginning to think that this might be an inside job. He would not have to interview the entire university. The cause of his death could be much closer to home.

The Inspector looked at Mr Forrester.

"Are there any other domestic tragedies connected to Dr Shawcross?"

Russell again hesitated.

"Well, I had one here - in my own office. I'd rather not mention it - but if this is now a murder investigation, it is probably better that you have the full story.

"The Vice-Chancellor's secretary was a lady whom I greatly respected. I have known her for years and I am very fond of her…"

He caught the Inspector's eye.

"… in a professional sense. Nothing more. She has had a very serious breakdown because of Dr Shawcross. He poured out all his emotional problems on her. He involved her in many hours of overtime and got her to type out all his private letters and reports to people in London. He took her to all sorts of conferences and meetings - often matters quite un-connected with the University. She spent days and nights in his company. Her marriage began to fall apart. It was alleged that the Vice-Chancellor was having an affair with her. She denies it. But the whole thing broke her up. I had to remove her from his office. I've put her on sick leave for four weeks - but she may need more time off."

"Was that Linda Hobbs?"

"Yes. How did you know about her?"

"Mrs Shawcross mentioned her. She said you'd replaced her with a Mrs Gordon."

Russell laughed.

"He won't get into any hanky-panky with her!"

"If he's dead, he won't be getting up to any hanky-panky with anyone!"

"No, of course not. But it's difficult to think that he's gone. He was such a dominating figure."

"Is Mrs Hobbs in Grasshallows at this moment?"

"Yes. She and her husband went to Tenerife on October 12 or 13. I felt they needed a holiday to put their marriage back on track. They would have returned by the 27th."

'In good time for the murder' thought Carlisle.

He turned to Mr Forrester.

"What's her husband's name?"

"Bill. Bill Hobbs. He's a good man. Excellent record. He works in the maintenance department. I imagine he must have been pretty hurt by the whole business."

Raynes asked: "Is there anyone else who might have had some personal grievance against the V-C?"

"Well," said Russell, "you can include the entire student community. They've been up in arms for several weeks. They're still absolutely livid that he forced them to pay rent for their building, together with all their costs of heating and lighting. It's cost them thousands. I did warn the Vice-Chancellor of the consequences. I saw it coming. But I never thought the reaction would have been quite so violent. Of course, we have one man to thank for all that!"

"Mr Krauss?"

"I really don't know why we let him back. He is a complete

firebrand. He knows how to work people up. He's put on this mantle of being a prophet; but he's the same old Rudy who burnt down the animal laboratory. We still haven't got our money back from the insurance company. They keep promising - but it's almost eighteen months since it all happened."

"I think it was the wax images which made it worse."

"That made it 100% personal. Encouraging people to stick pins into the Vice-Chancellor was the first step to killing him. Was he stabbed?"

Raynes did not answer the question.

"We're not saying anything about how he died. Not until we receive the full forensic report. We're maintaining "suicide" as the cause of death. I hope you'll go along with this?"

"Most certainly. Anything I can do to help."

Raynes smiled.

"Well, perhaps you could tell us where you were after the Senate meeting on Thursday night?"

Russell Forrester laughed.

"Me? You think I might be a suspect?"

"Well, you certainly disliked him. You described him as…"

He looked at his colleague.

Carlisle flicked back through his notes.

"… 'the most detestable man I have ever had to deal with'…"

"Thank you," said Raynes. "You have told us of the damage he has done to the University, the staff, the students… even to his own secretary. I imagine that you felt very bitter towards him. I'm sure you must have wished for the proverbial bus to crash into his car. For his wife to have put some deadly poison in his *foie gras*. Or some demented mistress to have stabbed him in the groin in a five star hotel?"

He looked inquiringly at the University Secretary.

"I'm sure such thoughts must have crossed your mind?"

Russell felt that it would be dangerous to withhold his deepest thoughts from the Inspector.

"I'm afraid many evil thoughts have crossed my mind in recent months. I have thought of electrocution. The electrics in the University House are very dangerous. I think they date back to the late 1920s. I have thought of lacing his coffee. I even thought of hiring a hit man. But I haven't done any of these things."

"Why not?"

Russell smiled more confidently.

"Well, because I thought that if we let him go on causing mayhem, he would self-destruct. Strangle himself with his own brassiere - so to speak. Upset all his chums in the Department of Education. Make such a complete hash of his reforms that even his deepest admirers would disown him. We were coming close to that point."

"Fair enough," said Raynes. "But you still haven't told me what you were doing after the Senate meeting."

Mr Forrester seemed happier.

"I had a very profitable weekend," he said proudly. "I went across to Salisbury to see a former member of Grasshallows University who lives in the Cathedral Close. He is now in his eighties and is thinking of down-sizing and moving into a residential home…"

Raynes interrupted the flow of conversation.

"Name and address?"

Russell Forrester picked up a letter on his desk and handed it over.

"I am just writing to thank him for his kindness."

Raynes passed the letter on to Carlisle.

"Did he put you up for the weekend?"

"No. But he has decided to give his fine collection of books and manuscripts to the University Library. He thinks they will be of more use to us than to him. So I went down to see exactly what treasures were on offer."

"They were quite valuable?"

"Some of them were unique. I should think the whole collection is worth in excess of two million pounds. It would greatly enhance the prestige of the University. We may decide to build an extension to the Library…"

"Or sell them?"

Russell looked wary.

"Not whilst the donor was alive!"

"But you may not be able to afford an extension to the Library?"

Mr Forrester's eye twinkled.

"The project would obviously take some time to reach fruition."

Raynes nodded.

"And where did you stay when you were in Salisbury?"

"The White Hart Hotel. It has quite a high reputation."

"And you returned… when?"

 "Sunday afternoon."

Raynes smiled - and stood up.

"We shall keep you on our list of suspects. But thank you for your help. We shall now move on and visit the other people on our list."

Carlisle drew a line under his notes, put away his pencils and handed back the letter to the University Secretary.

Raynes walked over to the window and stared out - at yet another rose bed! Mr Forrester joined him at the window. "It looks much nicer in summer…"

Raynes said to him: "How did you know that Mrs Shawcross was having an affair with the University Chaplain?"

"I have many contacts in the University - and outside. The information rolls in. People tell me what's going on. Several of the University lecturers live in the same street as Mr Latimer. Their wives have been keeping watch behind their net curtains! Even the taxi man who drives her to his house, tells me what is going on. You really cannot do anything in this University without people noticing."

Raynes turned and looked at Russell.

"Does that include murder?"

"I hope it does. The longer this investigation lasts, the worse it will be for the University. It's very bad publicity. We try to protect the University from scandal. You will need to find the murderer - or murderess - very quickly. I just hope it's someone outside the University. It would be very bad news if people thought we were a bunch of murderers."

Raynes turned back to the window - and the rose bed.

Very quietly, he said: "Perhaps you are?""

27: Visiting Peter Latimer

As they travelled down in the lift, Carlisle asked: "Where next?"

"I think it has to be Mr Latimer."

"Do you have his address?"

"No. Ask at the reception desk."

Carlisle came back with a chaplaincy brochure.

"41 Sandringham Crescent."

The journey took less than five minutes.

All the weekend, Peter Latimer had been like a cat on hot bricks. The article in the newspaper had rattled him badly; but, publicly, he had brushed it off, saying it was a private matter between himself and his wife. His marriage had irretrievably broken down. He was very distressed about it.

The University Secretary had suggested that he should have a couple of weeks off - to let the matter die down. He and Freddie had decided to go down to London for the weekend; but Timothy's death had put a stop to all that.

He was worried that there might be some letter - some accusation - in police hands which might cause him further embarrassment. But there was nothing in the newspapers to say what the police were doing.

The national papers were all full of praise for Dr Shawcross, featuring his distinguished career and 'the very real changes he had brought to Grasshallows University'. His death was not just a personal tragedy but also 'a great loss' - an 'irreparable loss' - to the city.

But perhaps help was on the way.

As he was sitting reading all this rubbish, he saw a police

car draw up at his gate. Two men were coming up the steps. The door bell rang.

"Detective-Inspector Raynes and Detective-Constable Carlisle."

"Come in."

He took them into his front room. There was a strong smell of coffee - and a heap of newspapers lying on the floor.

"Are you reading all about it?" asked Raynes.

"Yes. It's really quite sickening. They say he was a great reformer. A visionary. He was nothing of the sort. He was a mean, sarcastic bully."

"Did you have much to do with him?"

"More than I would have wished. We met at most university functions. He was determined to close down the Chaplaincy - and get rid of me. We clashed several times."

"Do you think he would have succeeded?"

"No. The Senate was dead against him. They opposed all his plans for cutting departments. He was in a minority of one."

"Why did he continue his campaign?"

"I think he was trying to convince his political masters that he was achieving something. He believed he could wear down the opposition. But people like Russell Forrester knew how to handle him. They gave him a very rough ride. He must have known he couldn't win."

"Do you think this was why he committed suicide?"

"Probably."

Peter Latimer's reply did not sound entirely convincing.

"You do not consider that you were in any way responsible for his death?"

Inspector Raynes stared at him intently.

"No."

His reply still did not sound convincing.

"You didn't think your relationship with Mrs Shawcross might have pushed him over the edge?"

"You've been talking to Russell Forrester!"

"I have - and he says this has been going on for some time."

Peter Latimer was silent.

"Do you think it might have upset him?"

The Chaplain recovered quickly.

"Nothing upset him! He thrived on hostility and conflict. He had a hide like a rhinoceros."

"But something personal which affected his wife? Something which might have become a public scandal?"

"They didn't have a good marriage. She was always leaving him and going back to London. She couldn't bear the claustrophobia of provincial life. She preferred the bright lights. She was a Madame Bovary sort of person."

"Who?" asked Carlisle.

"Female character in a French novel," said Raynes, annoyed at the interruption. "B-O-V-A-R-Y."

He turned back to the University Chaplain.

"Did he know about your relationship?"

"I think he did. Freddie... Mrs Shawcross... says he didn't."

"When did you last speak to her?"

"On Saturday morning."

"At what time?"

"About eleven o'clock."

"Just after I left?"

"Yes. She said you'd been."

"She was quite upset about her husband committing suicide."

"Yes. It came as a shock. But she had been warned..."

Raynes was surprised.

"Warned? By whom?"

"By Rudy Krauss."

Raynes groaned inwardly. Every time, he kept coming back to this wretched young man.

"How was she warned?"

"Well, apparently, she had asked Rudy to read her cards. Tarot cards. I didn't know about this. I certainly don't approve of people using Tarot cards. But she'd heard about his skills from the people in Palmerston - and she asked for a reading."

"When was that?"

"About ten days ago. He came round to the University House. She said he was very good. He was able to tell her about people in her family. People she had known in London. Very accurately. Information he could not have picked up anywhere else. That gave her confidence in him…"

Raynes was disappointed to hear that Mr Krauss did have some genuine gifts in reading cards. He had regarded him as an impostor right from the start. But perhaps he did have second sight. That could be dangerous.

"… so she asked him about Tim. He was able to tell her a lot about his career. But he said that Timothy was about to die - quite soon. That was what upset her. Rudy said it would happen before Christmas. He would die quickly, he said. But there was no doubt about it happening. It could have been a car accident - but I don't think either of us expected suicide. Did he leave any message?"

Raynes was about to say: "No" - but then he realised that a suicide note could cause Peter Latimer and Mrs Shawcross quite a lot of embarrassment. So he said:

"All the Vice-Chancellor's effects are being examined by the police surgeon. He will be going through all his pockets - and through the car - to see what he can find."

Raynes watched Mr Latimer like a hawk to see if he registered any awareness of the clothes Dr Shawcross had been wearing. There was no reaction.

He asked: "Were you frightened of what might appear in a suicide note?"

Mr Latimer did not reply immediately. But the Inspector was still watching him closely.

"Yes," he said, "It could be highly embarrassing for both of us."

Raynes smiled.

"If there is a suicide note, I will make sure that it doesn't appear in public."

He knew there would be no suicide note. It was murder.

The University Chaplain was surprised and grateful for this assurance. This was one burden less to bear. His spirits rose -

and his self-confidence returned.

But only for a moment! The Inspector's next question went straight to the point.

"Where were you last Thursday night?"

"I was here at home."

"Alone?"

Peter Latimer hesitated.

"No."

"There was someone here?"

The University Chaplain sighed.

"Freddie was here. But you probably knew that?"

"I know that you were planning to spend the weekend with Mrs Shawcross. When I arrived at the University House on Saturday morning, she had her bag packed and the car was waiting outside the front door. I'm afraid I interrupted your plans."

He looked at Peter Latimer's face. He could see drops of sweat on his forehead.

"When did she arrive here?"

"About 7.30. Once Timothy had gone to the Senate meeting."

"And she left... when?"

"About 1.00am. She normally leaves about that time."

"Did you take her back to University House?"

"No. She took a taxi both ways."

"When she returned home, did she find any sign of Timothy?"

"No. We've talked about this. There's no plates, mugs or glasses. His bed hadn't been slept in. Freddie said that she didn't think he had come back to the house. There was no sign of the car keys. They normally hang in the kitchen. She assumed that, after the Senate meeting, he'd just driven off to London on his own. That's why she didn't report the missing car."

Raynes sat back - and stared at Peter Latimer.

"You didn't help Mrs Shawcross to move the body?"

"Good heavens, no! We didn't even know he had died. We

decided that he must have been very upset by the Senate meeting; went away to think things over and then topped himself."

Raynes was not entirely convinced by the Chaplain's story. He was a self-confessed adulterer; he had abandoned his wife and children; and he had been exposed on both counts. He was not a man who could be trusted. He had a motive for murder. He had a powerful accomplice. And the two of them were together at the time Dr Shawcross disappeared.

As Raynes and Carlisle moved towards the door, the Inspector turned and asked one final question:

"Were you thinking of marrying Mrs Shawcross?"

Peter Latimer was lost for words.

"I don't know."

Raynes taunted him.

"She's a widow now. Probably a very rich widow. You could propose. Would she want you?"

Very sadly, the Chaplain said: "But I'm not free. I'm not divorced… No, I don't think she'd want me. She'll marry someone with money. Not a poor Chaplain. She prefers the bright lights… That's where she'll go."

28: Interviewing Rudy Krauss

They were back in the car.

"Rather a sad man, I thought," said Carlisle. "Nothing much to offer."

"Good looks," said Raynes, "but little else."

"Where would you like to go next?"

"Back to base. I sent a message to Mr Krauss asking him to pay us a visit once his morning lectures were over. I imagine he'll be with us by half past twelve."

"He should be more entertaining than Mr Latimer."

"Infinitely so."

"We shall at least be able to have a coffee."

Raynes sighed.

"It's a pity we weren't offered one by Mr Latimer. His coffee smelt excellent. We must return and find out what it was."

* * * *

They managed to have two cups of coffee before Rudy appeared.

He arrived at about 12.45pm, looking rather nervous.

"Am I being arrested?" he asked.

"Not yet," said Raynes. "That may come later. I daresay your friend, Miss Williams, would enjoy getting another juicy headline into this Friday's paper."

Rudy laughed.

"She's done quite well so far."

"That head-dress came out well in the photo."

"I believe it came from a theatrical store in London."

"You certainly looked the part."

The compliments were soon over. Raynes leant over his desk and looked hard at Rudy.

"Do you consider yourself responsible for Dr Shawcross' death?"

Rudy wriggled uncomfortably in his chair.

"No."

"You have driven this man to an early death. You and the rest of the students have hounded him relentlessly over the past few weeks. People have driven hundreds of pins and needles into his heart and brain. Eventually, he has succumbed."

Rudy looked coolly at the Inspector.

"You don't believe that - and neither do I. It wasn't suicide. It was murder!"

"How can you be so sure?"

"Dr Shawcross was enjoying himself too much. He'd got the whole University community running round the campus like headless chickens. He wouldn't have topped himself."

Raynes repeated himself: "How can you be so sure?"

"You should have bought one of my packs of tarot cards. They might have told you something."

Raynes drew back a little.

"Regrettably, I do not have the gift of second sight. But I believe you do?"

"Who told you?"

Raynes smiled.

"I have my secrets - just as you do. Shall we just say that I know you gave a reading to Mrs Shawcross, which impressed her greatly. You were extremely accurate about her past - and also her future. So perhaps you can tell me what you saw?"

"Secrets of the confessional!" said Rudy. "I couldn't possibly breach a penitent's confidentiality."

Raynes smiled again.

This man was as slippery as an eel.

"In normal circumstances, I would agree with you. But, as you have said, this is not a case of suicide; it is a case of murder and I need to know who killed the Vice-Chancellor last week."

"Is there any money in it?" Money for professional services and all that?"

"No."

"I think my services might be just as valuable as the fingerprints man - or the police surgeon. I would imagine both of them are being paid?"

"I'm afraid the Dark Arts would not qualify for repayment. And if they appeared on my expense account, they would be refused."

Rudy laughed.

"You expect it for free?"

"I do. Because you know things - and you have seen things which I have not. You are a witness to a murder - and that makes it very important that I should hear your evidence. When did you give Mrs Shawcross her reading?"

"Wednesday October 17th."

"You visited the University House?"

"At her request."

"Her husband didn't know anything about this?"

"I would imagine not."

"So what happened?"

"She gave me a nice cup of coffee and we sat in his study - and I dealt her four cards. They were mostly about her childhood. Some of the things I knew. But the longer I looked at the cards, the more I saw. I was able to describe the circumstances surrounding her mother's death and the death of her twin sisters. No one else could have known about that.

"It impressed her. It also impressed me, because it was the first time I'd seen anything in the cards. Normally, I paint a pretty picture. But, this time, it was for real.

"I dealt her four more cards. They were far more interesting. They were all her ex-boyfriends and lovers. One of them played a trumpet in a night club. Another was so angry with her that he hit her in the face. She had to have stitches. Another gave her a fantastic ring. I could see it."

Rudy looked at the Inspector.

"There were also one or two of her more recent conquests which I could see in great detail. It was embarrassing with her sitting there. But I promised never to reveal what I had seen…"

"Rev Peter Latimer!"

"Well, I warned her against him. That was before Emmy's article came out in the paper. I could see exactly what he was like. A complete bastard! He had deserted his wife and family because he was ashamed of them. One of his children is severely handicapped. He didn't want the folk in Grasshallows to know anything about her. But he will go back to his wife. I told Freddie; 'This man will let you down. Don't trust him!' I know he looks like a film star; but he's a complete shit."

Raynes nodded in agreement.

"I think it's the future we're interested in, Mr Krauss. What you told her about her husband's death."

"I told her he was going to die. I said it would be quite soon. I dealt seven cards for him. I don't know why. It was a horrible combination of cards. You could see it was going to be nasty. I found it terrifying…"

Rudy shuddered.

"I never want to see cards like that again. You may not believe me, but I actually felt sorry for the guy. Everyone was hating him."

"Who?"

"I saw hundreds of faces. All contorted with rage. They were shouting out things against him. I could feel them breathing out their hatred through me. It almost choked me. Freddie had to go and get me another cup of coffee. I was gutted."

"But did you actually see his death?"

"I saw the date of his death. It flashed past me. I realize now it was November 1 - but I thought it was November 11. It must have been a case of double vision."

"Wisdom after the event?"

"No, it's true. But so much was happening. I saw lightning crossing the card. It burnt my hand - my right hand. It was quite sore. Everything seemed to be going round and round. I saw a rope round his neck - tightening. I saw a stone mason's hammer crashing into his skull. I saw someone painting his body in lurid colours. He was stark naked - except for his shoes. He was lying in front of his car - the University car. I saw a brown wig being placed over the blood on his head. But I didn't tell Freddie any of that. I just told her that he would die quickly. Which he did. All those other things happened after his death."

Raynes nodded.

It tied in with what Dr Stewart had said.

"I saw Mrs Shawcross laughing - and raising a glass of champagne. Saying to the murderer: 'Well done!' It made me physically sick. I threw away my Tarot cards. I was so upset. Emmy had to go and rescue them."

"So you think the person who killed Dr Shawcross was someone close to him? Someone he knew?"

"I think so."

"A man or a woman?"

Rudy shook his head. "There were so many faces crying out. The women looked as vicious as the men. It could have been any of them."

As he stopped speaking, Rudy slumped back in his chair. Raynes thought he was going to faint. The experience continued to drain him. He looked like a limp doll.

In a feeble voice, he said: "Can I have something to drink?"

Raynes got up. He could imagine that Carlisle would have had some difficulty getting Rudy's story down in full. He would still be filling in the bits.

"I shall get you a cup of coffee. Sugar?"

"Two sugars. Cappuccino, if you have it."

Raynes went to the nearest machine. He'd be lucky to find cappuccino in a coffee machine in police headquarters. But he deserved the best.

What a fantastic story! What revelations! Rudy had seen every detail as if he had been there. Everything it seemed - except the murderer. He had seen the naked body of Dr Shawcross before he had been dressed up in those ridiculous clothes. He had seen the car. He was now sure it was November 1 - the night when Dr Shawcross returned home from the Senate - and Mrs Shawcross did not return to the University House till 1.00am.

Who had said that? The University Secretary. How did he know when she had come back from seeing Peter Latimer? Was he spying on her?

Raynes poured out the coffee and added the sugar. He found himself shaking - and spilling the coffee.

Rudy's evidence was vitally important. It put Mrs Shawcross at the very heart of the murder. He wondered how he could break through her icy reserve?

He returned to his office.

"One coffee. Two sugars."

He looked at Carlisle.

"Did you manage to keep up?"

"Just about."

Rudy looked at the Inspector.

"Is this when you produce an arrest warrant?"

"No," said Raynes. "You've been extremely helpful - and I believe you. However…"He looked at the elegant bearded figure in his white robes. "… However, I cannot ignore the fact that you have incited hundreds of students to attack the Vice-Chancellor. You encouraged them to attack him on a psychic plane. And he has in fact been killed by person - or persons - unknown. It may be that one of these people, whom you have incited, did the killing. I would like to know why the murderer killed Dr Shawcross before I give you a clean bill of health."

Rudy cheered up.

"So I can go?"

"Certainly. You are free to return to your studies. But if you remember anything more, please come and tell me. I should also be most grateful if you could maintain a discreet silence about Dr Shawcross' death. We should like to maintain the fiction of suicide for as long as possible."

Rudy nodded.

"My lips are sealed."

"And that includes Miss Williams!"

"She already knows."

Raynes uttered a silent groan.

Once that information was in the hands of the Press, nothing would be secret.

29: Clifford Brown

After a late lunch, Raynes and Carlisle went to see the chauffeur, Mr Clifford Brown. They found him at the University House polishing Mrs Shawcross' pale blue Mercedes.

"Is her ladyship at home?"

"She's speaking to the undertakers; after that, she is driving down to London. Then there will be nothing for me to do."

"I presume they'll be getting a new Vice-Chancellor and, perhaps, a new car?"

"There's nothing wrong with the present car - except that someone's died in it. But I'm told it was a peaceful death." Clifford crossed himself. "May God rest his soul."

Raynes was not sure whether Mr Brown was being entirely sincere.

"Did you like him?"

"No, sir. He was not kind to me. He accused me of terrible things."

Raynes raised his eyebrows.

"What terrible things?"

"He said that I was listening to his conversations in the car and reporting them to Mister Russell Forrester."

"Were these private conversations?"

"They were mostly about business - the business of the University - between him and his secretary, Mrs Hobbs. They were very close, sir."

"And did you report them?"

"No, sir. I did not."

"But he said that you did?"

"He said I was a liar, sir, and he sacked me. He told me that I would receive my P45 at the end of the month. I was in tears, sir; it was so unjust."

"So you went to Mr Forrester?"

"I did, sir, and he is a good man. He said that he didn't know anything about this - me being sacked. He said that I would not be dismissed and he would speak to Dr Shawcross."

"And when did all this happen?"

"It happened on October 12th, sir; and I spoke to Mr Forrester on the Monday the 15th."

"And how did Dr Shawcross treat you after that?"

"He ignored me, sir. Completely ignored me. He would say: 'The University' or 'Back home' - but nothing else. He never said: 'Good Morning' or 'Thank you'. He sat in the back of the car looking through his papers. Of course, sir, he was a civil servant - not a gentleman."

Raynes smiled.

"I wonder if you could tell me what happened on the Thursday evening - the night he died?"

Clifford bit his lip.

"I never saw him die, sir."

"No. I realize that. But I would like you to tell me what happened earlier in the evening."

Clifford cheered up.

"Well, sir, we left the house just after half past six. The roads were clear so we reached the front door of the University at about 6.40. His meeting was at seven."

Raynes nodded.

"And very long meetings they were too. Always two hours. Sometimes much longer."

"How long was this one?"

"He came out of the building at about 9.40pm. He was on his own. With his briefcase. He was very angry. As he always was when he didn't get his own way."

"And you brought him home?"

"I brought him home and he never said a word. I pulled up at the front door and opened his door. I said: 'Goodnight, sir' but he just walked straight past me into the house. He said nothing."

"And what did you do?"

"I drove the car round to the back of the house and put it in the garage beside Mrs Shawcross' blue one. I locked them both up and then I went into the kitchen and hung the keys on their hook. That's where I always put them. I had no desire to see him again, sir, so I went out quickly and went to collect my own car a little further down the road. Then I drove home."

Clifford sounded relieved.

"You left University House when?"

"About five to ten, I would say."

"There was no other car around?"

"No, sir. I would have noticed."

"No one lurking in the bushes?"

Clifford laughed.

"No, sir."

"Did you hear any voices when you put your keys back in the kitchen?"

Clifford shook his head.

"The walls are quite thick - it being an old house and all that. You wouldn't hear anyone talking at the front of the house."

"Was Mrs Shawcross at home when her husband came back?"

A rather shifty look appeared in Clifford's eyes.

"No, sir. She goes out with her... friends."

"Every Thursday night?"

"Usually."

Raynes could tell that he was choosing his words carefully.

"But you told me her car was in the garage by the time you returned."

"She doesn't use her own car, sir."

"I see."

"She uses a taxi, sir. She doesn't want to get done for drunk driving."

"Do you know where she goes? Would it be Sandringham Crescent?"

"Usually, sir."

"And when does she get back?"

"Quite late, sir."

"You've never collected her?"

"She wouldn't want me to know where she'd been."

"But you know. Who told you?"

"The taxi man. I asked him."

"Do you think Dr Shawcross knows where she's going?"

"I think so, sir. He said to me that he was her spiritual adviser. But there was more to it than that."

"You think so?"

Clifford grinned.

"She didn't get on with her husband any better than I did. She'll be glad he's gone. That's why she spent so much time in London."

Raynes thanked Clifford for all the information he had given and then asked to be shown the garage at the back of the University House. They were converted stables. Cobbled floor. There wasn't much to be seen. Not even a roll of green hose!

When they returned to the front of the house, they found Mrs Shawcross speaking to a man who was very smartly dressed.

She called out: "When are we getting Tim's body back, Inspector? Mr Ferguson says that he can't arrange anything till the body's released."

Raynes tried to look as agreeable as possible.

"We can't hand the body over until it's given up all its secrets."

"Secrets? There's not much secret in a suicide!"

Raynes inclined his head.

"Dr Stewart, the police surgeon, is still working on it. I expect we'll have some news by Wednesday. I'll let you know immediately. When are you coming back from London?"

"Tomorrow night."

"Well, that'll be all right. By the way, Mr Brown was telling me that you weren't at home on the Thursday night when your husband returned."

Freddie laughed.

"That's our girls' night out."

"What time did you get back?"

"About 1.00am. Perhaps later. I really don't know."

She looked down at the Inspector,

"Do get a move on with his body. The University want to arrange his funeral."

Raynes looked at the undertaker.

"Burial or cremation?"

"Cremation."

"I thought so."

Dr Stewart bustled in with his report early on Tuesday morning.

"I needed a couple of stiff ones to see me through this," he said.

"Was it very complicated?" Raynes asked.

"No. I just hated the man so much. He was insufferable in life - and even more repulsive in death. He lay there on the slab, still looking smug and complacent, as if he was expecting me to bow down and kiss his feet.

"But I said to him: 'They got you in the end! And so have I. It's your body that's on the line - not mine. So let's have a bit of respect before I slit you open.' That took the smile off his face! The mortuary staff thought I was bats. They often think that. But this one was a real stinker - in every sense of the word."

Raynes smiled.

"He really tested your powers of self-control?"

"He did that."

Raynes picked up his report.

"Were your first thoughts confirmed?"

Dr Stewart scratched his head.

"Blessed if I can remember what I said to you on Saturday morning! I was still half asleep."

"You said that the murder had a comic touch."

"So it did. Those awful clothes. The make-up. The variety of his injuries. The University car. Theatrical! That's what it was."

"So what killed him?"

"Well, the basic idea was electrocution. He must have plugged him in to the mains. That should have killed him; but the little creep had thick rubber soles. So it didn't finish him off - as you might have expected. It only stunned him.

"Then he was hit with a stone mason's hammer. That should have done the trick. But, apparently, his heart was still beating - or he was crawling around on the floor - or shouting for help. To put him out of his misery, our murderer friend whipped a piece of window cord out of his pocket and garrotted him. Three attempts before he succeeded."

"So he wasn't gassed?"

"No. That might have been a lot easier. The murderer wanted to make his departure as elaborate as possible. As I told you, he even poured a small quantity of sand down his throat. I think that was for your benefit! But the sand came later."

"Once he was dead?"

"Perhaps a day later. When he started mucking around with his clothes. There were some grains of the sand on the wig."

He looked down at his report.

"No fingerprints. We're dealing with a professional. We took Dr Treasman's dabs. His and the chauffeur's. But no one else." Dr Stewart laughed. "What a character! Wouldn't stop crossing himself. 'Oh, my God, what a catastrophe!' Have you met Mr Brown?"

"Yesterday," said Raynes. "He seems to have a great sense of humour. Do you think he could be the murderer?"

Dr Stewart shook his head.

"I don't think he's got the wit or the imagination to plan out something like this. He's a bungler."

"That's a pity."

"Well, he's also suffered at the Vice-Chancellor's hands. He told me the wretched man sacked him on the spot - for nothing. Told him to collect his P45. The chauffeur threw his keys at him - but missed. Then someone pinched the University car. He reported it but no one believed him. They thought Dr Shawcross had taken it down to London. But then it turns up as a hearse! Clifford thinks it's an act of divine judgement. And perhaps it is."

"What about the clothes?" asked Raynes.

"A job lot. Been lying around in a cupboard for quite some time. They all seem to belong to the same person. About five feet five. She had a cat and a budgie. Seed and touches of cat food on the skirt. Large pink knickers. Blouse. Old bra. Thick woollen skirt. Lisle stockings. Vintage 1950s.

"But no labels! All carefully cut off. With scissors. Every thread removed. No fingerprints. It obviously took some time. Our murderer took twenty-four hours to get Timothy ready for his final appearance. I would think he dumped the body in the University car and then drove it home; put it in his garage and worked on it during Friday or early Saturday morning."

"The make-up?"

"Also ancient. Pretty dried up. Powder, years old. No idea how to make up a face. Suggests a man. No finesse."

"And the Vice-Chancellor's clothes?"

"Binned or burnt - if he's got any sense. Judging by the evidence, I would say he's been pretty thorough. Nothing left to chance. Covered his tracks very carefully. I would say that he took the car up to Slipper's Hill very early on the Saturday morning. Arranged the corpse in the driving seat. Put in the green plastic hose. Switched on the ignition and said goodbye. He may have taken a taxi home. Or had an accomplice with a car. Of course, he could have walked. But he might have been seen."

He looked at the Inspector.

"Does that help?"

"A great deal."

"I don't know why I bother writing these reports…."

Raynes smiled.

"I always like to hear your own summary. There's always one or two useful insights which I might have missed."

"I hope there's more than one or two! I wrote that thing during the midnight hours - with a little help from my friends…"

"The Famous Grouse?"

"No. Whyte & Mackay! Neat of course!"

Raynes smiled again.

"I'll see if I can find some replacements."

"They would be much appreciated."

31: The Lady With The Golden Gun

Once Dr Stewart had left, Raynes and Carlisle set off for the Philosophy Department. The Inspector had decided that this was the main centre of opposition to the Vice-Chancellor. It was the spiritual home of the most violent students who had attacked the police on Wednesday night. They had come well-armed with fireworks, bottles and distress rockets. These were people who said they believed in principles, ideals and reason; but, in his eyes, they had behaved like drunken savages, threatening the lives of many ordinary students and - more importantly - the lives of his fellow officers.

The lecturers had been just as bad. They had encouraged them. They had also tried to stir up the rest of the students to mount a violent protest. But they had not succeeded. The large body of police and the presence of every police dog within one hundred miles of Grasshallows had seen to that. Otherwise there would have been many more serious injuries on the Wednesday night.

He was looking forward to meeting the blonde firebrand who had rained down abuse and hatred on the University and the police - calling for immediate revolution and insisting that heads must roll. Nor had he forgotten the Indian gentleman who had recommended de-capitation for Dr Shawcross and suttee for his wife.

But, at this hour of the morning, the Department seemed very peaceful. Many of the lecturers had not yet arrived; and their students had not yet rolled out of their beds. But Dr Treaseman was there to meet them.

"Good morning, Inspector."

"Good morning, Dr Treaseman. This is my colleague, Detective-Constable Carlisle."

"I've arranged for you to use our library. It's a quiet and peaceful place. I shall arrange for a continuous supply of fresh, black coffee."

Raynes cheered up.

He settled himself at the head of a well-polished table -

with Carlisle on his right. A nervous secretary came in with jugs of coffee, a tin of chocolate biscuits and plenty of sugar. She was nervous because this was the first time the police had visited the Department - and she realized that they could cause just as much trouble as Dr Shawcross and his dangerous ideas.

Dr Treaseman sat on Raynes' left.

Coffee was poured.

"What position do you hold?"

"I'm the Senior Lecturer?"

"What does one have to do to become a Senior Lecturer?"

Dr Treaseman smiled modestly.

"I owe my position entirely to having written an extremely long book on Jean-Paul Sartre, the French Existentialist. It was published just after his death. It was well-timed."

"Do have a copy in the library?"

Dr Treaseman pointed to the four books on a middle shelf.

"Good God! Four volumes!"

The Senior Lecturer laughed.

"That's what they all say."

"Is it still selling?"

"It is."

"Did you ever meet him?"

"No, but Dr Cooper did. She studied at the Sorbonne."

Raynes' eyes narrowed.

"Was she the blonde-haired… lady… who spoke to the students last Wednesday night?"

"She was."

"I shall look forward to meeting her."

Raynes turned to Carlisle to see if he was now ready. He returned to Dr Treaseman.

"Have you had time to think about what you saw on Saturday morning?"

"Yes. But I still don't understand about the clothes. They didn't make any sense. I can't see why they did it."

"You wouldn't have thought of it?"

"No."

"What would you have done?"

"Well, I hadn't made up my mind. I was hoping someone else might come up with a good idea. I might have pushed him down a flight of stairs. But I was sure something would turn up." He smiled. "As it has."

Raynes said: "Russell Forrester told me yesterday morning that people in this department had been discussing methods of killing him for several weeks."

"That's true."

"How did he know that?"

"I told him."

Raynes raised his eyebrows.

"I was sent to the University Secretary to report on the mood of the Department. It was one of despair. We all felt something must be done by the University before people exploded. We had already lost Professor Hampton. It was affecting our work…"

"Someone was going to shoot him."

"That was Dr Cooper."

"And someone was going to poison him."

"That was Miss Rabstead."

"And another person was going to kill him with a blunt instrument on a dark night."

"That was Dr Barnes."

"I heard an Indian gentleman at the Botanical Gardens recommending de-capitation. And suttee for his wife… A bit gruesome, I thought."

Dr Treaseman winced.

"That would be Dr Coomaraswamy."

"Were there any other suggestions?"

"Dr Venables had bought a crossbow. And I think Miss Smart had sent off for an African blow-pipe with a set of poisoned darts…I don't think they've arrived yet. She would have told us."

Raynes shook his head in disbelief.

"Many of suggestions were quite impractical. In fact, most of the staff were hoping the students would do their dirty work

164

for them. Then they could wash their hands of any responsibility. That's why they supported the Hallowe'en protest. But it achieved nothing. They were quite disappointed."

"You weren't there on Wednesday night!"

He made it sound like an accusation.

Dr Treaseman did not react.

"No," he said. "I avoid such things. I used to attend a lot of protest marches when I was a wild, young student; but now I have children of my own, I feel I have a duty to set a good example to my family."

'How very boring!' thought Raynes.

To the Senior Lecturer, he said: "And what were you doing on Thursday night?"

"We went to the cinema."

"And on Friday night?"

"We had a dinner party that went on till 1.00am."

Raynes smiled.

"You had your alibis carefully prepared?"

"I thought you might ask!"

* * * *

Miss Rabstead had no lectures that morning. She was quietly reading P.D.James' latest detective novel - with a pile of student essays waiting to be marked. They could wait.

She was delighted to be interviewed by a real live detective. Two, in fact… The younger man had a very sweet face. She suspected that Inspector Raynes was a wolf in sheep's clothing.

But he was polite. He stood up when she came into the room. And he invited her to have a cup of coffee. She accepted. It had been a busy morning!

But he immediately asked the all-important question:

"Did you kill the Vice-Chancellor?"

"No."

"But you intended to do so?"

165

"Most certainly. I had already chosen the date. Friday November 16."

Raynes looked at the cool, grey eyes behind the rimless glasses.

"And what is so special about November 16?"

"That's when we have the Bradbury Lectures."

She looked at the Inspector's blank face.

"Sir Ian Bradbury founded a special trust for the University so that they could invite famous figures - explorers, poets, philosophers, politicians - to give a series of public lectures on some contemporary issue. On the final night, there is always a reception after the Lectures, with drinks in the Senate Chamber. That would be on November 16."

"Could you be sure the Vice-Chancellor would be there?"

"It's a long-standing tradition."

"And how were you going to poison him?"

Her eyes twinkled happily.

"You see, he always drinks fruit juices. Not alcohol - at least in public. It is a perfect opportunity to add a small, colourless potion to his glass - but you have to be quick."

"What happens if it is given to the wrong person?"

"You have to deliver it personally."

"And which particular poison had you chosen?"

"Atropine. You only need a couple of grains."

"Do you still have it?"

"Yes. I was keeping it in my room. Just in case it was needed…"

"I think it would be better if we took it away. Dr Shawcross won't be needing it…"

"No, of course not. I shall go and get it."

Once she had left the room, Raynes said: "She's a bloody psychopath!"

She returned with a small bottle.

"It's already diluted." she said.

"Thank you," said Raynes. "I think it's probably safer with us. Removes the temptation…"

Miss Rabstead smiled happily.

"Oh, I wouldn't use it on anyone else. But he was an exceptionally evil man. And he deserved a particularly painful death."

"And you - as a woman - were willing to take the responsibility for killing him?"

Miss Rabstead said proudly:

"Every revolution needs a Charlotte Corday!"

* * * *

Having explained to Carlisle how Charlotte Corday killed the French Revolutionary leader, Jean Marat, by killing him in his bath, they turned to their next lecturer: Dr Ralph Barnes.

He was a cheerful little man, who looked rather like the elderly Richard Attenborough. He had rosy cheeks and horn-rimmed spectacles. Dr Treaseman said that he was one of the students' favourite lecturers. Raynes remembered seeing him in his duffle-coat laughing with the protestors.

Raynes said: "What branch of philosophy do you specialise in, Dr Barnes?"

"Hegel and Kant."

"The eighteenth century?"

"The *late* eighteenth century. You know where you are with these chaps. The Era of Enlightenment. No hallucinations; no repudiating French rationalism; no pursuing White Russian girls; not having your essays being re-written by that dreadful de Beauvoir woman. Just pure thought - clearly expressed."

Raynes smiled.

"I believe you had some impure thoughts about Dr Shawcross?"

"Many impure thoughts pass through my mind every day, Inspector! But you have to live with them."

"Do you have a conscience?" asked Raynes.

"Much better without one!"

Raynes agreed.

"So what did you intend to do to the Vice-Chancellor?"

"Something nice and simple. A snow shovel and a quick blow to the back of his head."

"That suggests snow."

"Precisely. I was planning something nearer Xmas. At that time, you see lots of people clearing their steps, sweeping their paths and pavements.

"The problem is that the Vice-Chancellor travels everywhere by car - door to door. He's not often seen walking. But I'd devised a nice little plan. I was going to pretend that I'd received a registered letter from the Department of Education. He had been out; but I'd left it in a red carrier bag beside his waste bin. It was too big for the letter box. He doesn't know my voice, so he'd probably fall for it.

"So, on a cold blustery night, he'd come out of the University House - and I'd be right behind him. One swipe and all our troubles would be over. He'd probably die of hypothermia.

"Now, on a winter's night, with the snow falling, there's a lot of people going around in balaclavas, thick coats and wellington boots. Difficult to identify such people. And the snow covers your tracks."

"So his death came a little too early for you?"

"I would say so. But I bought a really tough little shovel. Just my size. That would have stopped him in his tracks." He laughed uproariously. "The next Vice-Chancellor had better watch his step!"

* * * *

After he had gone, Carlisle asked: "Do you think he could have done it?"

"No," said Raynes. I think Dr Barnes is just a 'softie'. He wouldn't hurt a flea. Mark you, he would be quite a jolly person to be stuck with in a lift. He'd help to pass the time."

Dr Treaseman came back to say that Dr Venables, the crossbow enthusiast, was off sick. And there was still no reply from Dr Coomaraswamy.

"It's most unusual," he said. "Perhaps he too is sick."

Raynes smiled.

"I'd be more worried about his wife... Last night was Bonfire Night!"

Dr Treaseman ignored the joke.

Perhaps his mind was on higher things?

"Dr Cooper has just arrived. I'll bring her in."

* * * *

Charlotte Cooper may have had a good sense of humour. She might even have enjoyed Raynes' joke. But she really didn't want to speak to the Inspector whom she regarded as a 'Fascist pig'.

The argument continued for almost five minutes - most of which Raynes could hear through the half-open door. Eventually, he got up from his seat and went out into the corridor and looked Dr Cooper in the eye.

"This is not a theoretical discussion about some abstruse philosophical point. This is a murder inquiry and most of this department are prime suspects. I understand that you have an issue with the police, but I need to interview all the suspects. I would be glad if you could immediately step into the Library."

Breathing out fire and slaughter - and cursing under her breath - Dr Cooper conceded defeat. She refused the offer of coffee, but said she would drink whisky. Dr Treaseman, knowing her tastes, was able to find a half bottle in her room.

Raynes said: "I quite understand that you hated Dr Shawcross. Perhaps you could tell me why?"

Charlotte said: "Well, first of all, he was the wrong man for the job. He had no academic quailfications. He had no knowledge of university administration. He was a Government stooge appointed for the sole purpose of destroying this ancient University. I am sure you've read his C.V. He was just a jerk working in the Department of

Technology who specialised in time and motion studies. He was the person they sent into factories to see how much more the workers could be made to produce at less pay. And how many of them could be made redundant.

"That was why he was sent to British Leyland - to grind down the faces of the workers and secure higher productivity. Why do you think they had so many strikes at Longbridge? It was all his fault. The workers stood up and fought both him and the Government.

"Fancy sending a man like that to a University! He had no understanding of the purpose of a university education. To think, to research, to improve minds. To train skilled people like doctors, lawyers, scientists, politicians, foreign language experts, archaeologists. They can't be measured by time and motion! You just can't cut chunks off a university. It's like cutting bits off a living organism." Raynes was sympathetic to her views. But when she stopped, he said: "Does that justify your desire to kill him?"

"Of course. He was the class enemy. The traitor within the gates. A Government spy. A wrecker. He was probably hand in glove with the property developers. He would have got his cut."

"And you were going to shoot him?"

"I was."

"But why hadn't you done it already? Why have you waited fifteen months?"

Dr Cooper paused.

Why hadn't she done it earlier? Well, the answer was that it was more fun attacking the Vice-Chancellor than killing him. Once he was dead, the game was over. Whilst he was alive, you could shout and rage. You could convert the students from passive acceptance of the status quo to raging fury. (Which takes time.) You could build up solid opposition in other universities - establishing solidarity right across the whole spectrum of Higher Education.

It gave you a reason for living. For getting up every morning, knowing there was fresh excitement ahead. That justified your existence.

After a significant pause, she said: "It takes time to build up an effective opposition."

Raynes was watching her closely. He said: "Do you need to build up an opposition? You are a talented and charismatic person; you are both perceptive and practical. Once you saw what he was like, should you not have acted immediately - before he could do any damage to the University? Would it not be true to say that, but for the efforts of Rudy Krauss, there would have been no opposition?"

Dr Cooper angrily tossed her head.

"Krauss is just a brainless anarchist!"

Raynes said: "Most people seem to think that he raised the political temperature very quickly. He made his campaign 100% personal. 'You stick the pins into the Vice-Chancellor!' He'd already burnt down the animal laboratory. You've got to admit that he's a man of action - not just a talker."

"He's a complete phoney!"

"That still doesn't explain why you have waited so long. I believe you have a pistol?"

"A Beretta."

Almost immediately, Dr Cooper realized that she should not have admitted possession of any weapon. But it was too later. She had been thinking about Rudy Krauss when the Inspector casually mentioned the pistol. His next question was inevitable:

"Have you got a licence for the gun?"

Charlotte said nothing.

Raynes said: "We have no record of you having a licence. Is it still in your possession? Here or at home?"

Dr Cooper remained silent.

"We need to know whether it was your pistol that killed him."

"It was suicide!"

"No, it wasn't. We received the police surgeon's report this morning. It was definitely murder."

"He was gassed."

"Who told you that?"

"Dr Treaseman. He said that he saw the hose going into the car through the back window. That would suggest suicide."

"That was what the murderer wanted us to think. In fact, he had been electrocuted. He had a blow on the back of his head; and a rope tied round his neck."

"Really?"

Dr Cooper was clearly surprised.

"Did it take all that to kill him?"

"Don't you think a bullet would have been quicker and kinder?"

The lecturer shook her head.

"He needed to suffer. A bullet would have been too easy."

Raynes continued to pile on the pressure. "Now you have told people what you were going to do. When would you have done it? Where would you have done it? At a Senate meeting? Passing him in the corridor? In the staff toilet? Whilst he was sitting in his car?"

Dr Cooper shrugged her shoulders.

"I hadn't decided."

Raynes looked at her.

"All talk; no action."

"If you say that again, I shall kill you!"

"Promises! Promises!" said Raynes. "I don't think you are capable of such a thing. You are willing to stir up the students - as we saw last Wednesday night - congratulating them after they had attacked the police! But you weren't willing to put your career or your liberty at risk. You didn't kill your real enemy. You tried to kill us!"

The Inspector sounded justifiably angry.

"Anyway, we're not going to waste any more time talking to you. We need to remove that illegal pistol."

"It belonged to my uncle. It's a family heirloom."

"If it hasn't got a licence, you are obliged to hand it over. You can apply for a licence - and we shall consider it. But you can't possess an illegal weapon and threaten people."

There was silence.

"Is it in this building…"

He paused.

"… Or do we have to search your home?"

Carlisle looked at his notes.

"15 Sandringham Crescent."

Raynes waited.

He waited a long time whilst Dr Cooper considered the full implications of giving way to a police demand. People would expect her to stand firm. Not to weaken. It would be better for her to refuse. But if they searched her house… that would be disastrous. Her address book… with all her Left-wing contacts. They would seize that. Her contacts would blame her if they were arrested.

Raynes watched and waited.

She hated him. She wished she had shot him outside the Botanical Gardens when she had had the chance… When the pistol was in her pocket. Then she would have been hailed as a hero of the Revolution. But to meekly hand it over…

Raynes said quietly: "If you don't hand it over, I shall arrest you immediately."

"It has nothing to do with the murder!"

Raynes smiled.

"But we may prevent another!"

Dr Cooper had thought it might be fun to be arrested - but her arrest would have serious consequences for her Communist friends. She could not put them at risk. There were secret contacts based all over Europe. If the British police passed over her address book, the CIA would have a field day.

It would be better to give way.

Charlotte Cooper looked directly at the Inspector.

"I will hand it over."

"And where is it?"

"It is in the bottom drawer of my filing cabinet in my office."

"We shall come with you to collect it."

Raynes realised that she must have a great deal more secret

material hidden at home. If she got off lightly - merely handing over the pistol - she would count herself fortunate. But the Special Branch could always pay a private visit to her house. The incriminating material would still be there.

Raging with silent anger, she handed over the Beretta and its ammunition.

"Thank you," said Raynes. "It is always much easier when people co-operate."

The blonde firebrand longed to say: 'When the Revolution comes, you'll be the first to go'.

Her look said it all.

32: The Delectable Mrs Hobbs

After lunch, the Inspector decided that it was time for him to meet the 'delectable Mrs Hobbs' and her husband, Bill. They had been away in Tenerife for a fortnight, but they had been back in Grasshallows at the time of the murder.

The house looked very well-maintained and the garden was immaculate. Raynes imagined that the interior would be much the same. So, as he sat down on the sofa, he was careful not to derange the cushions or the antimacassar.

"Did you have a good holiday?"

"We did. It was all the better because it was unexpected."

"That was Russell's idea?"

"It was. He felt that we needed to get well away - and he was right."

Linda looked to her husband for his agreement.

"We couldn't go on the way we were."

"No."

Raynes nodded.

"Your working relationship with Dr Shawcross had become impossible?"

Mrs Hobbs chose her words carefully.

"I realize now that I had got too emotionally involved. I was not just supporting his projects, I was supporting him as well. Trying to maintain his morale. But it was getting more difficult every day."

Bill said: "It was really breaking us both up. I hardly ever saw Linda. When we did see each other, we did nothing but row. We never had rows before he came."

"Of course, he was tremendously unpopular."

"He had no friends…"

"And the Senate completely rejected his plans."

"Russell felt he had to intervene."

Raynes said: "He intervened very quickly. I believe you were away before Dr Shawcross realized you had gone. And Russell gave him a much less sympathetic secretary - Mrs Gordon."

"How did you know that?"

"Mrs Shawcross told me. She said that he complained bitterly about the change. He kept trying to phone you - but it was too late."

Bill Hobbs said: "Things seemed to get worse after we came back. That huge protest outside the Botanical Gardens! People firing rockets at the police."

Raynes said: "It wasn't very pleasant."

"That Rudy Krauss has a lot to answer for!"

Raynes could not let that pass.

"He didn't cause us any trouble. He actually tried to calm down the more violent students. And I was very grateful he did because, although the students didn't know it, the Vice-Chancellor was there!"

"Really?"

"I didn't want him there; but he insisted on being there. He kept begging me to stop the violence, but I told him it was his fault!" Raynes laughed. "Eventually, we had to lock him in a police car - for his own safety."

"He wouldn't have liked that."

"He would have liked it even less if the students had got their hands on him. Several of them were carrying knives."

"It must have been a very expensive operation."

Raynes smiled.

"Well, at least nothing happened to the glasshouses. Repairing them would have cost the University a large amount of money."

Raynes felt there had been enough small talk.

"Now about the murder…"

"Murder?" exclaimed Linda Hobbs. "I thought it was suicide. That's what the papers said."

"They were wrong."

Bill Hobbs did not look surprised.

"He deserved to die."

Raynes said: "Did you have any dealings with him?"

"Not really. I was in his house a few times but he never spoke to me. He didn't know who I was."

"You had a key to the house?"

"We had to have one when we were repairing his roof."

"When was that?"

"Last winter. Quite a lot of water came in through one of the ceilings."

"And you're in the Maintenance department?"

Bill nodded.

"He was going to close that down, wasn't he?"

Bill laughed.

"Once the water came pouring into his house, he was glad to get it dealt with so quickly. After that, he moved on to other things. I think we saved the department from getting the chop."

Linda Hobbs was still coming to terms with the news that someone had killed her boss.

"So he didn't gas himself…? Can I ask what did happen?"

Raynes didn't see much point in hiding the facts. They would soon be in the papers.

"He was electrocuted. There was a savage blow on the back of his head. And he was garrotted."

Linda burst into tears.

Bill looked white-faced.

"Where did all this happen?"

"In the University House."

"Well, I never." Bill was silent. "I never thought the

electrics in that House were safe. They've been arguing about how to replace them for years."

"Well, they'll be done now!"

Linda wiped away her tears.

"He didn't deserve that! No one deserves to be treated like that."

But her husband disagreed.

"I think he deserved all he got. He rode roughshod over everyone. He threatened people. Bullied them. He had no conscience about throwing people out of their jobs. He had no feelings for other people."

But Linda still felt some affection for him.

"What will his wife be feeling at this moment?"

"She is delighted," said Raynes.

Bill cheered up.

"Did she have a hand in the murder?"

"We don't know. That's why we're conducting our investigations."

Linda Hobbs said: "But we were away."

Raynes said quietly: "You were back a full week before he died."

"You don't suspect us - surely you don't suspect us?"

"Well," said Raynes, "I would say that you two suffered more than most. You had something approaching a nervous breakdown." He looked at Bill. "And you blamed him for almost destroying your marriage…"

Bill said firmly: "I still do."

"Well," said Raynes, "you have a motive."

Linda broke in. "But we would never have killed him! Never! I felt sorry for him. Bill may have felt differently. But we're not the sort of people who go round killing people." She paused. "If he was murdered, I would blame those people in the Philosophy department, the staff at the Botanical Gardens and the University Chaplain. They were all the people whose jobs were most at risk. And, of course, the students. There are a lot of angry people out there."

"Were you thinking of anyone in particular?"

"Yes. But she's my friend."

Raynes had been keeping an eye on the University House, waiting for Mrs Shawcross to return from London. It was not till after 9.00pm that a patrol car reported that there were now lights on in the building. Raynes was there within fifteen minutes.

She opened the door.

"Oh, it's you. I'd forgotten you were coming."

"Did you have a good time in London?"

"Mostly shopping. I had to get something suitable for the funeral."

They went into the sitting room.

"Do sit down."

Raynes sat down.

"Now when is Timothy's body going to be released?"

"Next Monday."

"Not till then?"

"Well, the police surgeon has had to do quite a lot of work on it. It wasn't straightforward."

Mrs Shawcross looked surprised.

Raynes said quietly: "It wasn't suicide."

"Not suicide?"

"No, it was murder."

She was silent.

Raynes said: "You knew that…"

"I most certainly didn't!"

Raynes looked at her more critically.

"You had your cards read by Mr Rudy Krauss on Wednesday October 17. He told you that your husband was going to be killed by those who hated him. He told you it would be a quick death - and that it would happen very soon. Whilst you were with Mr Krauss - before you got him his second cup of coffee - Rudy felt a burning sensation in his right hand. He said that something like a flash of lightning crossed the card and burnt into his hand. This told him that Dr Shawcross was going to be electrocuted."

"Electrocuted?"

Raynes nodded.

"Where?"

"In this house - after he came back from the Senate meeting. You told me that you were out that evening. You said you were having 'a girls' night out'. You were not back till after 1.00am."

Raynes watched Mrs Shawcross rapidly re-arranging her alibi.

"When you returned home, did you find Timothy dead on the floor or in one of the rooms?"

Freddie's confidence returned.

"No, I did not. When I came back there was no sign of him. I thought he had gone off to London for that meeting."

"I'm afraid that, by that time, he was dead."

"But he was killed here?"

"Yes. But the body was moved elsewhere. That's why it wasn't found till Saturday morning."

"Up at the golf club?"

"Yes."

"But someone killed him here?"

"Yes. The police surgeon thinks that he put his right hand on a door knob - or a tap - or some other metal object, which had been wired up to an electric plug…"

"They were in the house waiting for him to return?"

"Yes."

Mrs Shawcross at last showed some emotion.

"Oh, poor Timothy! How dreadful!"

Raynes waited till she had had time to absorb the first blow before proceeding.

"Dr Stewart doesn't think that the electricity killed him. So he was hit on the head - probably whilst he was still writhing on the floor. But even that didn't kill him. So he was finally choked with a rope round his neck. That finished him off. But it all happened very quickly."

Mrs Shawcross wept as the whole picture was laid before her. Raynes could imagine the impact of her hearing this for

179

the first time. He sat silently in his chair and made no effort to comfort her. He waited till he could fill in the final part of the story.

"The body was then removed by the murderer - or by the murderer and his accomplice. It was another twenty-four hours before the body was taken up to the golf club. Dr Shawcross was found in the front seat of the University car - behind the steering wheel. There was a green hose attached to the car's exhaust - pouring gas into the car. The engine was still running when the car was found. But Timothy was not gassed. He did not commit suicide. The murderer wished us to think that was what happened. But it didn't. It was a cruel hoax - on the back of a murder."

There was obviously a great deal that the Inspector left out. The sand. The old clothes and the make-up. It was perhaps better that they should remain a secret - though of course Dr Treaseman knew.

Mrs Shawcross was now visibly angry. She had red patches on her wet cheeks. Her lips were quivering.

"And have you arrested Rudy Krauss and the other students? Are they in custody?"

"No."

"And why not?"

"We have no proof that they killed your husband. I didn't even know till yesterday that Rudy had read your cards. His evidence has been most helpful."

"They've been planning it for weeks. You must have seen the signs they were carrying outside the Botanical gardens: 'Kill the V.C.' You can't deny that. You were there!"

"Indeed I was. It was a very unpleasant evening for all concerned. But the students did not attack your husband. They jeered at him. But they didn't throw any stones in his direction. I think your husband deliberately provoked their hostility. He was lucky to get off so lightly."

Mrs Shawcross shook her head in disgust.

The Inspector looked more hopeful.

"Of course, we shall have to consider your movements

more carefully - now this is a murder enquiry."

"My movements?"

"I would like you to tell me where you were on Thursday night. You have said that you were having 'a girls' night out' which you do most Thursday nights. It would be very helpful if you could give me the names and addresses of these girls so that we can check your movements."

"I'm telling you nothing!"

Raynes smiled - one of his dangerous smiles.

"There is nothing to tell, Mrs Shawcross. I know exactly where you were on the Thursday night. You were at 41 Sandringham Crescent seeing Peter Latimer - your 'spiritual adviser'. The University Secretary told me that the residents of Sandringham Crescent - most of them lecturer's wives - have been watching your comings and goings. They have seen you arriving by taxi and leaving at 1.00am. I am sure they will be able to provide full information about your movements - and so will your taxi driver."

He waited till she had fully absorbed these unpleasant facts. Then he added: "And just for the record, it was Peter Latimer who told me about Rudy Krauss and the Tarot cards. You told him."

Mrs Shawcross must have thought her misery was complete, but Raynes had one final, crushing blow in store.

"You will appreciate that now I have the forensic report from Dr Stewart, this house has become a crime scene. The police have been waiting all day for the opportunity to seal off the house and begin a minute search of the premises to find out exactly where the murder was committed. I'm afraid you will not be able to remain in the house, whilst all this is going on.

"However, I have booked a comfortable suite for you in the *Green Man*. I have also arranged for a police car to take you to the hotel." Raynes looked at his watch. "That will be in about half an hour's time when you have packed your clothes. You will not be able to return to the house until the police investigation is complete. Carpets and articles of furniture may have to be taken away for further examination."

Raynes rose to his feet and walked over to the window. He pulled back the curtain and gave a formal wave to the officers standing outside on the gravel drive. The Inspector turned and looked at Mrs Shawcross, wondering how much more she could take.

"I did wonder whether you might have preferred to stay with Mr Latimer. But his future is a little dodgy at this moment. So it might be better not to add to his troubles."

Raynes went out into the hallway and opened the front door for the police. He said to the solitary policewoman: "You'll find Mrs Shawcross in the sitting room. Don't let her move anything except her clothes - and her toothbrush!"

34: A Funeral Is Arranged

Inspector Raynes picked up the phone.

"Yes?"

"There's a Mr Hayward wanting to speak to you."

"Put him on."

"Is that you, Inspector? This is Tom…"

Raynes was still not feeling very charitable towards the local Press baron. Especially when he was encouraging his Welsh dragon to stir up trouble in the University.

"What is the problem?"

"Well, I'm not sure it is something we should be discussing over the phone. I've received an intimation for publication in this Friday's paper, which concerns you personally. I've checked to see if it came from the undertakers - but it hasn't. Do you want me to read it?"

"Please do."

Raynes could detect hesitation at the other end of the line.

"Get on with it!"

Mr Hayward coughed nervously.

"RAYNES, Richard.
Suddenly, in Grasshallows on Sunday, November 11.
Dearly beloved partner of Mrs Deborah May.
Former husband of Brenda Whelks and Doreen Chalmers.
Much loved father of Sidney and Cecil.
A funeral is arranged for Wednesday November 21
at Grasshallows Crematorium at 12.30pm.
Donations to the Donkey Sanctuary."

Raynes was silent.

Stunned.

"Are you still there?"

"Yes, I am." The Inspector was trying to make sense of what he had just heard. "When did this reach you?"

"By post, this morning. It contains six five pound notes to cover the cost of the intimation."

"Have you got the whole thing?"

"Everything except the envelope. But we should be able to find that in the mail department downstairs."

Raynes said: "I should like to see this remarkable document immediately. Would it be convenient for me to come round and see it?"

"Of course."

Raynes put down the phone.

Carlisle looked across the room at his boss.

"What was all that about?"

"A funeral has been arranged…"

"Whose?"

"Mine! I'm scheduled to die on Remembrance Sunday. And then to be cremated ten days later. I think we should go down and see Tom Hayward immediately."

"Shall I get the Granada?"

"No. We'll walk. It'll only take a few minutes."

* * * *

Seated in Mr Hayward's comfortable office, Raynes looked

down at the single sheet of paper bearing the news of his death.

It was typed neatly - with no mistakes. Forty-nine words if one included the dates. It was surrounded by a thin black line. The document was a photocopy so it was impossible to examine the impact of the typewriter keys on the original paper.

Raynes looked up.

"How many people have touched this?"

Mr Hayward looked apologetic.

"Probably two or three people in the mail department. They open things up and then pass them on to the relevant department. In this case 'Classified Ads'."

He looked more optimistic.

"We've found the envelope…"

He picked up the remains of the envelope - torn and crumpled.

Raynes noted that the address was on a label. Probably photocopied as well.

"… and the thirty pounds."

The Inspector said: "We shall have to test this for fingerprints. Yours - and members of your staff."

"Of course."

"Detective-Constable Carlisle has some plastic bags."

The material was collected together.

Mr Hayward looked at the Inspector.

"At first, we thought it might be a bit of a joke. Then we decided it might be more serious. A threat. We thought you ought to know."

"You've done the right thing. We do get poison pen letters from time to time; but some of the correspondents are easily recognised. Their handwriting. Their colour of ink. The things they complain about. The words of abuse they use. We shall have to compare this letter to see if it matches any of them."

Mr Hayward smiled.

"Do you have any enemies, Inspector?"

"Plenty! But most of them are safely behind bars.

Though…" He paused. " … you have one of them working for you at this moment - in the University."

"You mean Emily Williams?"

"I do. I would imagine she is still breathing out fire and slaughter against me. I wouldn't put anything past that young woman."

He looked at the proprietor of the *Echo* more thoughtfully. "I hope she's not been involved in this. We don't like people playing stupid games. It could have serious consequences for her future career."

* * * *

Raynes and Carlisle walked back to the police station.

"We should find out who it is."

"We may. But I think this person knows what they are doing. They're cocking a snook at us because we haven't solved the crime. We haven't caught the murderer. I know it's early days; but this chap is twisting our tail."

"Do you think it could be the murderer who sent it?"

"Could be. Dr Stewart said he - or she - had an odd sense of humour. It fits."

Detective-Constable Carlisle felt that he had to ask one further question: "Were you ever married to someone called Brenda Whelks?"

"No," said Raynes. "I was married to neither Brenda Whelks - nor Doreen Chalmers. And my sons - if I can remember their names - were certainly not Sidney nor Cecil. Our invisible friend was having a little more fun at my expense."

"It was a nice touch to suggest that all donations should be given to the donkeys."

Raynes smiled.

"At least he got that bit right. I've already included the Donkey Sanctuary in my will!"

Rudy and Emily were sitting in a quiet corner of the Union coffee bar, waiting for their afternoon lecture: "Fascism in Britain". They had already endured a gruelling tutorial with their politics lecturer, who had given Rudy very low marks for his essay on General Franco. "Too much prejudice; too few facts," he had said. "If you are going to present your case, you must build up a solid argument. Provide plenty of ammunition. Then hit hard."

They were on their second cup of cappuccino.

Rudy's mind was on other things.

"It's nearly a week since the murder and no one's been arrested."

"I am thinking the Great Inspector, Richard Raynes, has hit a brick wall."

"Are you proposing that we should help him?"

"Certainly not! He is paid to pursue the ungodly. I am thinking that he is very well paid for this. He must try harder."

Staring into middle distance, Rudy said: "I could give him a reading… See if we could bring up the murderer…"

Emily said: "I do not think that the Inspector operates on the psychic plane. It is one of his many failings. If he did, he would know how important it is to arrest Mrs Shawcross. I am sure it was her and that detestable Mr Latimer who killed her husband. I am told they have been fornicating for many months."

"Who told you that?"

"My friend, Tom Hayward. But he did not tell me that when I was writing my article on the Chaplain. It would have completed the picture - perfectly."

"Perhaps he was trying to protect him?"

"But why?"

Emily was extremely annoyed that, for the first time in five weeks, there would be no contribution from 'our University Correspondent' in this Friday's *Echo*. The death of Dr Shawcross had already produced five pages of copy, all written by Mr Hayward's full-time reporters. They had had a field day. With the benefit of back copy and photographs, they would be telling the people of Grasshallows all they could possibly wish to know about Dr Timothy Shawcross - and much, much more!

There was even a picture of Inspector Raynes standing beside the University car. Emily was surprised to find how angry it made her. But there was nothing she could do about it. However, one idea had been buzzing around in her mind during the politics tutorial.

A seance! Could Rudy handle a seance?

That way, the initiative could pass back to the students. Emily imagined a huge gathering of students in Halifax College chapel. Rudy, of course, would be presiding at the altar, invoking the spirit of Dr Shawcross. Begging him to return to this world to tell the students who had killed him.

It would be drama on the grand scale. They would invite photographers to try and catch an ethereal blob of white ectoplasm which might be Dr Shawcross materializing in the darkness of the sanctuary. A tape-recorder might capture his voice. Great gusts of wind might blast through the nave. Candles might mysteriously gutter or catch fire. There would be clouds of incense surging about. And deep groans of remorse rising from the gratings.

She, of course, would write it up for the Echo. It would be her story. Rudy would once again be the hero. Mr Haywood had refused to print her article about Mrs Shawcross having her Tarot cards read. But this would be a spectacular follow-up. She would demand full copyright and a huge fee.

She turned to Rudy: "Have you ever thought about conducting a seance? Getting the Vice-Chancellor back from the dead to speak to us? To tell us what happened - and who killed him? I am thinking it might make rather a fine article."

Rudy rose to the bait. (As he always did.) Anything was better than brooding about Fascism. He was bored by their antics. By their feeble policies. Posturing pygmies - that was all they were. The thought that one hour of his life was being given over to Sir Oswald Mosley was utterly depressing. With the benefit of hindsight, he knew the Fascists were born losers.

Anarchists might have been more exciting. Including that Catalan terrorist he had just been reading about, who dropped a bomb on King Alfonso and his new bride. He had missed both of them but had killed quite a few of the royal guard. He was dreaming of such joys when Emily popped the question.

"A seance? I've never done one; but it might be worth trying. How would we organise it?"

Emily said: "I am remembering a play by Noel Coward. 'Blithe Spirit' it was. I saw it on television with Margaret Rutherford - a most irritating woman. She brought back the man's first wife in order to torment him and his second wife. They found that they couldn't get rid of her. It was quite amusing. He could see her - and speak to her - but his second wife couldn't see who he was talking to."

Rudy laughed.

"We wouldn't want the Vice-Chancellor back permanently."

"Heaven forbid! But I was thinking of you conducting the seance in Halifax College chapel."

She described the scene as she had imagined it. But Rudy was realistic:

"They'd never let us use the chapel. Just think what would happen if it went on fire! It'd be far worse than the animal laboratory."

(But he added: "I like the idea" just in case she thought he had got cold feet.)

There was brief silence.

Then Rudy said: "I'm not sure that a lot of students would be a good idea. They might chatter amongst themselves and shuffle their feet. I think a seance should be a more intimate thing. Perhaps just five or six people round a table. I remember a chap saying you had to create a warm, hospitable atmosphere where a spirit would feel welcome. Somewhere he would like to be. Dr Shawcross wouldn't want to see us

188

students again. He'd run a mile! Especially after all we did to him. They might shout and jeer at him. He'd tell us nothing.

"I think if you were going to do it properly, you'd have to make it a private gathering. With incense - if you like. Low lights. Bring together a few of his friends..."

"He didn't have any!"

"There must have been someone..."

There was a silence.

"OK. He had no friends! We'll probably need to get some of his clothing. Did any of the students bury anything at the University House?"

Emily shrugged her shoulders.

"I've no idea."

"Perhaps his Vice-Chancellor's gown might still be in his office? Or a book he was reading? Do you think Inspector Raynes might lend us his shoes? He was wearing them when he died, wasn't he? Would you be willing to go and ask him?"

"I could ask. But he would probably say 'No'. They might turn out to be vital evidence. And if we lost them..."

"Yes, that would be awkward."

However the plan was still maturing..

"Where could we do it then - if you don't like Halifax?"

Rudy looked thoughtful.

"What about Palmerston? There were good vibes at the Symposium, weren't there? We wouldn't need Mr Dawkins' gravestone..."

"I'm not digging that up again!"

"No. But it might be just the right place to have contact with the Hereafter. It is University property. They may even have a photo of Timothy..."

"You've got that nice round oak table in your room."

"Yes, that'd be fine. You could get five or six round that. Do we need a table cloth?"

Emily could tell he was getting excited. She was thinking that even a small seance could be written up and dramatised. Only those who had been present would know what actually happened. And, if something did happen, they couldn't complain. She could already see the headlines: 'Psychic Triumph brings Vice-Chancellor back to Life'. Or for a follow-up: 'Shawcross speaks from the Grave. Rudy Invokes Underworld in Police Hunt'."

It was a wonderful idea. And he was going to do it.

Rudy looked at his watch.

"It's five to four. We'll have to go."

Beside their earth-shattering plans to reveal the murderer and make a financial killing, a Blackshirt march through Limehouse in October 1936 seemed very small beer.

36: Raiding The Vice-Chancellor's Office

Emily got up at about 7.00am and headed into the city. By 8.00am, she was in the main administrative building of the University. She reckoned that the cleaners would probably have dealt with the Vice-Chancellor's office fairly quickly. She hoped that they might have left the doors unlocked.

Rather than use the lift, she walked up the back stairs to the fourth floor. The map in the main entrance told her that Vice-Chancellor's office was directly above the front door. So she had to make her way down a long corridor to get there.

She could hear the sound of voices, the rattle of mops in buckets and the roar of vacuum cleaners as she passed the Senate Chamber and the University Secretary's office. She moved on quickly.

The Vice-Chancellor had a large outer office leading to the *sanctum sanctorum*. Both doors were open. Emily passed through into his private chamber. A light and airy room with a splendid view over the city. To her right there was a bookcase, filled with impressive, leather-bound books. Not the sort of books anyone would read! But they looked good. In the middle of the room, there was a large desk and another highly-polished table with a lavish flower display. Nearer the windows, there were several comfortable chairs where the Vice-Chancellor could entertain his guests.

Emily was sorry that Rudy was not with her. He might have been interested to see the lay-out of the main building in case he ever decided to make an attack on what was clearly the heart of the University's administration.

Emily set to work on the desk drawers and then the cupboards, looking for the Vice-Chancellor's ceremonial robes - or any item of property which specifically belonged to him. It seemed that she was too late. There was nothing left from the previous regime. No books, no diary, no pens, letters or clothes. Not even his Security badge.

Whilst she was at work on the cupboards, she suddenly became aware of a small, rather ugly-looking woman standing in the doorway between the two offices, effectively blocking her escape route.

"Who are you?" she asked. "And what are you doing?"

Emily had decided that if she was challenged, it would be best to tell the truth. There was a reason for her being there; but her explanation would seem so utterly bizarre that there would be no justifiable reason for punishing her.

"I am looking for any personal property belonging to Dr Shawcross."

"Do you have any permission to be here?"

"No."

Emily was pleased to note that the woman challenging her also had a distinct Welsh accent. They were sisters under the skin.

"And who are you?"

"I am Emily Williams from Pwddldwc in Gwynedd. I am a first year Politics student in Salisbury."

"And why would you be wanting some of the Vice-Chancellor's property?"

Emily brushed back a lock of her dark hair.

"We are having a seance to call up the spirit of Dr Shawcross. We wish to ask who killed him and why. In such circumstances, it is customary to have an item of clothing belonging to the deceased, something that he used or something he has written. I came here early to see if I could find any such thing. It would of course be returned."

Mrs Gordon was taken aback by her explanation.

"And who is to conduct this seance?"

"Mr Rudy Krauss."

Her reply immediately set alarm bells ringing.

"Are you a friend of Mr Krauss?"

"We are both first year Politics students."

"I asked if you were a friend?"

"We are both determined to find out the truth about his death. We are trying to help Inspector Raynes."

Mrs Gordon felt that she must have been told a lie. She could not imagine that the Inspector would agree to this girl rummaging through the Vice-Chancellor's office.

"Do you know Inspector Raynes?"

But she did.

"The Inspector has stayed in our house in Pwddldwc when he was working on the branch line murder in our village in June this year."

"Does he know that you are helping him?"

The answer was 'No' but Emily battled on:

"Rudy has been to see the Inspector. He has told him that he has read Mrs Shawcross' Tarot cards in which he has seen her husband's death. He was able to tell him things that he did not know. I am thinking that this will have been of some importance to him."

Mrs Gordon was somewhat mollified by the explanation, but the girl was certainly trespassing - and if she had taken anything, she would be regarded as a thief.

The reason why she had found nothing belonging to Dr Shawcross was because Mrs Gordon had already cleared out all the dead man's property, boxed it up and sent it to the University House.

She looked at Emily with a quiet admiration. Her quest was hopeless but she had not been frightened of penetrating to the very heart of the University to get what she wanted. Mrs Gordon herself came the valleys of South Wales so she could understand the ruthless determination that motivated this

192

young woman.

"I'm Mrs Gordon," she said, "The Vice-Chancellor's secretary. Even though he's dead, there's still a lot of routine work that has to be done. I like to come in early. Would you like to join me for a cup of coffee and tell me about this seance?"

Emily decided that this was an olive branch worth accepting. So, within five minutes, they were sitting in Mrs Gordon's office talking about Dr Shawcross and drinking some of his favourite coffee.

"Where are you holding this seance?"

"In Palmerston."

"Is that where Rudy held his Symposium?"

"He thinks the building has good vibes."

"I've never been there."

"Would you like to come to the seance?"

Mrs Gordon immediately said 'No'. As a good Welsh Presbyterian, she abhorred spiritualsm. 'Meddling with things you know nothing about'. But as a woman, her natural curiosity tempted her to say 'Yes'. But the thought of being in any way connected with Rudy Krauss made it impossible to accept the invitation.

But she did know someone who might be interested... who might help... Someone who had been to seances before. She knew this because she had told Mrs Gordon all about them. It had been suitably scary.

"And who would that be?

"A Mrs Linda Hobbs. She was the Vice-Chancellor's former secretary."

Emily's eyes lit up.

"Was she a friend of Dr Shawcross?"

Mrs Gordon shook her head.

"Dr Shawcross had no friends. He treated her like a slave. She won't have any happy memories; but she might have a card or a book - some trifling memento. She'll probably be glad to get rid of it." She smiled. "Shall we give her a call?"

Emily nodded.

Mrs Gordon picked up the phone. It was still only half past eight; but she should be up.

"Linda? It's Bryony Gordon. Yes… Are you back from holiday…? Did you have a good time…? Was the weather OK?"

Once the preliminaries were over, she came to the point.

"Linda, I've got a young woman here who's organising a seance… i know you like such things… No, not me… I'd be terrified! But I was wondering if you could help her. Would you like to speak to her?"

Mrs Gordon handed over the phone.

"I think she's interested."

"Hello, Mrs Hobbs. I'm Emily Williams - a student in the University. We're hoping to have a seance to try and find out who killed Dr Shawcross…"

There was a sudden silence at the end of the line. Emily gathered that Mrs Hobbs was not exactly willing to help.

She decided to press on: "As you probably know, the police are getting nowhere in their investigations. We wondered if we could help on the psychic plane. Just a small group of us - four or five at the most…"

It was still proving difficult.

"Mrs Gordon says that perhaps you may have some items previously belonging to him. A book? A card? A gift…? You have a gift…? And you'd be willing to get rid of it? That's excellent!"

Progress! She had one or two things.

"Do you think I could come round to your house and collect them? We could discuss the matter further… This afternoon…? I will see you then… Thank you."

She handed the phone back to Mrs Gordon.

"I think she's interested. But she says that she's already suffered too much because of him. She says she has no desire to meet him again - in this world or the next!"

Mrs Gordon smiled.

"She'll come. You know the old saying: 'Curiosity killed the cat. Satisfaction brought it back!' Let me know how you get on."

37: A False Accusation

Detective-Inspector Raynes was not in a good mood that morning. He felt the case was dying on its feet and, for once, he did not know what to do. He had interviewed all the most likely suspects. None of them had lied. Everyone now knew it was murder - not suicide - but no one seemed to care. He had read Dr Stewart's report five times; but there were no clues, no clear leads, no brilliant insights.

He still thought the Philosophy department were sheltering a murderer; but they were such nice people that it seemed heartless to break through their vow of silence. And there were another 736 members of staff that he had not seen and 2998 students who did not want to see him. Where should he go? What should he do?

Carlisle did not press him. He knew that something would turn up - and, whilst he was rustling up two cups of strong black coffee, it did. But it was not exactly a person the Inspector wanted to see - certainly not at this moment.

He said: "You have a visitor."

Raynes stopped twirling his biro.

Carlisle put the coffee down on his desk.

"Miss Emily Williams is in reception wanting to see you."

"What does she want?"

"I have no idea; but I promised to pass on the message. Do you want me to get her a cup of coffee?"

"No. Tell her we'll see her in ten minutes. Let us at least have a few minutes of peace whilst we drink our coffee."

He would not grant her any favours.

When he had finished his coffee, he said to Carlisle: "Bring her in."

When she came in, he did not stand. She deserved no respect. He pointed to a nearby chair.

Carlisle raised his pencil.

Emily smiled. A rather nervous smile.

"I wonder if you would be willing to do me a favour?"

"I doubt it."

He looked at her. She was so damnably pretty; but he knew she was as treacherous as hell.

"Well...?"

"I was wondering if I could borrow Dr Shawcross' shoes? The brown ones he was wearing at the time of his death. Rudy saw them when he was reading his Tarot cards."

"Why on earth do you want them?"

"Well," she said, "Rudy and I have decided to hold a seance. A private seance. Rudy is going to try and get in touch with Dr Shawcross and ask him if he can tell us how he was murdered - and by whom."

"Everyone knows how he was killed."

"No, they don't. Rudy says you have only told people part of the story. You haven't told them about the electrocution. But Rudy saw the blackened mark on his hand. And he felt it."

"And he has told you all this?"

"Of course."

"Since I spoke to him on Monday?"

"No. After he did the reading for Mrs Shawcross. He didn't want to tell anyone. But he couldn't keep it to himself. He was quite distressed. Well, you saw what he was like..."

"Yes," said Raynes grimly.

Rather unwisely, Emily continued: "I was thinking that since you seem to have come to a standstill in your investigations, our seance might help. We shall let you know what Dr Shawcross says - and we shall return the shoes."

Raynes was curious.

"Why does Rudy want them?"

"Well, I didn't know anything about this, but apparently it helps if you have some item belonging to the deceased with you at the seance. An item of clothing, a letter, a photograph... something which helps the person re-connect with his earthly life. Rudy felt that the one constant factor in Dr Shawcross' death was his shoes."

Raynes found it easy to get out of that one.

"The property of the deceased belongs to the court. It is Crown property which may be used as evidence in a future court case. It can be produced to assist either the prosecution or the defence. Such things cannot be lent out.

"If I was to lend them out - and they went missing - your friend, Mr Hayward, would plaster it all over his front page. You would write one of your nasty articles and collect a few hundred pounds. And I would be made to look a complete fool!"

Emily looked shocked at the vicious way the Inspector spoke to her.

"You sound completely paranoid!"

"I think I have every reason to be. I'm afraid I just cannot trust you. And, anyway, I haven't got the shoes. Dr Stewart, the police surgeon, has all his clothes - and his body. And he is even less likely to give them to you than I am."

He looked at her.

"So I cannot grant your request."

There was silence.

Raynes said: "Have you seen Mr Hayward lately?"

"No. Why?"

"I saw him yesterday. He was very upset by a classified ad which was sent to his office. An anonymous note about a death which has not yet occurred." He looked at Emily. "And I believe it came from you!"

Emily's face reddened.

Raynes immediately assumed that she knew about the intimation.

"It was beautifully done. Deliciously wicked. Most people would have found it extremely funny. But I didn't. It was a malicious attack and I could get you for breach of the peace!"

Emily looked at him in amazement.

"I do not know what you are talking about."

"Don't you?"

Raynes took the plastic folder out of his drawer and extracted the obituary. He threw it down on the desk in front of her.

Emily read it.

It was extremely amusing - and she wished she had written

it. But she realised that the Inspector was in a towering rage; and that was why he had been so rude to her. It would not do to smile or laugh. Besides, she herself was angry at being accused of writing it.

She pushed the obituary to one side - and stood up.

"Inspector Raynes, I am thinking that you would be better spending more time trying to find who killed Dr Shawcross - as I am doing - rather than making false accusations for which you have not one shred of evidence. I did not write this. I have never seen it before.

"I am sorry that you are unable to help me with the shoes. I understand why you do not trust me. But you are making a big mistake. We are both pursuing the same objectives, you and I - the search for truth and justice."

Raynes shook his head angrily.

"The only reason why you are doing all this is to make money out of Dr Shawcross' death and to promote your friend's dealings with the underworld. You are not interested in truth or justice. All you want is cash!"

Emily pointed a reproving finger at the Inspector.

"But you are being paid to find the murderer. It is your job. And I am thinking that you are not doing it very well!"

She strode out of the office without a single backward glance. At least she did not slam the glass door.

There was a deep silence.

Carlisle sighed.

"I think you owe her one for that!"

"Do you?" Raynes was sarcastic. "You think I should lend her the shoes?"

Carlisle shrugged his shoulders.

"It might help. You could at least say you had tried… All avenues explored… It's been done before… I believe British Intelligence examined Adolf Hitler's horoscope…"

Raynes looked at Carlisle.

It was not a friendly look.

Carlisle felt that the Inspector found it difficult to admit that he was wrong.

After another long silence, he said: "Find out when that bloody seance is being held, and I'll let her have the shoes for an hour!"

Then he too stormed out of the office.

38: Black Underwear!

Mrs Hobbs gave Emily a warm welcome.

She was a very kind, motherly sort of person and, after her bruising encounter with Inspector Raynes, Emily was willing to be extensively mothered. With a slice of freshly-baked pizza in one hand and a cup of cappuccino in the other, the two women settled down to have a good chat.

"You were very lucky Mrs Gordon didn't report you. Students are not allowed in that part of the building - and certainly not going through the Vice-Chancellor's drawers. She could easily have called in Security and made it very unpleasant for you."

"I think us both being Welsh helped."

"And the fact that you were trying to find out who killed the V. C. It's something we all want."

Emily said bitterly: "I don't think the police have any idea who did it. It's now almost two weeks since Dr Shawcross died. You would think they would have arrested someone before now."

Linda nodded.

"Inspector Raynes came round to see us on Tuesday. He was very sympathetic, but there wasn't anything we could do to help him. I haven't seen Timothy since Thursday October 10. We left the following day to go on holiday. We didn't come back till the 25th. I still have another fortnight of sick leave. But I was dreading going back. Now he's gone, it'll make things a lot easier."

She smiled.

"Now what about another cup of coffee then we can talk about this seance? Whose idea was it?"

"Mine, really. It just came into my mind during a tutorial. Rudy had given Mrs Shawcross a reading on his Tarot cards - at her request. And it was then that he discovered that he had the power to see into other people's lives - through the cards. So I thought that if we had a seance, we might be able to bring back Dr Shawcross and ask him a few questions."

Mrs Hobbs looked anxious.

"It's frightfully brave - both of you. But do you really know what you're doing? You don't know how the spirit will react. Some of them can be quite sweet and helpful. But if you start messing with someone who doesn't want to come back, they can do a lot of damage. If you approach a murderer - or someone who has committed a really horrible crime - they could be quite dangerous. There are stories of people being invaded by evil spirits - having terrible dreams, severe headaches, suffering from schizophrenia, having violent depression - and even attempting suicide. You do have to be careful."

Emily looked at the older woman.

"Mrs Gordon said that you'd been to seances before. What happened at them?"

"Oh, they were very much under control. We had a very experienced medium. The people whom she called up were very willing to answer our questions. I found out a few things from my grandmother that I found most comforting. You see, my mother was adopted. She didn't know who her real mother was. But I was able to speak to her real mother and she was able to tell me the circumstances - why she gave her away. She knew who had adopted her. She kept an eye on her and now they've both been re-united on the other side of death. So - a happy ending."

She looked at Emily.

"But I don't think it could possibly be the same with Timothy. He was so full of anger and resentment. He was bitter, spiteful, willing to hurt people. I can't imagine that he would have changed much on the other side of death. I think he'll be even more angry to have been prevented from carrying out his plans. He regarded them as his life's work. He'll be absolutely blazing."

"Don't you think he'd be glad to tell us who killed him?"

"Would he actually know? The Inspector told us that he'd been hit with a stone mason's hammer and then garrotted. A rope was put round his neck. He may never have seen his assailant." Emily did not agree.

She was sure the Vice-Chancellor would know. She felt he would co-operate with Rudy - determined to get his revenge on whoever it was.

She smiled at Linda.

"He'll be glad to see you again!"

"I doubt that."

"But you did so much to help him."

"Yes, but I allowed myself to be spirited away by Russell. He would regard that as treachery."

"But he must have had some affection for you?"

"It was sheer lust!" She looked at Emily. "You know what men are like. But he never got anything from me - except sympathy. And a bosom to cry on. He certainly wanted much more than that. But I was only prepared to help him with his work. I could never have faced my husband if I'd done anything with him. As it was, Bill was extremely angry. I walked out on him. It was terrible. Russell was right to spirit me away. He's a good man."

She laughed.

"But if you're going to use me as live-bait, I've got something that I think will help you." She stood up. "I'll go and get it for you."

She returned with a shocking pink carrier bag and put it down on the kitchen table. She pulled out a set of lacy black underwear.

"No?"

"Yes! He bought them for me. He had no idea of my bra size or my waist measurements. They were far too small. I could never have worn them. Bill would have asked where I had got them. So I had to hide them away. I would probably have given them away to some charity shop. But they came from Timothy. He probably ran his hands over them - and dreamt of me. I think they might still excite him."

Emily felt the material. They were soft and silky. They would be lovely against her skin. And they were probably more her size.

"I am thinking they were probably quite expensive?"

"Very. Just look at the labels."

"Italian."

"He thought he could buy me; but he couldn't. I'd have been more impressed if he'd have chosen the right sizes." Linda put the underwear back in its pink bag. "But that should prove quite an incentive!"

"I shall look after them. We'll see what happens."

"What exactly are you planning?"

Emily said: "Well, I was thinking of a big public event in Halifax College chapel…"

Linda shook her head.

"… but Rudy said it had to be a much smaller and more intimate gathering. Two hundred students would be quite disastrous…"

"He was right."

"So now we have decided to have just a small meeting in his room at Palmerston. Around his table. A little incense. Take it gently. Explain why we want to speak to him. What we want to know. I think that if Dr Shawcross knows you are there, he won't be violent. You cared for him. You did your best to help him. I am thinking that should calm him down. If it was just the three of us, we can handle things in a nice way. Rudy was very good with Mrs Shawcross. He didn't tell her all the terrible things he saw. I am sure he will be very respectful to her husband."

Linda looked at Emily.

"Would you mind if I brought someone with me?"

"Your husband would be most welcome."

"Oh, he wouldn't come to a thing like that. No, I was thinking of a friend of mine. From the University. A lecturer.

Nothing frightens her. She didn't like Timothy one bit. In fact, she told me just recently that she was planning to shoot him! She's a frightfully brave person. She was John-Paul Sartre's lover - just for a short time. She understands men. We've been to several seances together. She's always very practical. I'm not quite sure how it squares with her beliefs… She's a complete atheist. But I'd be very glad if you'd let her join us."

Emily nodded.

"She'd be most welcome. We'd be glad of her advice." She looked at her empty mug. "And we'll make sure we have some decent coffee on the night. It makes such a difference. Better than any amount of incense!"

39: Bill's Confession

Whilst Emily was tucking into freshly-cooked pizza and discussing the finer points of how to organise a seance, Raynes received a phone call from the University Secretary.

"Inspector, I wonder if you could help me? I have a very distressed person with me, who wishes to make his confession."

Raynes cheered up.

"And what is he confessing?"

"The murder of Dr Shawcross."

"I shall come round immediately. Where is he?"

"In my office."

"And who is this person?"

"Bill Hobbs."

"I've already spoken to him and his wife."

"He says he didn't tell you the full story."

"I'll be there in fifteen minutes."

* * * *

Raynes walked across Mr Forrester's office with a smile on his face and an outstretched hand.

"Bill!" he said. "Good to see you again."

He drew up a chair so that their conversation could be as intimate as possible.

"Now what's all this about?"

"I didn't want to say anything about this in front of Linda. She's suffered enough... But I'm afraid my conscience is troubling me and I thought I'd come and speak to Russell. But he said I must speak to you."

Raynes nodded helpfully.

"I didn't kill the Vice-Chancellor; but I planned to kill him. I've been planning it for the past couple of months - long before Linda and I went away to Tenerife."

Tears came into Bill's eyes.

"I believed that Dr Shawcross was having an affair with my wife. They were always away together - for days at a time.They went to conferences and meetings. She was hardly ever at home. And one of my work-mates told me they had been seen together in a compromising situation in the University House."

He looked at Raynes.

"I know now that it wasn't true. Linda and I had a long talk before we went away on holiday. But, at the time, I believed it was true. I decided that I had nothing more to live for. So I worked out a plan to kill Dr Shawcross.

"When I read in the papers that he had committed suicide, I was delighted. Really delighted. I didn't say anything to Linda but I was relieved that my plan had not been necessary. His death had been self-inflicted.

"But when you said, on Tuesday, that it was not suicide - but murder; and when you said that he had been electrocuted in the University House, I realized that it was my plan that had been used to kill him."

Raynes said: "Tell me exactly what you planned to do."

Bill looked deeply uncomfortable - and looked at the University Secretary who was sitting anxiously behind his desk.

"Well, as I said, I know the University House rather well. I did quite a bit of work on the roof last winter. Timber and slates. For a couple of months, I had the key to the House. I was free to come and go. There was a lot of rotten wood to be replaced - and couple of new ceilings to be installed. When I had done the job, I returned the key to its hook in the Maintenance department. But when I made my plan, I borrowed it again and made a copy, so that I could get into the House whenever I wanted.

"Now, I didn't want to do Mrs Shawcross any harm, so I knew it would have to be a night when she was away. I'm told she often goes down to London for the weekend. I didn't fix any actual date but that was when I was going to do it.

"I had plenty of old cable lying around. It wouldn't take long to fit a jump lead and a plug. I thought the best way of electrocuting the brute was once he came in through the front door. I didn't want him collapsing on the front step. The chauffeur might have seen what had happened.

"I thought about the toilet, the kitchen and the study. I hadn't really made up my mind; but I knew the job could be done quickly and efficiently and it would take only a few seconds to remove the cable.

"We all know the wiring in the House is pretty ropey. But I reckoned that if I used a transformer, I could get enough power going through a brass knob to polish him off. It would probably fuse all the lights; but I could deal with that.

"I guessed the Vice-Chancellor might be wearing rubber-soled shoes, but I'm told he often uses fancy leather shoes. So I considered what I would do if I just stunned him.

"They have a bathroom downstairs in the University House - with a large old-fashioned bath. I had thought about that. I was going to fill the bath half-full of water, drag him over to the bathroom and then push him in. Then I could drop the jump leads into the water to finish him off."

It sounded quite ruthless.

"But you didn't do it?"

"No. It wasn't necessary."

"But you believed it would have worked?"

"Certainly."

"And what happened to the key?"

Bill again looked distressed.

"I forgot all about it. I've been off work for the past four weeks - thanks to Mr Forrester. But I hid it in a tin box in my garden shed. I only realized - after your visit on Tuesday - that it was still there. So this morning, when I went back to work, I took it into the maintenance department and put it back on its hook with the other keys. But it didn't match! It was a different key!"

Raynes looked at Bill.

"You think someone used that key to get into the University House?"

"It wouldn't have worked. It was the wrong key."

"So do you think they took the copied key and left that one in its place?"

"But nobody knew I had a key! And nobody knew where it was hidden."

"You don't think someone - even your wife - could have changed the key to prevent you committing the murder?"

"She didn't know. I told her I wanted to kill the man; but I didn't say how - or where."

Bill shook his head sadly.

"I felt it was best to come and tell Mr Forrester right away."

The University Secretary nodded.

Raynes said: "Well, Bill, I think you've done the right thing." But, despite the denials, the Inspector still wondered if he had been told the whole truth. Bill Hobbs had been back in Grasshallows by November 26. At that time, he was still in possession of the key. Had it been given to anyone? Had he talked to any of his work-mates about his plan? Did they hate the Vice-Chancellor as much as he did?

Was this half a confession? Bill Hobbs had a strong motive. He had the means; and he had had no hesitation in telling both the University Secretary and the police that he had intended to commit a brutal murder. Could he still have done it? Could he have invented this story about the second key to direct attention away from him? Would the rest of the confession come later?

Unfortunately, Carlisle had not been with him, taking his usual detailed notes. He was often very useful in picking up pauses and hesitations during an interview.

Certainly, the Inspector was quite sure he had been told no lies. But Bill must have spoken to someone - and that person, with good reason, must have switched the keys before murder could be committed.

He decided that he would return to Bill a little later. Perhaps he would then hear the full story. But he felt he was getting closer to the truth.

40: The Praying Hands

The phone rang in the office.

Carlisle picked it up.

"Ferguson's - for you."

Ferguson's were the most prestigious - and the most expensive - undertakers in Grasshallows. They had their main premises in Riverside Road.

Raynes assumed that this would be the University arranging Dr Shawcross' funeral.

"Inspector Raynes speaking…"

There was a silence at the other end of the phone. Then a voice said: "Are you still there?"

"I think so. Why?"

"Well, we've just had someone ordering a coffin for your funeral…"

"An expensive one?"

"No. Our cheapest model. But they have asked for the 'Praying Hands' on top."

Raynes smiled grimly.

"Was this a phone call or a written order?"

"Written. With a £100 deposit in five pound notes. We were told to obtain sizes and weight from this number." There was a pause. "Do you think this is a hoax?"

"Very much so."

He looked across at Carlisle who had realised what had happened and pressed the recording button on his phone.

"I'm very sorry, Inspector."

"That's all right. We get these nuisance phone calls from time to time. Would you mind if we came down to your office and looked at the letter, the envelope and the notes?"

"Not at all. We have them here."

"We'll be with you in the next hour."

Raynes put down the phone.

"Our funeral friend," he said. "This time he's ordered a coffin and paid a deposit. Again in five pound notes."

He looked thoughtful.

"I don't think Emily can be held responsible for this one. I don't think she'd pay out £100 just to annoy me. I think this is a deliberate provocation. Someone is trying to rile me…"

* * * *

Within the hour, they were standing inside Ferguson's private showroom, surrounded by pictures of the Ferguson family and impressive certificates for embalming and funeral directing. "Good morning, Mr Ferguson."

"Good morning, Inspector. I'm so sorry to upset you in this way."

"I thought it was perhaps about the Shawcross funeral?"

"No. That's happening next Monday. We've been asked to pull out all the stops. There are one or two Government ministers and several civil servants coming up from London."

"I don't think the staff or students will be shedding many tears."

"No."

They were taken through to a comfortable sitting room where the Fergusons entertained their clients. Mr Ferguson handed over the letter he had received that morning. Raynes recognised the same photocopied text, the envelope with a sticker containing the address and the £100.

208

"He certainly likes five pound notes," said Carlisle.

"Have you had them before?"

"Once before," said Raynes. "Last time he used gloves. I imagine this will be the same."

Carlisle put all the documents and money into a plastic bag.

"It's very embarrassing," said Mr Ferguson. "We don't like to upset people."

"Of course not," said Raynes. "Has anyone been in to look at the coffins? Just recently, I mean. Have you noticed anyone looking at this… Pennine model?"

Mr Ferguson was apologetic.

"We get people coming in all the time. Many of them are making future arrangements for their own funerals. Drawing up their Golden Charter Plan. It saves their families a great deal of trouble when everything's been arranged and paid for."

A solitary thought flashed through Raynes' mind.

"How far back do your records go?"

"Back to 1922," said Mr Ferguson proudly.

"Would you be able to look back - over the last thirty or forty years - to see how many people have ordered a Pennine coffin with 'Praying Hands'?"

"The Pennine model has only been used since 1971."

"Well, that will make it easier. Perhaps one of your staff could look back and see who it was. It would probably be for an elderly woman."

Mr Ferguson was eager to help.

"I shall do it myself. I will let you know by lunchtime."

"Thank you."

* * * *

Carlisle was quite excited.

"You think he may have used Ferguson's before?"

"Yes. Our friend may have slipped up there."

"D'you think he's deliberately twisting your tail?"

"Of course he is. The next thing will be the wreath, delivered by the flower shop to police headquarters. I think we

209

need to deal with this one right away."

"What about Dr Shawcross?"

"He can wait."

* * * *

Once they were back in the office, Raynes started to assemble his thoughts about this comedian - whom he suspected might also be the murderer.

The man had now paid out £130. It was an expensive sort of joke. But he must have a curious sense of humour. He was a lone wolf. Probably, since his mother had died, he had been living on his own. He had kept her clothes; he couldn't be bothered to get rid of them. They might have been kept in a box in his garage. He had carefully planned one murder; he could easily be planning another. Raynes noted that date of his proposed death - November 11 - had already passed. Had the man already tried and failed? Was he perhaps asking to be caught? Had he made any mistakes so far?

Raynes was going to say 'No'. But he suddenly remembered the last line of the obituary notice.

He looked up from his desk.

"I think I may have overlooked one clue!"

"You said it didn't give us any clues."

"I was wrong."

He smiled cheerfully.

"You remember the names of my ex-wives and children? Dear Sidney and Cecil? They were all made up. He didn't know their names. But he did know that I was giving money to the Donkey Sanctuary! That was right."

Detective-Constable Carlisle sat bolt upright in his chair.

"Yes!"

Raynes noted his reaction.

He looked at his colleague.

"You're quite close to me and you don't know anything about my will. Mrs May doesn't know what I'm leaving her." He smiled. "Mark you, she might have wiped me out before I die… But someone knew I was leaving money to the Donkey Sanctuary. I must have told them."

"Can you remember who it was?"

"Yes. It's just come to me. He's not on my list of suspects… He's not a member of the University… He's a lone wolf… He also has a curious sense of humour… Mr Tom Hayward!"

"The publisher?"

"Yes." Raynes looked thoughtful. "I remember him asking me if I would like to give a donation to the Puddleduck Railway Preservation Society. I said no. I felt I was doing quite enough for them finding their murderer. But, later, he asked me if I would leave them a legacy in my will. And I'm almost sure I said to him that all my worldly goods were going to the Donkey Sanctuary! So he must have known that fact which nobody else knew…"

"Surely he wouldn't have sent an obituary to his own newspaper? He looked very embarrassed about the whole business."

"So he did. But he might have remembered whom he told about the Donkey Sanctuary… And that's what embarrassed him."

"It could have been Emily - but I think not. She was so angry at being accused. But he has spoken to someone. And that indiscretion has been used against me. If he can remember who that person was, we've got the comedian - and probably the murderer as well."

The telephone rang.

It was Mr Ferguson. He sounded excited.

"I think I may have the answer to your question. There was a lady - an old lady - whom we did a funeral for in 1978 - twelve years ago. A Mrs Elizabeth Morton. Does that ring a bell?"

"Not yet."

"She had a Pennine coffin and her son asked for the 'Praying Hands' to be placed on the lid of the coffin. He wanted brass - but, of course, when it goes to the crematorium, it has to be plastic."

"Have you got an address?"

The undertaker was happy to oblige.

"Thank you so much."

Raynes put down the phone.

He smiled.

"Our gamble has paid off. Once we have spoken to Mr Hayward, I expect the whole thing will fall into place. We can jog his memory. We're looking for a Mr Morton - son of the late Mrs Elizabeth Morton. But…" He paused. "… I think we'll wait till the flowers arrive before we pounce."

Raynes looked supremely happy.

The telephone rang again.

Carlisle took the call. It was from Emily.

"The seance will take place in Rudy's room in Palmerston College at 7.00 tonight."

"Excellent!" said Raynes. "Tell her ladyship that I will deliver the shoes to the College front door at 7.00pm. He looked at Carlisle. "And you will return to collect them at 9.00pm."

41: The Seance

When Emily arrived at Rudy's room, she found everything was ready for the seance. The room was warm; and there was a single table lamp burning in the corner. The round table contained the alphabet and the numbers 0 - 9 arranged in a circle about two inches in from the edge of the table. In the centre stood a solitary glass upside down - and three more on the mantelpiece.

"In case we break any. I got a set from Debenhams this afternoon."

"It looks very professional," said Emily.

"Dr Cooper was a great help," Rudy said. "She came in this morning to tell me what I needed to do. She also brought the cards with the letters and numbers. She had them at her house but she said they'd be of more use to me."

Emily was impressed.

"Well," she said, "I've brought the black silk underwear which the Vice-Chancellor gave to Linda Hobbs. And Inspector Raynes has sent me a letter apologizing for his rudeness. He has given us the shoes; but they must be returned immediately after the seance. Detective-Constable Carlisle will be at the front door at 9.00pm to collect them."

"He's not coming to the 'do'?"

"No. I asked him - but he said 'No'." She smiled. "You know, I think he is very sorry he accused me so falsely. It was very wrong of him."

Rudy said: "Perhaps he now realizes that we are trying to help him."

Emily agreed. "He now believes you have the spiritual power - which he does not have. But he still believes I am only doing this for the money - which is true. But it is all very exciting. I would not miss it for the worlds."

Rudy admitted: "I am a bit frightened about what may happen. We are dealing with a very dangerous and unpleasant person."

Emily laughed.

"Be careful what you are saying. He may be listening to you!"

"Well, he's not exactly my ideal guest. If I could summon up someone I would really like to meet, I'd have chosen Marilyn Monroe."

"Not General Franco?"

"Certainly not. Who would you choose?"

"Jane Austen. I think she would enjoy this." She looked round the room. "You really have made it nice and cosy. What do we actually do?"

"Once we're all here, we sit round the table - silently for a little while. We create an atmosphere of tranquility. That's what Dr Cooper says. She has the reputation for being a bit of a firebrand; but she says that, where spirits are involved, you have to be polite and well-behaved.

"She told me that she had a pistol ready to shoot Dr

213

Shawcross - but the opportunity never arose. But he may be aware of her attitude - and it might deter him from joining us. I told her to leave her pistol at home."

"You can't shoot a spirit!"

"No. And since I am the medium, I don't want her shooting me! She tells me that if I have a genuine gift, I should be able to know what Dr Shawcross is thinking. It's a bit frightening really."

"What are the letters for? And the glass?"

"Well, apparently, when we think the spirit is present, we ask it questions. We probably say who we are. We introduce ourselves before we ask the questions. And we've got to be very patient. Dr Cooper says we mustn't rush things. Spirits can be very sensitive. If we are rude, they will just go away.

"Once we start feeling a presence, one of us puts a hand on the top of the glass and, if our question is being answered, the glass will move from one letter to another. Dr Cooper told me to polish the table to make the glass move smoothly - but not too much in case it slides off the table." He laughed. "We may break a few glasses. If we break them, we shall have to use coffee mugs."

"So the glass spells out the word?"

"Yes. If I ask: 'Are you with us in this room?' the glass will move to Y-E-S. If the answer is 'No' then obviously nothing will happen. That's why some people use an ouija board. Oui and Ja. That's what they use in France and Germany."

Emily looked at the clock.

"Twenty minutes to go."

She looked back at the table.

"Rudy," she said nervously, "the glass has moved!"

It was now standing by the letter Y.

"Perhaps he is here already?"

Rudy shivered.

"I told you it was frightening. We're dabbling in something we don't understand. I've read about how we should treat a spirit. But it's something completely alien to my nature."

Emily looked at Rudy.

214

"You said you believed in primitive religions. Their rites and customs. I challenged you to live according to your beliefs. To put them into practice. You got in touch with Mr Jeremy Dawkins. He caused you no trouble."

Rudy nodded - and moved the glass back to the centre of the table. Both of them watched to see if it would move again. Nothing happened.

Rudy continued: "I felt terrible after reading all those Tarot cards. I felt complete drained psychically. I felt I could never use them again. It's terrifying to get involved in some power which you can't control."

The glass remained static in the middle of the table.

Emily said: "I've brought a bottle of wine. Do you think we should give everyone a drink before we start?"

"Better afterwards," said Rudy. "We'll probably need it."

"Where shall I put Linda's underwear? I can't put it on the table, can I? There wouldn't be any room."

"You could put it on your lap - and touch it."

As they stared at the table, the glass moved to L and then to H.

Emily looked at Rudy.

"I am thinking Dr Shawcross has spoken. Linda will have to put them on her lap. Perhaps he wants her to wear them?"

The glass moved to Y.

Emily looked again at Rudy. "You're not doing anything to make it move, are you?"

Rudy shook his head.

"I don't like it. I find the whole thing quite intimidating. Even before they've arrived, Dr Shawcross is already dominating the meeting."

Emily moved the glass back to the centre of the table. "Stay there!" she said. "Wait till everyone arrives."

They stood there silently, waiting to see if the spirit would obey them.

Rudy's clock reached 7.00pm.

He said: "They should be here in a few minutes. I'll go and let them in."

"Are you going to leave me alone with him?"

"I don't think he'll hurt you."

"Remember to collect the shoes from Inspector Raynes. He'll be downstairs too."

"Hell! I'd forgotten about him."

Emily stood calmly watching the table and the glass.

"Dr Shawcross," she said, "you've given my friend, Rudy, a nasty shock. But I want him to conduct this seance properly. I don't want him collapsing or breaking into tears. We're only doing this because we want to find out who killed you. We want justice - as I am sure you do.

"We are very inexperienced in this sort of thing. We shall probably make mistakes. You must be patient. We don't want to hurt anyone. We want your soul to rest in peace after this is over. And we don't want any of us to be hurt. Is that understood?"

Very slowly, the glass moved to Y.

Emily inclined her head.

"Thank you."

Even if Rudy could not control the spirit, she felt she could. Generations of Welsh women would not be intimidated by a mere immortal!

* * * *

Very soon, she heard the sound of cheerful voices coming down the passage. The door opened and in came Linda Hobbs and Dr Cooper. Rudy followed them, carrying a pair of smart brown shoes. Detective-Constable Carlisle had polished them before they were handed over.

"So Inspector Raynes will not be joining us?"

"No," said Rudy. "He says that he doesn't believe in all this mumbo-jumbo; but he is willing to be proved wrong."

"How very brave of him!" said Emily.

Introductions needed to be made. Rudy had never met Linda Hobbs and Emily had never met Dr Cooper. "Call me Charlie," she said. "Everyone does."

Rudy put the shoes and Linda's underwear on the bed.

"Is that all right?"

Linda nodded.

"I hope I've done the right thing giving them to you."

"I am thinking it will help proceedings," said Emily.

"We've got some wine," said Rudy, "but we thought it might be better afterwards. We may need it."

"Did Dr Shawcross drink?"

The glass promptly moved to Y.

Both women screamed.

"Is he already here?"

"I'm afraid so," said Rudy. "We were just talking about ouija boards. When we looked back at the table, the glass had moved."

Emily moved the glass back to the centre.

"I've never seen anything like that before," said Charlie. "Normally, you have to focus on the person for quite some time before you get any response. Dr Shawcross must be quite desperate."

She looked at the table; but nothing happened.

"Perhaps he doesn't like me?"

The glass moved to N.

Emily looked at Rudy.

"You should never have polished that table!"

Charlie said: "Just leave it till we get settled - and begin to do it properly." She looked at Linda. "is it worrying you?"

Linda admitted: "It is a bit. It's different in a big public gathering. You feel there's safety in numbers. Here it seems a little too close for comfort."

"Well, at least it's nice and warm," said Charlie. "It's quite cold outside. They say it may be snow before the weekend."

She placed her handbag on the floor and rested her two hands on the edge of the table.

Rudy sat beside her - with Emily on his right.

Emily squeezed Linda's hand.

"We will look after you."

* * * *

"Now," said Charlie, "Rudy is going to be the medium. He must put his fingers lightly on the glass."

Nothing happened.

"Perhaps the spirit's not ready?"

"Perhaps Rudy's not the right medium?"

Suddenly the glass moved towards Emily. The letter W was close to where she was sitting.

"It's your voice," said Linda. "He knows you are Welsh."

"Perhaps he likes Welsh women?"

Emily laughed. "More than Inspector Raynes does!" More seriously she said: "But I haven't got any spiritual powers. None at all."

Rudy said: "He thinks you have."

"He trusts you," said Charlie.

"Well," said Emily, "I don't mind."

She moved the glass back to the centre and kept a a light touch on it.

Charlie said: "Perhaps Rudy should ask the questions?"

The glass remained static.

"Right!" said Rudy. "Are we all settled?"

He looked intently at the glass.

Nothing happened.

"He's being sulky," said Charlie.

"Perhaps he doesn't like you?" said Linda. "After all, you did threaten to shoot him."

Unmistakably, Emily felt the glass moving under her fingers towards the numbers 4-6-2. Everyone looked at the strange combination.

Charlie twigged. "It's my pistol. A Beretta 4.62."

The glass moved to Y.

Charlie shrugged her shoulders.

"Well, I can't forgive him for what he did to Professor Hampton and the rest of the department. He caused us untold misery."

After a long pause, the glass moved to S-O-R.

218

"He's saying sorry."

"And so he should!"

Emily looked up. "Do you think we should ask him about the murder?"

The glass moved determinedly to N.

"He doesn't want to talk about it."

The glass moved to N-O-T-Y.

"Not yet."

Rudy said: "What do you want to talk about?"

There was no hesitation. L-H.

"Me?"

"He wants to speak to you."

S-O-R.

"Sorry again."

Linda said: "Well, I did care for you. I did everything I could do to help you."

The glass moved to U-D-I-D.

"Well, at least there's someone he wants to talk to," said Charlie.

The glass moved to U-N-D.

"Underwear," said Emily. "Perhaps he wants you to put it on your lap?"

Linda went over to the bed and picked up the black, silky material and put it on her lap.

"It feels lovely," she said.

Very rapidly, the glass moved to W-E-A-R-I-T.

"I'm not putting it on, you dirty old man! Just to give you a cheap thrill. I didn't want the gift and it was the wrong size anyway. My boobs would be bursting out if I wore it."

Emily tried to resist the movement of the glass but it moved to G-O-O-D.

"It's not good," she said to the spirit. "We're not here to satisfy your earthly lusts. We're here to find out who murdered you. You can look at Linda any time you want. But she's a married woman and she loves her husband. What's his name?"

"Bill."

Emily said: "She's going to give the underwear to Oxfam."

The glass moved busily to Y-R-S-I-Z-E.

Emily said: "Well, it may be my size, but I'm not putting it on for you."

P-I-T.

"Yes, I know it's a pity. But please concentrate on what matters. Your murder."

2-P-A-I-N-F-U-L.

Everyone looked sadly at the letters on the table. The spirit of Dr Shawcross clearly regarded it as too soon to reveal the murderer. They all looked at each other.

Rudy had been very silent. He could see what the others could not see - and it frightened him. First of all, he had seen a dark blue shadow standing behind Charlie. There was no doubting who it was. As she talked about the pistol, the shadow bore down on her and shrouded her face. At the mention of S-O-R, it lifted.

Now when the talk had moved to Linda, the shadow had been replaced by a sort of glow in the shape of a head. A brightness where the eyes might have been. He was conscious of joy. The brightness seemed to envelop her. Nothing hostile. He thought he could hear music.

But the spirit was fickle. It did not want to pass from joy to the painful memories of Thursday night. The purple shrouds fell over everyone around the table. Heavy, smothering, deadening.

Rudy could understand what Dr Shawcross was feeling. His emotions and reactions were very clear.

The glass moved sharply to W-A-I-T.

Charlie said: "We can't wait all night. How long does he want us to wait?"

The glass moved to 8.

"Eight minutes…"

"Or eight hours?"

"Heaven forbid!"

Everyone relaxed. The glass stayed firmly planted in the middle of the table. Emily removed her fingers delicately.

They felt quite sore.

"It must be difficult," said Rudy, "Having to communicate from his side. He has to come to terms with things that hurt him. It's his memory that's shackling him to this world. He needs release; but he can't get it. Perhaps his death involves people he knows. People he loves…"

"He doesn't love anyone except Linda."

"I don't think he knows what love is."

"Well, that doesn't help him!"

Charlie looked at Rudy. "Did you see anything?"

Rudy nodded.

"He was behind you when you were talking about your pistol. You were in shadow - a sort of dark blue. He seemed to be trying to smother you. When he was asking Linda to wear his underwear, there was a real brightness all around her."

"That was because I refused," said Linda.

"And quite right too!" said Emily.

Charlie looked at Emily.

"You were doing it really well. I've never seen such quick reactions. He must find it very easy to communicate through you."

Emily looked at Rudy.

"You did say I was the daughter of Blessed Osiris!"

"I'm beginning to believe it!"

* * * *

They gave Dr Shawcross ten minutes to prepare himself for the next stage of the seance.

With some reluctance, Emily returned to the glass in the middle of the table. Linda took charge of the Vice-Chancellor's brown shoes.

Rudy asked: "Are you still here?"

A reluctant Y.

"The police think you died at home. In the University House. Is that right?"

Y.

"You had just come back from the Senate meeting. You entered the house… Which room did you enter first?"

Y moved to T.

"I think we can guess that one. Which room did you go into after that?"

S-T-U-

"The study. And was that where you received an electric shock?"

Back to Y.

"What happened next?"

C-A-N-T-R-E-

"He can't remember."

Linda stroked Timothy's shoes. But to no effect.

Rudy continued: "Did you see anyone?"

N

"What happened after that?"

M-Y-H-E-

"Your head? You were hit on the head?"

Y

"What do you remember next?"

N-O-T-H-

"Nothing? That's not very helpful."

G-R-E-Y

Just greyness?

"Did you try to fight your way back to consciousness?"

T-H-I-N-K-S-O.

"What did you want to see?"

M-Y-W-I-F-E.

"Freddie? And was she there?"

L-A-T-I-M-

"Yes, we know about Peter Latimer," said Emily, taking over. "Do you think he was involved in the murder?"

There was a long pause. Then P-E-R-H-

"Perhaps? You're not sure? Do you think she wanted to kill you?"

N

"It couldn't have been an accident?"

222

A faint move - ending up with N

Linda lifted up the shoes.

"Where did your shoes take you next?"

I-N-2-C-A-R.

"The University car?"

Y

"And who was driving the car?"

I-W-A-S-I-N-B-O-O-T.

"I see. And when were you taken out of the boot?" Emily was very authoritative.

I-N-A-G-A-R-A-

"Garage! You stopped at a garage for petrol?"

N

"No. Was the car hidden in someone else's garage?"

Y

Charlie said: "Ask him if he'd ever been in that garage before?"

Dr Shawcross must have thought this was a stupid question. Nothing moved.

Emily resumed: "Were you taken out of the car?"

Y

"Were you laid on the floor?"

No reply.

"What did the person do to you?"

T-O-K-O-F-F-M-Y-C-L-O

"Took off your clothes and your shoes?"

Y

"So you were naked on the floor of the garage?"

Still Y - but moving to C-O-L-D.

"Did you see the person who took your clothes off?"

Y

"Getting better," said Linda optimistically.

"Did you recognise the person?"

N

"A complete stranger?"

On to Y

Emily said: "That won't help Inspector Raynes."

But suddenly the glass became much busier.

O-T-H-R-C-L-O-

"He put you in other clothes? What kind of clothes?"

W-O-M-A-N.

"Woman's clothes?"

O-L-D-W-O-M-A-N-S-

"Really?"

H-I-S-M-O-T-H-E-R-S.

Emily looked round the table in amazement. Was this true?

Charlie said: "I was sworn to secrecy; but Dr Treaseman did tell me that when the body was found, the Vice-Chancellor was wearing women's clothes and was heavily made up. Dr Treaseman found the body - so the police will know that."

Rudy nodded.

"I didn't understand that bit. When I was doing the cards, I saw a hideous old woman sitting in a maroon-coloured car. I didn't know who it was."

The glass resumed its path to M-E.

"But why?" asked Emily.

H-U-M-I-L-

"To humiliate you? But you were dead!"

"How horrible!" Linda was so upset, that she dropped one of the shoes. "Fancy doing that to him!"

"Why should he do that?" asked Rudy.

I-H-U-R-T-H-I-S-F-R-I-E-N-D.

Everyone watched the letters spelling out.

"You hurt his friend?"

Y

"Who was his friend?"

I-D-O-N-T-K-

"He doesn't know."

Conversation stopped. It was proving much more difficult than they had expected. They had assumed that Dr Shawcross would have seen his killer. In the next world, if not in this. But even if he had seen him, the person was a stranger, who had apparently done the murder to avenge someone else.

Emily tried to go a little further.

"Then he took you up in the Jaguar to Skipper's Hill?"

Y

"And Dr Treaseman found you?"

Y

Rudy said: "That doesn't get us much further."

Charlie said: "Are you seeing anything?"

Reluctantly, Rudy said: "I could see a garage floor. I saw the shoes. I could see the steering wheel and the body in the car."

"That's quite a lot," said Linda.

"But most of it was grey."

"No purple shadows or shining lights?"

Rudy shook his head.

Emily looked from left to right. People were running out of ideas and her fingers were getting sore. She decided to go back to the one point in the discussion when the spirit had shown some hesitation.

"Dr Shawcross, when we asked you whether your wife was involved in your death, you said you were not sure. Do you think she would have known the person who killed you?"

Y

That was promising. The glass moved briskly.

4-1-S-A-N-D-

"Yes. That's Mr Latimer's house. Do you think the murder was planned there?"

D-O-N-T-K-

"Could it have been Mr Latimer's friend?"

"He hasn't got any friends," said Rudy. "That's what you wrote in your article."

C-L-O-S-E-R.

"Well, Dr Shawcross seems to think he had one. But how would he have got into the University House?"

K-E-Y-S.

"He had access to the keys. Someone working at the University House?"

Y

The glass moved on.

C-H-A-U-

"Clifford Brown? The University chauffeur? You think he had access to the keys?"

K-I-T-C-H-

"The keys are kept in the kitchen?"

Y

Linda Hobbs intervened: "He wouldn't give anyone those keys. He's a very kind man. Very considerate."

Dr Shawcross began to get very animated. Very rapidly, the glass buzzed from left to right.

H-E-S-P-I-E-D-O-N-U-S.

"He did no such thing!"

Linda seemed to have taken over.

H-E-R-E-P-O-R-T-E-D-U-S-T-O-R-U-S-S-E-L-L.

"He wouldn't do anything like that! There was nothing to report!"

Charlie said: "Calm down! You're getting him all worked up."

"But it's not true. I won't have him telling lies!"

H-E-T-H-R-E-W-H-I-S-K-E-Y-S-A-T-M-E.

"I never heard about that!"

I-S-A-C-K-E-D-H-I-M.

"When?"

D-A-Y-A-F-T-E-R-U-L-E-F-T.

"I never heard anything about that. Russell would have told me."

Emily said: "Well, Clifford is still working at the University. I spoke to him yesterday morning when I went to the University house and tried to pinch Freddie's wedding photograph."

There was a sudden silence round the table.

Even Dr Shawcross seemed shocked.

Charlie asked: "Why would you want to do that?"

"I wanted it for tonight. Like the shoes and the underwear, I was thinking it might jog Dr Shawcross' memory."

Linda smiled.

"I think the underwear was probably quite enough to get him going."

Emily returned to the vexatious spirit.

"You think he killed you?"

Y

"Took your body back to his own garage?"

Y

"Dressed you up in his mother's clothes?"

Y

Linda said: "I just don't think he'd do a thing like that." She turned to her friend, Charlie: "I remember when we employed him. He had excellent references."

Dr Shawcross made one final effort to get his message across.

I-T-E-L-L-Y-O-U-I-T-W-A-S-T-H-E-C-H-A-U-F-F-E-U-R.

Rudy said: "I think he's gone!"

Everyone seemed very relieved that it was all over. It was not an experience they would repeat in a hurry. Rudy seemed particularly sad.

"I don't think we handled that very well."

"Well, I am telling you, my fingers are extremely sore. I felt I was fighting against him at the end."

Linda said: "I will not have him telling lies. Of course, I see now that he lived his whole life in a world of fantasy and self-delusion. He believed what he wanted to believe. But why he should turn against Clifford, I cannot understand. He had no grounds for sacking him."

Rudy said: "Was it really worth bringing him back from the dead just for that?"

Charlie was collecting all the letters and numbers and putting them back in a white envelope. Emily put the glass with the other three on the mantelpiece.

She said: "I am thinking it was a valuable experience for all of us. I had never truly realized that we could communicate with the dead so easily."

Linda Hobbs put the Vice-Chancellor's shoes on the table and then handed her black underwear to Emily.

"I think he may have been right about the black underwear!" She laughed. "It is more your size than mine. Try

227

them on and see if they fit."

Emily said: "I wouldn't dare. I would always be thinking that I was bearing Dr Shawcross close to my bosom. It would be far too scary!"

Charlie screamed: "The shoes are burning!"

Everyone turned to look.

Smoke was rising from the left hand shoe.

Emily lifted her eyes heavenwards.

"Dr Shawcross! Not the shoes! Anything but the shoes!"

There was a moment's silence.

Then, one by one, the four glasses on the mantelpiece exploded, sending flying shards of glass across the room.

Everyone ducked - but it was too late.

There was a coarse laugh.

Then a final, brief pop as the table light went out, leaving them in pitch darkness and their feet crunching on broken glass.

Emily said: "I am thinking our tormentor is still here. Dr Shawcross, go!"

42: The Wreath

"How did it go?"

Emily was sitting in Raynes' office the following morning. The brown shoes were still lying on his desk.

"It was terrifying."

"He turned nasty?"

"Just at the end. Because we wouldn't believe what he was saying. He set your shoes on fire; he destroyed four wine glasses and then fused the lights. I still have cuts from the flying glass."

She showed him her arm.

The pinpricks of blood were still visible.

"How long were you able to speak to him?"

"About thirty minutes. We had a break in the middle for about ten minutes."

"So it was possible to speak to the departed?"

Raynes remained dubious.

"We asked the questions. Well, Rudy asked most of them. I had my hand on a glass which moved from letter to letter giving us his reply."

"Wasn't it rather slow?"

"Most of the replies were 'yes' or 'no'. But longer answers were spelt out letter by letter."

"Did he see the murderer?"

"Yes."

"Did he recognise him?"

"No." Emily shook her head. "But he seemed to recognise him later. He said it was the chauffeur…"

"Clifford Brown?"

"Yes."

"Surely he'd have recognised him immediately?"

Raynes looked at Carlisle who was struggling to get down the first questions and answers.

He returned to Emily.

"Start at the beginning," he said, "and tell us all you can remember."

Emily said: "We sat round a small table. Rudy was on my left and Mrs Hobbs on my right. The only other person there was her friend, Dr Cooper."

"From the Philosophy department," murmured Raynes.

"Yes. Dr Shawcross didn't like her being there. He knew she had a pistol - and that she had planned to kill him. But he did apologise for all the misery he had caused her department."

"A bit late for that."

"Then he wanted to talk to Linda. He had bought her some underwear which was too small for her. He wanted her to wear it at the seance. She refused. He was annoyed - and we were annoyed because all he wanted to talk about was lingerie. But he said that talking about his death was too painful. That's why we had the break.

"After we got going again, he did answer most of our

questions. He told us that when he came back from the Senate meeting, he went to the toilet - and then to his study. That's where he received the electric shock. He knew that he had been hit on the head - but after that 'greyness'."

"He told us that he was put in the boot of the University car, which took him to a garage, where he was stripped naked. Then the murderer dressed him up in his mother's clothes."

Emily looked at Raynes.

"He also had some make-up and painted his face. Dr Cooper confirmed that that was true."

"Where did she get that from?" asked Carlisle.

"Dr Treaseman," said Raynes. "He found the body."

"Rudy asked him why the murderer had humiliated him after his death? He said it was because he had hurt his friend."

"Exact words?"

"'I hurt his friend'."

"Thank you. That's interesting. We have a motive."

He looked at Carlisle.

"Rudy asked him who the friend was; but he didn't know. He wondered if it was Peter Latimer …but he didn't say anything…" Emily paused thoughtfully. "One thing he did say when we were talking about Peter Latimer… He said we were getting closer…"

Raynes thought about it. He had the beginning of an idea.

But Emily was still speaking: "He said that the murderer had got the keys from Clifford Brown, the chauffeur. He knew that the keys were in the kitchen… Well, he would, wouldn't he? But then he said that Mr Brown had spied on him and Linda when they were travelling to meetings in the University car. He said that Mr Brown had reported them to the University Secretary. He said that Mr Brown had flung the keys back at him when he got out of the car - so he sacked him."

"Was that on the night of the murder?" asked Raynes.

"I don't think so. It must have been earlier… But Mrs Hobbs said that she knew nothing about it. She was insistent that Mr Brown was a good man and wouldn't have spied on them. She said it was a lie.

"Then Dr Shawcross got very angry with her. And that's when he he printed it out on the table: 'It was the Chauffeur'. He spelt it out quite deliberately."

Raynes said: "I don't think it was Mr Brown."

Emily said: "Well he did. And that's when things began to go wrong. We thought he'd gone. But as we packed up our things, the shoes started to smoke; all four glasses exploded and the main light went out. It was quite awful. I ordered him to go - and he went."

A satisfied smile passed over her face.

"I wish I'd been there," said Raynes.

"You had the chance."

"I know. But I don't believe in invoking the supernatural. I prefer to deal rationally with things."

Emily shrugged her shoulders.

"I don't think we achieved as much as we had hoped…"

She looked at the shoes.

"I am wondering whether perhaps Rudy could do some more Tarot work on the shoes. He might pick up something else."

But Raynes was not in a mood to give any more concessions.

"No more shoes," he said. "They're going back to Dr Stewart."

Emily's eyes pleaded for the Inspector's help.

"One shoelace?"

Raynes succumbed to her charm.

"One shoelace? Yes. But get it back to us as quickly as possible."

* * * *

Once Emily had gone, Carlisle said: "They tried to beat us!"

Raynes smiled triumphantly.

"But they didn't succeed! Dr Shawcross told them: 'It was

the Chauffeur'. But it wasn't. We think it was Mr Morton; but we have no direct proof. But they are equally sure it wasn't Clifford Brown. So there is an element of uncertainty in their evidence."

Carlisle looked out of the office windows.

"But he said there was a connection with Sandringham Crescent…"

"… but it wasn't Peter Latimer."

"And it wasn't his wife, Freddie."

"No."

"Was there any other connection with Sandringham Crescent? Mrs Shawcross took a taxi, didn't she?"

"She didn't take her own car."

Carlisle continued to speculate.

"But she did take a taxi. I suppose a taxi-driver is a sort of chauffeur?"

Raynes nodded.

"The taxi-man would have known where she was. He took her there. He brought her back. So he would have known the coast was clear…"

"…And whilst he was waiting for Freddie, he could have pinched the house keys. He could have put them back before he went to collect her at 1.00am?"

Raynes said: "I think we're still ahead of the game. We have our suspicions about Mr Morton. We have his address. We think he may be a friend of Mr Hayward. Have you looked him up on our files?"

Carlisle said: "He has no criminal record. But quite a few fines for speeding."

"What kind of car?"

"Vauxhall Cavalier and Vectra."

Carlisle went back to his notes to see what else had been said.

"There was a friend who had been hurt. Who would that be?"

Raynes shrugged his shoulders.

"Bill Hobbs?"

"It fits."

"It most certainly does."

"He took over Bill's plan? Added a few details of his own?"

Raynes nodded quietly.

"I think it's time to wrap up this case. We'll go and see Mr Hayward and see if we can fill in some of the blanks. We still have very little to go on - but the indicators are all pointing in one direction."

There was a knock at the door.

"Come in."

A rather nervous young policeman from reception stood in the doorway.

"Inspector Raynes?"

"Yes."

"Someone's just left something for you from the flower shop. A wreath…"

The Inspector smiled.

"We were expecting it. Please bring it in."

The wreath was small and disappointing. More greenery than flowers. Carlisle had the feeling that it had been taken from the graveyard or the crematorium - and re-cycled. But it contained a personalised note, again typed on a label and stuck on a card.

"In memory of the late Inspector Raynes.
Given by his grieving colleagues in the
Grasshallows police.
Never to strike again!"

Raynes laid the wreath down on his desk.

"A little premature, I think. But beautifully timed!"

43: The Murderer's Friend

Within fifteen minutes, Raynes and Carlisle arrived on the front steps of the *Grasshallows Echo*. There was a look of

233

grim determination on the Inspector's face and a marked unwillingness to put up with any obstacle.

"Mr Hayward?" he said.

"He's at lunch."

"Send for him."

The two officers walked up the main stairs and sat down in the publisher's office. Fortunately, Tom was not dining out at the *Green Man* - or any similar establishment. He was having a sandwich and a beer in his own canteen, discussing possible articles for the Friday paper.

He came upstairs very quickly.

"Inspector?" he said. "I wasn't expecting you. Have there been some developments? Have you caught the Vice-Chancellor's killer?"

Raynes shook his head.

"I'm afraid not. But we are somewhat closer to discovering the comedian who sent in my obituary and gave you £30."

Tom Hayward was disappointed not to have anything more exciting to put in the paper.

"Well, I suppose that's something," he said. "And it wasn't Emily Williams?"

"No," said Raynes. "I'm afraid I did that young lady an injustice - accusing her. But she has proved quite helpful of late. She and Mr Krauss held a seance in Palmerston last night. They were trying to see if Dr Shawcross could help them catch the Vice-Chancellor's killer."

"Did they succeed?"

"Almost. But just as they were getting closer, Dr Shawcross got very upset. He started smashing things up and throwing things around the room. I believe it was quite frightening."

Mr Hayward was amazed.

"They actually got in touch with Dr Shawcross?"

"For about half an hour. I'm sure she'll tell you all about it. It'll provide a dramatic story for your readers."

Tom cheered up. At least there would be something interesting in this week's newspaper. It would stir up a whole sheaf of *Letters to the Editor*. Every crackpot in the city would want to express their opinion.

"But to return to the other matter," said Raynes. "The gentleman who was arranging my funeral. He has also been in touch with Ferguson's to order my coffin. And, this morning, he sent a wreath to the police station. So he seems to be quite serious. I think it's about time we reeled him in."

Tom laughed.

"He certainly rattled your cage!"

Raynes looked at the publisher more critically.

"But only with a little help from his friends… That's why we've come to see you this afternoon. There has been a small indiscretion on your part."

"On my part?"

Raynes nodded.

"There was one item in that obituary that only you could know."

Mr Hayward looked rather alarmed.

"I had nothing to do with it!"

"I wouldn't say that."

Mr Hayward became quite agitated.

"You're quite wrong, Inspector. I had never seen or heard of that obituary until it arrived on my desk. I phoned you immediately."

Raynes paused.

"So you did. But perhaps you failed to notice the last line? 'All donations to the Donkey Sanctuary…'."

"That was a joke!"

"Indeed it was. But it also happened to be true. It is part of my will."

"I didn't know that."

"No one knows - except my lawyer. But I expect he's forgotten about it by now. However, I did tell one other person. I told you that I was leaving my money to the donkeys…"

"I don't remember that."

"Cast your mind back! About six months. To an evening in Wales, when you were talking about the Railway. You asked me to give a donation towards *Lady Ermintrude…*"

Mr Hayward tried hard to remember.

Raynes continued: "… I refused to give you a donation. I felt I was doing quite enough to help the Railway. But later, just before we returned to Grasshallows, you suggested that I might leave a legacy to the Puddleduck. And I said to you: 'all my worldly goods are going to the Donkey Sanctuary'."

Mr Hayward said hesitantly: "I think I do remember that. I spend my life trying to raise funds for the Railway. It's the sort of thing I say to all my friends."

"Well, you must have spoken to someone. One of your employees… or one of your mistresses…"

"I don't have any mistresses!"

Raynes looked at Tom with a mocking smile.

"You might even have spoken to Miss Williams! But I am sure you told someone what I was doing with my money. And that indiscretion turned up in my obituary notice."

Mr Hayward was still in denial.

"I'm sure I haven't spoken to anyone about it."

"Try harder!" said Raynes.

There was a long silence.

"Mr Morton?"

Realization dawned in Tom's eyes. Yes, he had made a sneering reference to the Inspector. He had said something like: 'He's leaving all his money to the donkeys. They're the only friends he's got!' It was not something he wished to repeat.

Very apologetically, the publisher conceded: "Yes. I do remember saying something to Mr Morton."

Raynes smiled.

"And Mr Morton was the man who ordered my coffin from Ferguson's. The cheapest model in the funeral parlour! And if I make a few enquiries at the florist, I shall doubtless discover that he is the man who sent the wreath."

Raynes' eyes twinkled.

"It has been a very expensive joke. It must have cost him at least £160. I wonder why he wants me to die? I think this little joke may cost him even more - if it comes to Court."

"Are you going to charge him?"

"I am thinking about it. He deserves it." Raynes paused. "But as you will appreciate, I have other, more serious matters on my mind at this time."

Raynes appeared to relax.

"However, whilst I have a few moments to spare, perhaps you could tell me something about Mr Morton. Is he one of your employees?"

Mr Hayward sat down in his editorial chair.

"Part-time. He fills in as and when we need him. Loads the vans. Delivers newspapers. Gives people lifts."

"And you pay him cash? Five pound notes?"

Raynes was being provocative.

"No. He gets more than that. We pay his expenses. We don't pay his National Insurance or anything like that."

"Do other people use his services?"

"All the time. Andy is a jack-of-all-trades. He's had many jobs in his time. Soldier, military policeman, security officer, taxi-driver, bar man, bouncer, children's entertainer…"

"Did he ever do any work for the University?"

"He used to drive the University car for Dr Bulman. But not for long. He found the job far too boring. But I believe he still brings the University Secretary in to work each morning…"

"Mr Forrester?"

"Yes. I think Andy keeps him up to date with all the things that are happening in the University. People tell him all sorts of things. He passes it on."

"Does he tell you what's going on in the University?"

"He tells us where to look."

"And you tell your University correspondent?"

"She does her own thing."

"So I noticed."

"And she does it rather well."

Raynes did not disagree.

He asked one final question: "Does Mr Morton have a good sense of humour?"

"He has an excellent sense of humour."

"So you think I should treat him kindly? Even if he is trying to arrange my funeral?"

Tom Hayward laughed.

"He's always trying to help people."

"But not always in the way they expect!"

Raynes stood up.

"Well," he said, "that clears up one problem. But now, I'm afraid, it's back to the grindstone."

He looked down at his colleague. Carlisle had already drawn a neat line under his notes. Game. set and match! He knew where their next call would be.

44: The Comedian

Not a word was spoken on the road to Ambleside Crescent. Both men were hoping that Mr Hayward would not have phoned Mr Morton to warn him that the Inspector now knew about the practical joke and was on his trail. They hoped that they would catch Mr Morton entirely unprepared - which they did.

Andy had just had a couple of tyres replaced on his car. He was now in the kitchen, making up a sandwich and a mug of coffee before sitting down to watch the racing on TV.

So he did not see the police Granada pull up on the other side of the road and two well-dressed men walking up his driveway. One of them looked at his tax disc; the other looked beyond the car to the garage. Like everything on Ambleside Crescent, it looked solid and respectable.

"Mr Morton?"

"That's right. What can I do for you?"

"I am Inspector Raynes and this is Detective-Constable Carlisle."

"Well, you'd better come in."

Andy led them into the front sifting room and switched off the television.

"Do sit down."

Mr Morton was a small, cheerful-looking man. He was wearing a leather bomber jacket over a white Arran sweater. He had brown cords and brown shoes.

"Now what can I do for you gentlemen?"

The answer was: 'Quite a lot' but Raynes played his hand carefully.

"Have you got anything against the police, Mr Morton?"

Andy shook his head.

"I've had a few speeding fines in my time; but nothing serious. I prefer to keep out of trouble - having been a military policeman myself."

"In the Army?"

"In Aden."

"Quite a dangerous place?"

"It was when I was there."

Andy was proud of his Army record.

Raynes looked at him thoughtfully.

"Have we met before?"

"I don't think so. But I've seen your photo in the paper quite a few times."

Raynes smiled pleasantly.

"Well, perhaps you can tell me why you seem to be interested in arranging my funeral?"

"Your funeral?"

"Yes. An obituary notice was sent to the Echo, saying that I had died on Sunday November 11 and my funeral would be held in the crematorium on Wednesday November 21."

"I didn't see that."

"It was never published."

Andy laughed.

"Well, you're still alive!"

"I am. But someone also ordered a coffin from Ferguson's."

"I wouldn't know anything about that."

"I believe you bought a coffin from Ferguson's for your mother's funeral in 1978?"

239

"I went there for my wife's funeral two years ago."

A tear or two came into his eyes.

"But I think you bought a rather special coffin for your mother. A Pennine coffin - with praying hands."

Raynes thought he could see a touch of mischief on Andy's lips.

"It's a long time ago, Inspector. I really can't remember."

Raynes said: "Well, you ordered a similar coffin yesterday. Or it may have been on Monday. You paid a deposit of £100. And even if you can't remember what coffin you bought for your mother's funeral, Mr Ferguson remembers it quite well."

"I haven't been into Ferguson's since Maureen died."

That at least was true.

Raynes smiled.

"And, this lunchtime, I received a wreath which you sent to police headquarters. It didn't look particularly fresh. My colleague, Detective-Constable Carlisle, thinks you picked it up at the crematorium - and re-cycled it." He paused. "Saved you a few five pound notes!"

"It's news to me, Inspector."

Raynes looked at Andy.

He was a wily, old devil.

"Can you tell me why you should have this obsession about my death?"

He looked at Mr Morton, sitting relaxed and comfortable in his favourite chair.

"Tom Hayward told me you had a great sense of humour…"

"So you've been to him?"

"He told me all about you. He said you had lived a very active life - soldier, security man, bouncer, barman, children's entertainer… He told me you've been a driver for the University. You run your own taxi service."

Andy nodded.

"I have had a good life, Inspector, but I don't get involved with the police. You've come to the wrong place. There's no connection between me and this funeral business. But I think it's a pity you can't take a joke."

Carlisle, taking full notes of the conversation, thought it was going to be a long, hard slog getting information out of this man. He would deny everything.

But Raynes was patient.

"I'm afraid you can't wriggle out of this one. There was information on that obituary notice which was known to only two people. One was my lawyer; and the other was Mr Hayward. He admits giving this information to you. So I have every reason to believe that you wrote the obituary, ordered the coffin and sent the wreath. Same technique. Same £5 notes. It has to be you. And I would like to know why?"

Mr Morton sighed sadly.

"I should have thought you chaps would have more to worry about than a practical joke. There are plenty of other problems troubling our city. Crime... drugs..."

Raynes said: "You are referring to the murder of the Vice-Chancellor?"

"Well, yes..."

"I shall be coming to that. But I felt that we should deal with this personal matter first; because it has wasted a lot of police time - and the evidence points to you."

Andy said nothing.

Raynes too was silent. Deliberately silent. It lasted long enough to get Mr Morton worried. But the wretched man continued to look totally unconcerned.

He decided to change the subject.

"Since you want to talk about the Vice-Chancellor's death, I believe you were quite friendly with his wife?"

"I wouldn't say that."

"You took her quite regularly from the University House to visit her lover, Peter Latimer, at 41 Sandringham Crescent."

Mr Morton said nothing.

"Your car has been seen regularly on Thursday nights, delivering Mrs Shawcross to his front door at 7.00pm and collecting her at 1.00am. Many University lecturers live in Sandringham Crescent. They have taken note of your number plate and your taxi badge."

"I have my job to do."

"Indeed you have. But I would like you to confirm that you took Mrs Shawcross to Mr Latimer's house most Thursday nights."

"I'm not confirming anything."

Raynes' voice took on a harder edge.

"I am particularly interested in your taking her to that address on the night of November 1 - the night Dr Shawcross was murdered. Mrs Shawcross told me that you delivered her there - and collected her at 1.00am. So you can't deny it."

Mr Morton also sounded more aggressive.

"I'm not saying anything to you chaps. You can ask as many questions as you like, but I'm not answering any of them. Now, if you don't mind, I would like to get back to watching the racing. I have a few quid at stake."

Raynes realised that Mr Morton was playing a very tough game which had every chance of success. He didn't think there was any point in threatening him. He would just dig in his heels. So he tried a different approach.

"Your friend, Bill Hobbs, has told me that he planned the murder of the Vice-Chancellor…"

Andy nodded.

He had thought this might come up.

"He told you his plans?"

"I believe he did."

"He told you early in October that he was going to electrocute Dr Shawcross. He had the key to the University House and he planned to do it on a night when his wife was out. He told you his plan in the *Kirby Arms*…"

"I believe he told quite a few people."

"… He also told you where he had put the key. In his garden shed. But, before he could commit the murder, the key was removed - and a quite different key was put in its place. It was only when he returned the key to the Maintenance department that he realised it was the wrong key. Would you know anything about that?"

242

Andy smiled.

"Didn't want him to do anything stupid."

"But did you take the key?"

"I don't know what happened to the key."

Inspector Raynes was expecting to be told a lie - but Andy's reply rang true.

"Perhaps it is still in your garage?"

A slight tremor of anxiety passed through Mr Morton's body. He had meant to add the key to the key ring in the University car. But had he done so? He couldn't be sure.

Raynes noted his reaction.

"I should like to have a look at your garage."

"There's nothing to see."

"Not at the moment... But a great deal of activity has happened there. This is where you brought Dr Shawcross' body on the night of the murder. You put his body in the boot. You laid him on the floor. You stripped him; then you dressed him up in your mother's clothes. That is where you painted his face. Was that another of your practical jokes?"

Mr Morton did not look quite so cocky. He was wondering how Inspector Raynes could know all these things. There had ben no witnesses... How could he be so sure?

Very reluctantly, he handed over his keys.

"Thank you," said Raynes "And which is the one for the garage?"

Andy pointed to a Yale.

"The police forensic team will be coming along later this afternoon to examine the garage; but I would like to do a preliminary search."

The sudden change in the conversation began to worry Andy. He had felt that all he had to do was to say nothing. No one could shake his story. But clearly the Inspector knew a great deal more. He could not think how.

He had worn rubber gloves all the evening. There were no fingerprints in either the University House or the car. Dr Shawcross' clothes had been disposed of in a black plastic bag out at Henslea. But where was the key? He hadn't seen it since that Thursday night. Surely he must have left it in the car?

"Shall I come with you?"

"No. You can stay here with Detective-Constable Carlisle and watch the racing. I hope you win a few quid."

But would he ever be able to collect his winnings?

Raynes went out to the garage and opened the lock. The first thing he noticed was the well-oiled hinges. The next was the space. It was a very wide and deep garage, built in the 1930s. There would have been plenty of room for the University car - and still space to lay out the body on the floor.

He walked back and forth across the garage looking for any specks of blood. There were none. He suspected that the garage floor had recently been swept. But if there were any micro-sized flecks of blood, Dr Stewart would find them.

He looked around for any sign of clothes belonging either to Andy's mother or the Vice-Chancellor. None. He looked in every box. He looked inside two toolboxes. Hammers, wrenches, chisels. There was only one item that caught his eye. A stone mason's hammer - hidden under a couple of spanners and a pair of pliers. It too seemed to be suspiciously clean. He laid it out on the work top. Dr Stewart could have a look at it.

He went through the contents of all the boxes on the higher shelves. He pulled down one cardboard box which seemed to be quite full. Inside, to his amazement, there was a roll of yellow cable with a plug at one end and a large metal claw at the other end - the sort of thing you clamp on to a battery when it is flat. To start a car, there are normally two claws - one positive, one negative. But here there was just one claw quite large enough to go around a brass door knob.

Raynes smiled.

The vital clue.

Andy had been very careful to cover his tracks. He had cleared all the evidence from the University house, the car and the garage... He had taken the labels off all his mother's clothes. He had disposed of all the Vice-Chancellor's possessions. But he had never expected anyone to suspect him. So he had kept the cable in case he needed it again. But he had forgotten to remove the claw.

He had also forgotten something else. As he brought the cardboard box down to the work top for Dr Stewart, he heard a small rattle inside the box. He turned it upside down and a small silver key dropped out. Bill Hobbs' key to the University House. Andy had just popped it into the box - with the cable - and forgotten about it.

The garage revealed no further secrets. But there was now more than enough to call in the experts. Raynes walked out to the police Granada and put through a call to Dr Stewart and his forensic team. He said:

"I've found our man."

"The comedian?"

"Yes. 10 Ambleside Crescent. Could you come right away? I've found some vital evidence and the garage floor needs an intense search for any micro-organisms which may have survived. He's tried hard to cover his tracks but he's made some glaring errors."

Raynes put down the phone and walked back to the house. As he had expected, both Andy and Detective-Constable Carlisle were watching the racing. It was the beginning of the new season and Andy still had some hope of winning.

Raynes went over to the television and switched it off. He turned to the cheerful, little man in his bomber jacket and said: "Mr Andrew Morton, I am arresting you for the murder of Dr Timothy Shawcross. Anything you may say will be written down and used in evidence against you…"

45: The Invisible Man

Raynes sat down and Carlisle picked up his notepad and pencils. "I have phoned Dr Stewart, the police surgeon. He will be here with the forensic team, who will find your garage most interesting. Before they arrive, I would like to tell you why you are being arrested and why I suspect you of murder.

As you have said, you are a man of immense experience. You are a brave man - an ex-soldier - who served in one of the most dangerous parts of the world - in Aden…"

"And Cyprus!"

"Doubly brave. In the course of your life, you may have had to kill people. People who were a danger to your colleagues. You are not a natural killer, but you realised that many people would be glad to see the back of Dr Shawcross, who was a very spiteful and stupid man. No one will grieve for him. Not even his wife.

"Because of your long association with the University, you still do quite a lot of taxi work for them. I believe that you transport Russell Forrester into work each morning. You act as his eyes and ears around the University. You let him know what is going on… what people are saying.

"You probably told him what was going on between the Vice-Chancellor's wife and the University Chaplain, Peter Latimer. A scandal which was likely to cause the University great embarrassment. Forewarned is forearmed.

"But you were not personally all that interested. It was just part of life's rich drama. It only began to upset you when it affected your own close friends. You have been a lifelong friend to Linda and Bill…"

"I was his best man."

Raynes nodded.

"So you were very fond of them both. When you heard of the stress that Linda was under, working for Dr Shawcross, and the terrible rows they were having, you must have been very distressed and anxious to help them.

"Bill was talking of suicide. I know that because he told me - as he told you. So you began to wonder what you could do to help them. To your surprise, you discovered that Bill had already concocted a plan to kill Dr Shawcross by electrocuting him. You thought that it was a good plan, but you had your doubts as to whether Bill could carry the plan through to a successful conclusion. He might bungle it - or his conscience might trouble him."

"Your first idea was to stop him doing the murder by changing the key to the University House which he had hidden in his garden shed. You put in a substitute which you knew would never work.

"The situation was saved by Russell Forrester sending Linda and Bill away on holiday. and removing her from her post as the Vice-Chancellor's secretary. That saved their marriage - and also postponed the murder. After Russell's timely action, there was no longer any need to protect Bill; but once you had started thinking about murder, you developed your own plan.

"No one would suspect you. You were a complete outsider. Not one of the University staff. You had no motive. But you had opportunities other people did not have. You had once been the driver of the University car. Not for very long, but long enough to know your way round the University House - where they keep the keys and where the lights go on and off.

"There was also some advantage in that the University House's electrics were in poor shape. Years of argument between the modernisers and the conservationists meant that there was delay in installing a new system of wiring. So electrocution was the perfect solution.

"You realized that once you took Mrs Shawcross to visit her lover, the coast would be clear for the next three hours. And you chose the night of the next Senate meeting which was on Thursday November 1st. The Vice-Chancellor would not arrive home before nine o' clock, giving you plenty of time to prepare for his murder.

"By the time of the Senate meeting, Dr Shawcross was in deep trouble. Opposition to his plans was growing. The students were up in arms - and already making wax dolls and sticking pins into them. On Wednesday night, there was a big demonstration outside the Botanical Gardens with protestors shouting 'Kill the V-C!' The following evening you struck.

"You took Freddie to Sandringham Crescent. Then you drove back to the University House and waited for Mr Clifford Brown to bring Dr Shawcross home. It was a long wait - because it had been a long meeting. Once he had been to the toilet, the Vice-Chancellor went to his study where the door handle was connected to the mains. But it failed to kill him. Dr Shawcross was wearing rubber-soled shoes and, underneath the carpet, there was rubber underlay. So he was doubly protected. But, even if he did not die, he was badly stunned.

"There was a danger that the Vice-Chancellor might cry out. Mr Brown was at that moment putting the University car in the garage, but he would be bringing back the keys to the hook in the kitchen. He might hear the cry and rush through into the hall. So, whilst Dr Shawcross lay stunned, you hit him with your stone-mason's hammer which, I see, is still in your tool-box all nice and clean."

Mr Morton immediately reacted. He sat up in his chair. He looked as if he wanted to do something about the hammer; but there was nothing he could do. Raynes was pleased to see some reaction.

"But even the hammer did not kill the wretched man. So you put a length of cord round his neck and strangled him. I would imagine it took some time to tidy things up after the murder. You had to remove the yellow cable from the plug and put it back in its cardboard box…"

Mr Morton looked at the Inspector.

"Yes, I found that too. You shouldn't have kept anything connected with the murder. You should have thrown the whole lot into the river…."

Andy shook his head.

"Once the coast was clear, you would have had to get the University car out of the garage, bring it round to the back door and load the Vice-Chancellor's body into the boot. Then you brought it back to your own garage and locked it away from prying eyes. But there was a witness - and he has told us what happened.

"You laid the body out on the garage floor and took off all his clothes. You had your mother's old clothes ready. You had cut off all the labels. And you proceeded to dress him up and pop an old wig on his head. Once you had kitted him out with some ancient lisle stockings, you put him back into his own shoes. The make-up you used was so weird and so badly done that Dr Stewart knew it must have been done by a man.

"You then put the Vice-Chancellor back into the University car. You put him in the passenger seat because you knew from your Army experience that *rigor mortis* would shortly take place and his limbs would go rigid. You put a length of green hose into the car with a rubber attachment for the exhaust, which would make it look like suicide. And for good measure, you also poured some sand down his throat. I imagine that you were mimicking the death of Allan Foster in Picton Dale - one of my recent murders. Dr Stewart was amazed at the number of different possibilities you had incorporated into one murder.

"Having dealt with the Vice-Chancellor's body, you returned to your own car in order to collect Mrs Shawcross from Sandringham Crescent. You knew that she would not be particularly worried about her husband's absence - or that of the car. She knew that he was going to a conference on Friday - and might already have gone. She was intending to spend a naughty weekend with Peter Latimer. When I turned up at the University House on the Saturday morning, she had her bags packed and was ready to go.

"So the murder had been committed; but there was no public outcry. You waited twenty-four hours and then, in the depths of the night, you drove the University car and its distinguished passenger up to Skipper's Hill and left it at the far end of the golf club car park, with the engine running and carbon monoxide pouring into the car through an open window. For some reason, you moved the body to the driver's seat. I noticed that you had adjusted the seat to make the deceased more comfortable. And there it remained until the body was found at 7.00am.

"You will appreciate that it took about three days to produce an intelligible report on all that had happened to the corpse. The methods of death, the clothes, the timing and the

249

motive - which seemed to be humiliation. The police surgeon told me that the person who had done the job had a strange sense of humour. I think that has been one of the hallmarks of this case.

"The reaction to Dr Shawcross' death was also quite interesting. There was no public call for vengeance - no hue and cry for the murderer to be found. Rather, there was a sense of relief that the Vice-Chancellor could do no further damage to the University. In fact, people seemed to think that whoever had killed Dr Shawcross was a public hero."

Mr Morton looked a little happier.

Raynes continued:

"So there we were - in an impossible situation. Thousands of avowed enemies among both staff and students, but only a small handful of suspects, most of whom could produce a suitable alibi. Where should we start?"

"If you had got on with your daily life, we should never have caught you. But as Dorothy Sayers once said: 'Murder Must Advertise'. And for some reason, you felt a need to provoke me, to remind me that you were still at large. I'm afraid that it was your perverse sense of humour which has led to you being arrested.

"When I was shown the obituary which you very kindly sent to Mr Hayward, I wondered who could have sent it. Not someone who knew me - my family details were pure moonshine - but someone who happened to know that my money was going to the Donkey Sanctuary - which was true."

Mr Morton grimaced.

Raynes said: "You got that from Mr Hayward!"

He nodded.

"But I didn't see it at first. It was only when Ferguson's phoned up about the coffin, that I started thinking: 'Who is this screwball arranging my funeral?' Could it perhaps be the murderer having a little fun at my expense? So my object became: 'Find the comedian - discover the murderer'."

Raynes looked at Andy.

He was showing every sign of frustration. He could have

got away with it. But he had been too clever - too clever by half. He had left no clues in the University House; none in the car. But the obituary and the praying hands had got him.

"I don't know why you re-ordered your mother's coffin."

Mr Morton said sadly: "I don't know either."

It was a confession of sorts.

Raynes wondered if he should say any more. The next part would sound almost like fantasy. But he decided that it might be better to hit Mr Morton with everything he had got. It would bring a swifter collapse and a full confession.

He said to Andy: "The chief witness against you was Dr Shawcross."

Andy looked startled.

"But he's dead!"

Raynes smiled.

"Not as dead as you think! What you did to the Vice-Chancellor was seen by a student on Wednesday October 17. Mr Rudy Krauss was reading his Tarot cards for Mrs Shawcross. She wanted to know what was going to happen to her husband. He saw all the people who hated him. But he also saw him being killed. He saw the flash of electricity and felt it burning in his hand…"

"On October 17?"

"Yes. He also saw the Vice-Chancellor dressed up in an old woman's clothes - with a painted face. He saw the hammer blow to the head - and the body sitting in the University car, long before you even committed the murder. At the time, he didn't know what it all meant. But it was clear to him that Dr Shawcross was going to die a violent death. But, later, he realised what he had seen. Even the date of the murder - November 1 - flashed in front of his eyes. He thought he had seen the eleventh. But the information was all there."

"Blimey!" said Mr Morton.

"And since then," said Raynes, "the students have held a seance - with two members of staff, including Linda Hobbs - and they have questioned Dr Shawcross."

Andy looked up in amazement.

251

"You can't arrest a chap on rubbish like that! I'm not going to admit to anything. I'm innocent. I want to see my lawyer!"

"Too late!" said Raynes. "Dr Shawcross was able to speak to the students - and Linda - for almost half an hour. He told them everything that had happened from the moment he returned to the University House. Going to the toilet; heading for the study; receiving the electric shock; feeling the hammer blow on the back of his head. He remembers being put into the boot of the University car. He remembers lying naked on your garage floor. He remembers being dressed up in your mother's clothes - and you painting his face. He said he saw you - but he did not recognise you."

Mr Morton cheered up.

But only for a moment.

"He saw the yellow cable - which you rolled up and put in a cardboard box."

Raynes smiled.

"And it's still there. In its box. In your garage! Dr Stewart will find it there when he arrives."

Mr Morton put his head in his hands. He had made too many mistakes. The yellow cable would finish him off. He had never reckoned that a departed spirit would testify against him.

Raynes completed the story:

"Even though he didn't know who you were, he recognised you as the taxi man who took his wife to Sandringham Crescent. But someone must have told him that you had once been the University chauffeur - because he was most insistent that 'It was the Chauffeur' who killed him.

"He spelt it out on the table.

"But the people who were present at the seance didn't believe him. They thought he was accusing Clifford Brown, the present chauffeur. Dr Shawcross would have recognised him immediately. But that was the last thing he told them.

"Now I checked the facts with Mr Hayward and he told me that you had worked for Dr Bulman, the previous Vice-Chancellor. And here we are!"

Mr Morton did not receive this information with any grace.

"Damn your ****ing eyes! I wish I'd killed you as well - while I had the chance."

Raynes was serious for a moment.

"You may still have that chance," he said. "It may be that when your case comes to court, there may be a wave of public support for what you have done. Dr Shawcross was so unpopular and ruffled so many feathers in the University that there may be an appeal for your release. You may be able to write a book: 'How I killed the Vice-Chancellor'. As I said earlier, you might become a public hero. You may even get an MBE. You may be thankful I caught you…"

"I doubt it."

"So do I. But I feel that without Dr Shawcross, the University will be a cleaner and a happier place. You also helped Linda and Bill… They won't forget what you did."

Raynes looked out through the front window. Dr Stewart had arrived with his team of experts. They were already donning their white overalls. They would discover all the hidden things in the garage. And they would enjoy doing it.

Raynes turned to Carlisle.

"The cuffs."

He slipped them on to Andy's wrists. As he undid the buttons on his shirt and rolled up his sleeves, he looked at the tattoos painted indelibly on his arms. They had probably been done on some warm night in Egypt or Cyprus after a couple of drinks. After he had escaped from Aden and the terrors of the Krater. He had escaped then; but he had been caught now.

The man seemed to have crumpled before his eyes. He said nothing.

Dr Stewart breezed into the room.

"So you've caught him?"

"Mr Morton."

Dr Stewart looked down at the small man in the dark brown bomber jacket.

"But I know you! It's Andy. He used to drive the University car. We've had many a pint together in the *Kirby Arms*! I should have guessed it might be you!" He turned to Raynes. "He's got a wicked sense of humour."

He turned back to Andy.

"You should have known better than to take on Mr Raynes. The Inspector always gets his man!"

46: From Our University Correspondent

Dr Stewart provided excellent results, but the report still took another two days to arrive on the Inspector's desk. It confirmed his suspicions that there might be invisible specks of blood and tiny grains of sand still lying on the garage floor - along with minute traces of thread and fluff from Mrs Morton's ancient clothes.

Brushing and sweeping had not destroyed the evidence. It had just heaped it up in the corners, providing valuable evidence for the prosecution. The stone mason's hammer was not the murder weapon; but the yellow cable, claw and key added dramatically to the case being built up against Mr Morton.

He himself had pleaded guilty - even before his lawyer, Mr Derek Coates-Smythe, arrived to defend him. He told the Inspector that he could not face a long drawn-out trial. He hoped that his family, who now lived in Australia, would find an immediate plea of guilty less harrowing.

Inspector Raynes decided not to inform the publisher of the *Grasshallows Echo* - even though Tom Hayward had provided the final pieces of the jigsaw which led to Andy's arrest. Instead, he announced the news through the University's public relations department and Reuter's Press Agency on the Thursday morning.

After they had completed their morning lectures, Inspector Raynes gave a private briefing to Emily Williams and Rudy Krauss. They had made a stupendous effort to find out who had killed Dr Shawcross. The evidence of the Tarot cards and the seance were overwhelming.

Although the national newspapers published the latest information that a man had been arrested for the murder of the Vice-Chancellor of Grasshallows University, it was not exactly "news". The story had already been fully covered ten days before. Fortunately, there was still time to get the latest developments into the *Echo*.

Raynes had removed two photographs of Mr Morton from his house in Ambleside Crescent. One was of Andy as a young soldier in Cyprus; the other with his wife at a party to celebrate their 30th Wedding Anniversary. Armed with these two pictures and having the full investigation at her fingertips, Emily was able to provide an exclusive article on the student side of the story, which Mr Hayward graciously printed on the front page of the *Grasshallows Echo* on Friday, November 16:

STUDENTS PLAY VITAL PART
IN ARREST OF KILLER

From our University Correspondent.

Emily had been given her chance - and she made full use of it:

"It is just over a year since Dr Shawcross became Vice-Chancellor of Grasshallows University. It was hoped that his experience in business would strengthen the financial position of the University. But, instead, the new Vice-Chancellor embarked on a cost-cutting crusade which alienated both staff and students.

The first body to feel the full force of his reforms was the Students' Union which, for the first time in its history, was made to pay both rent and heating bill. This led to an immediate rise in the cost of student services - particularly food and drink. (No mention of beer.)

The reaction of the student body to these reforms was understandably hostile and the campaign against the Vice-

Chancellor was led by Rudy Krauss, the President of the Pagan Society. In the space of a week, he was able to mobilise the student community and deliver a hard-hitting attack on Dr Shawcross.

This culminated in a tense stand-off between the students and the Vice-Chancellor outside the Botanical Gardens at Hallowe'en. It was a massive display of anger, attended by almost a thousand students; but the confrontation was peaceful. The strength of popular feeling was increased by the knowledge that Dr Shawcross intended to sell off the property for new housing developments.

The Vice-Chancellor died in the University House the following night; but his death had already been anticipated. Mrs Shawcross, his wife, was deeply distressed by her husband's unpopularity. She invited Mr Krauss to the University House to use his occult powers to see what the future might hold.

In a tense and dramatic reading of his Tarot cards, Mr Krauss revealed that the Vice-Chancellor was about to die a violent death. All the stages of his murder were foreseen - the attempted electrocution, the hammer blow to the skull followed by strangulation. Mr Krauss was able trace the movements of the University car to a garage in Ambleside Crescent.

He was also able to describe the bizarre clothing in which Dr Shawcross was transported on his final journey to Skipper's Hill Golf Club. The only thing which was uncertain was the date. Mr Krauss thought it was November 11. In the event, it was November 1.

When police investigations came to a halt a few days later, Rudy Krauss proposed a seance in Palmerston College to raise the spirit of the late Vice-Chancellor and find out directly what Dr Shawcross had seen.

Members of the University staff and student body attended the seance, where Mr Krauss was able to communicate with the departed spirit for almost half an hour. During that time, he was able to discover many aspects of the murder which, until then, had been shrouded in mystery.

Dr Shawcross was willing to help the students in their investigations, but later became violent when they refused to accept his insistent allegation: 'It was the chauffeur'. Staff members knew it could not be the present University chauffeur, Mr Clifford Brown, even though he had recently been sacked by Dr Shawcross - and re-instated by the University authorities.

However, it was subsequently discovered that Mr Andrew Morton, the murderer, was indeed a former University chauffeur to Dr Bulman. He was still driving the University Secretary to work every morning. He also drove Mrs Shawcross to secret meetings with Mr Peter Latimer, the disgraced University Chaplain, who has recently been suspended by the University. Because Mr Morton knew that he would not be collecting Mrs Shawcross till 1.00am, he knew that the coast would be clear and he would be able to get into the University House and murder the Vice-Chancellor that Thursday night.

The information received at the seance was rapidly passed to the police - enabling Detective-Inspector Raynes to make an arrest on Wednesday afternoon. Inspector Raynes has said that he was extremely grateful for the help given by the students, which could not have been obtained from any other source.

It is hoped that the death of the Vice-Chancellor will relieve the tension and distress felt by so many within the University community. Now the murderer has been arrested, both students and staff may be able to work together peacefully to heal the many wounds Dr Shawcross inflicted. One thing is *certain. The future of the Botanical Gardens is now safe and secure. There will be no new housing developments in that part of Grasshallows."*

* * * *

Having just sacked Peter Latimer and told him to go back to his wife, the University Secretary was faced with a barrage of questions from a second wave of investigative journalists.

Was it true that Rudy Krauss was an ex-jailbird? How had he managed to get back into the University? Was it true that the Vice-Chancellor's wife was having an affair with the University Chaplain? Had Mr Morton ever been a member of the University staff? Was it true that he drove the University Secretary to work every morning? Did the University permit its premises to be used for seances, spiritualism and black magic? Had he ever stuck pins into one of Rudy's wax dolls? Were Tarot cards still on sale in the Students' Union?

With a gracious sweep of his hand, an apology on his lips and displaying complete ignorance of anything that might have been happening in the University, Russell Forrester dismissed all suggestions of impropriety and immorality. He shook his head sadly.

"You gentlemen should know - only too well - that you can never trust a reporter to tell you the full story. They will always embellish the truth."

And, with that, the barriers slammed down.
